If Not for the Duke

The Duke's Lost Treasures
Book 3

LANA WILLIAMS

Dragonblade Publishing, Inc. is an imprint of Kathryn Le Veque Novels, Inc.
P.O. Box 23
Moreno Valley, CA 92556
ceo@dragonbladepublishing.com

Produced in the United States of America

First Edition November 2022
Trade Paperback Edition

ARE YOU SIGNED UP FOR DRAGONBLADE'S BLOG?

You'll get the latest news and information on exclusive giveaways, exclusive excerpts, coming releases, sales, free books, cover reveals and more.

Check out our complete list of authors, too!

No spam, no junk. That's a promise!

Sign Up Here

www.dragonbladepublishing.com

Dearest Reader;

Thank you for your support of a small press. At Dragonblade Publishing, we strive to bring you the highest quality Historical Romance from some of the best authors in the business. Without your support, there is no 'us', so we sincerely hope you adore these stories and find some new favorite authors along the way.

Happy Reading!

CEO, Dragonblade Publishing

Chapter One

London, England
May 1878

LENA WRIGHT SHRUGGED in an attempt to dispel the familiar but unwelcome sensation that threatened to sweep over her. The middle of the Barrington Garden party was not the time to have one of her spells. Yet a familiar chill ran along her scalp and down her spine, a telltale sign that something unfortunate was about to occur. Or had just occurred. Or might occur.

She heaved a frustrated sigh, trying to will the feeling away before someone noticed her acting oddly.

"What is it?" Norah, her older sister by two years, asked as she handed Lena a glass of lemonade.

"Nothing." Never mind that a glance at Norah's expression confirmed that she already knew. "Just a feeling." She took a sip of the cool, tart drink, still hoping the sense would go away.

Why Lena bothered to try to dismiss these moments was a source of disagreement between her and her sisters. Lena had explained that having the feeling that "something" was amiss wasn't helpful. After all, she rarely knew the exact nature of the problem. It wasn't as if she had a vision along with it that explained the details. Sometimes there wasn't even a problem. Too often, her supposed "gift" of intuition was misleading and upsetting.

Wrong as often as it was right.

Unreliable at best.

Nonexistent at worst.

The sense had failed her when she needed it most—the day her father died. Guilt from that terrible time was something she struggled with daily.

And she hated how the feeling made her different from other people. She couldn't share it, nor was it easy to hide. Not when it took over her mind and blocked out all else. For those few moments when the sensation swept over her, she didn't see or hear what was happening around her. It made friendships difficult and the chance of marriage unlikely. No wonder she tried to hide the sense, even from her sisters.

"Do you know what's causing it?" Norah asked quietly as she glanced around the numerous guests spread amidst the elaborate garden where conversation and laughter flowed.

The afternoon sunshine was warm and lovely. The brightly colored gowns of the ladies in attendance added to the picturesque scene with the vast array of blooming flowers, bubbling fountain, and sculpted shrubbery. Gentlemen dotted the area as well, their brown and beige suits lending a somber tone to the vivid color palette.

Lena heaved another sigh and reluctantly returned her attention to the question. This was the difficult part—attempting to identify the potential issue. She studied the guests, noting the increase of her heartbeat as her body seemed to insist she take action. If only she knew what action to take.

She worried her lower lip as she considered the possibilities. Movements caught her eye. A gentleman gestured with his hand. A woman spun to greet a friend, causing her skirts to flare. Parasols tipped forward and back as guests moved along the garden paths. She knew most or was at least acquainted with them. In truth, nothing looked out of the ordinary.

Still, the nagging feeling persisted, so she continued to study the scene. The cause might not even be at this gathering. Something could be amiss at home, or with their eldest sister, Ella, who wasn't in attendance as she was expecting her first child. It might also be Norah's husband, the Marquess of Vanbridge, since Lena had experienced previous inklings of danger threatening him, which had proven true.

Lena's gaze caught on a young lady who stood some ten feet away, and the sense heightened, her chills increasing. Lena watched her for a moment, having noted her earlier as she was unfamiliar.

The young woman couldn't be more than eighteen years of age and seemed uncomfortable based on the awkward way she moved with her hands slightly out before her as if to keep from bumping into anything. She stood near a fountain and didn't seem to be enjoying herself in the least.

That was something to which Lena could relate. It had taken her well over a year to appreciate any of the social events they attended, partly because she and her two sisters had been the center of attention, a novelty of sorts.

As the granddaughters of the Duke of Rothwood, Lena and her sisters were invited to more functions than they could possibly attend. During their first Season in London three years ago, everything seemed overwhelming and unfamiliar compared to their previous life on a remote island in Nova Scotia. The attention had made Lena uncomfortable, a sharp contrast to their quiet childhood.

The unfortunate young lady, with dark brown hair and a thin face, seemed to be in a similar situation. Her gaze darted about, not settling on anything. Her lips were pressed tight, whether from worry or in a grimace, Lena couldn't tell.

An older woman stood beside the girl, possibly her chaperone, and looked about with interest. Both were dressed fashionably, the younger in a pale-yellow muslin with a floral underskirt in the latest princess-line style, which had replaced bustles with a slim look created by using vertical tucks. The older woman wore a fashionable, green-striped gown with red trim.

Lena watched the young lady, noting how she lifted her gloved hands out before her only to drop them and take a step back. Then another.

"Good heavens," Lena whispered. "She's going to topple into the fountain." In an instant, she knew that was the cause of her distress.

"Oh, dear!" Norah gasped, suggesting she could easily envision the woman falling in, too.

The large water feature consisted of a life-size stone mermaid whose cupped hands spurted water. The base of the pool was knee-high, making it easy to fall into. Stone fish circled the shallow pool around the figurine with mouths open, spraying water as well.

Without hesitation, Lena handed Norah her lemonade and then weaved through the guests along the path, moving toward the lady as quickly as she dared. Though the woman wouldn't suffer a great deal of harm from falling in the fountain, doing so would be terribly embarrassing and cause a scene. Lena didn't wish that experience on anyone.

The squint of the woman's eyes made Lena wonder if her vision was somehow impaired. Her chaperone seemed oblivious to the potential risk. She spoke to her charge but kept her gaze fixed on something in the distance, perhaps the refreshment table. Then she walked away, leaving the young woman alone. The lady took another step back, bumping into the fountain wall before teetering alarmingly.

Lena lunged forward to grab hold of her outstretched arm and managed to steady her in the nick of time, relieved neither of them had ended up in the water.

"Oh!" The lady stared at Lena in surprise, eyes wide, clearly startled by her sudden presence. Then she glanced down at Lena's tight grip on her arm.

"I feared you might fall into the fountain." Lena kept hold of her arm to make certain she had her balance.

"Fountain?" The woman looked over her shoulder, seeming to just now realize it was there. "I thought I heard the sound of running water."

Lena frowned, astonished that she hadn't seen it. She eased them both forward and out of harm's way before releasing her.

"Drat." The lady reached into the cuff of her sleeve and pulled forth a pair of spectacles. "Aunt Edith insisted I shouldn't wear these, but honestly, I can't see a thing without them."

She settled them on her nose, then turned, gasping at the large pool of water behind them. "My goodness, but that was close. I thought it was a statue." Her attention shifted to Lena, and she touched her arm. "Thank you so much. Floundering about in the fountain was not on my agenda this afternoon."

Before Lena could reply, she caught sight of an angry gentleman striding toward them.

"You there. What are you about?" he demanded, his expression fierce enough to cause Lena to take a small step back.

Everyone knew that Sterling Dunworth, the Duke of Renwick, was no one to be trifled with. Lena had never been formally introduced to His Grace but mentally referred to him as His Grumpiness. The man never smiled and glared at anyone who drew close. He had a sharp blade of a nose and defined cheekbones that lent him an austere look. While handsome, with thick, golden blond hair that held a hint of wave and dark brown eyes, his sober demeanor was less than appealing.

"Sterling." The young lady took his arm and gave it the smallest shake as if to gain his attention. "You should be thanking this kind lady, not berating her." Then she looked at Lena with a bright smile. "She saved me from an embarrassing dip in the fountain."

The explanation didn't seem to be enough for the duke. He continued to glare at Lena, his eyes chilly, clearly suspicious of her intent.

Lena felt heat climb in her cheeks under his close regard. Any time Lena attempted to explain herself after an incident like this, she struggled. It was often impossible to make excuses for what she knew.

She switched her focus to the lady, doing her best to ignore the duke. "I-I happened to see you backing toward the fountain and feared you weren't aware it was behind you."

"Happened to?" he asked, his tone dubious.

She told herself not to feel guilty. She'd offered a reasonable explanation and managed to save the lady. This time, anyway.

He couldn't possibly know about her ability. But if anyone might see through her, it would be His Grumpiness. He seemed to suspect everyone of something.

STERLING WATCHED HIS sister, Bernice, to make certain she was all right. When he'd seen this woman place her hand on Bernice's arm from across the garden, his heart had nearly stopped. Especially since Aunt Edith was nowhere to be seen. What sort of chaperone was she?

He knew he was overprotective with his younger sister, but he couldn't help it. She had been ill often as a child, and health issues had plagued her into adulthood.

She'd only just returned home from a year in Switzerland at a prestigious finishing school. Though she insisted the experience had strengthened her, he still worried. She would always seem fragile to him and in need of extra care.

Bernie was the one and only person in his life he could trust. She was his guiding light, a compass to navigate by. He'd learned long ago that everyone else wanted something. Kind acts were only a cover for ulterior motives.

The title of duke was an honor and one he took seriously, having been groomed from childhood to fulfill his duties and responsibilities. But the title brought disadvantages as well. He never knew if he was liked for himself or for what he could do for someone.

Sterling shifted his attention to the pale-haired beauty who'd supposedly come to his sister's rescue. He wondered if the woman had somehow managed to cause the near miss. The pink in her cheeks and the way she glanced away roused his suspicions even more. She looked vaguely familiar, though he was certain they hadn't been formally introduced.

"I can't thank you enough," Bernie was saying to the lady. "Allow me to introduce myself. I'm Lady Bernice Dunworth."

"It's a pleasure to meet you, my lady." The woman dipped into a graceful curtsy. "I'm Miss Lena Wright."

"Wright?" Sterling turned over the name in his mind. "Rothwood's granddaughter?"

"Yes, Your Grace." Her tone was polite, but a hard glint flashed briefly in her eyes. Disapproval, perhaps? Or anger that he hadn't expressed more gratitude.

He didn't care if she was a relation of Rothwood's. She still might have reason to orchestrate the incident. Movement nearby had him glancing over to see a lady approaching from several feet away, who looked remarkably like her. "You noticed my sister's potential mishap from across the garden?"

Miss Wright's cheeks deepened in color. "Yes."

"That's quite a feat." So unlikely that he had to wonder if it was possible. He could think of several reasons someone would want to give his sister a shove only to save her. The things people did to try to get into his good graces knew no bounds.

Sterling had learned from an early age to trust no one. A pair of pretty blue eyes wouldn't change his mind. Neither would her heart-shaped face or those long lashes. Certainly not that glitter of defiance in her eyes.

"Is all well?" the other lady asked when she joined them.

"Very well," Bernie said as she looked between the sisters as if entranced by their similarities.

"May I introduce my sister, the Marchioness of Vanbridge."

Lena Wright completed the introductions, allowing Sterling

to study her a few moments longer.

"A pleasure, Your Grace." The marchioness was a petite version of her sister with blue-green eyes that shone with intelligence and curiosity.

"I'm acquainted with your husband, though I haven't seen him for some time," Sterling said. "I trust he is well?"

"Yes. Quite well, thank you." Lady Vanbridge smiled. "I shall mention to him that I had the pleasure of meeting you."

"Your sister was kind to assist me," Bernie said. "My aunt thinks it terrible that I require spectacles and would rather I didn't wear them." She tapped a gloved finger on the edge of them. "But from this point forward, I refuse to go without them."

"A wise decision, my lady." Lady Vanbridge pressed a gloved hand to her heart as if to calm herself. "I feared Lena wouldn't reach you in time."

Sterling noted the look the sisters shared, certain it communicated more than he could discern. The fact that they talked about the possibility of his sister falling into the fountain only made him wonder all the more.

"Wright?" Bernie's focus shifted to Sterling and then back to the sisters. "But of course. You're the daughters of David Wright, the treasure hunter."

"Yes, we are." Lady Vanbridge nodded. "May I ask how you're familiar with him?"

"My sister has been devouring all she can find about Oak Island and its hidden treasure." Sterling sent a warning look to his sister, though he knew it would do no good. Her enthusiasm for the topic was boundless.

"Truly?" Miss Wright's expression suggested she was not as thrilled to hear that as her sister was.

"Oh, yes," Bernie replied with enthusiasm, her brown eyes sparkling. Nothing gave him greater joy than to see her happy. "You see, I love to read. Especially travel journals. I came upon *Rambles among the Blue-noses* by Andrew Learmont Spedon. Are you by chance familiar with it?"

Sterling nearly shook his head. No matter how many people she asked about that book, none had heard of it.

"Of course." Miss Wright nodded, much to his surprise. "It mentions my father's work on Oak Island, though not his name."

"Exactly. The author's description of Nova Scotia and the surrounding area was fascinating. Of course, few realize bluenoses refer to people from the area. But the idea of treasure on Oak Island started me on a quest of my own."

Lady Vanbridge frowned. "Have you visited the island?"

Bernie smiled, albeit ruefully. "Unfortunately, not. Travel is difficult for me. But that doesn't mean I can't venture anywhere I want to go in the pages of a book."

Miss Wright's slow smile appeared to be almost reluctant. "I enjoy reading as well. I don't read many travel journals, but I can tell you that Mr. Spedon's account of the area is fairly accurate, if a bit dramatic at times."

Bernie's eyes rounded with excitement. "I don't suppose you'd be willing to share some of your personal experiences with me?"

Miss Wright looked uncomfortable once again, her smile quickly fading as she shared a look with her sister. "I suppose that would be possible."

Sterling was tempted to reveal what Bernie's latest hobby had driven him to do if only to see Miss Wright's reaction. But he would wait and allow Bernie to tell her if she chose to. He was happy to keep it a secret. After all, he'd done it to please his sister. No one else.

Granted, he had always longed to have the freedom to explore the corners of the globe and discover lost artifacts. But that had been impossible. His father would never have allowed him to shirk his duties for such an idle pastime. Now that his father had passed, it seemed he'd have the chance to do a little treasure hunting, even if it was indirectly.

Discovering that David Wright's partner, Mr. Johnson, was selling the property he and Wright had owned on the island had been a stroke of luck, considering his sister's interest in the stories that surrounded the place. Sterling had bought it under the name of a company he'd formed to keep the matter private for as long as possible. Bernie had agreed to secrecy as well, preferring the endeavor to be something the two of them shared for a time.

As a member of the Royal Geological Society, which focused on exploration of all forms, including treasure hunting, Sterling was well aware of the mixed opinions on whether any treasure was truly buried on the island. Continuing the treasure hunt using modern techniques and deeper pockets would surely bring quicker results than anything Wright and Johnson had managed.

"I would be honored." Bernie clapped her hands in delight. "Would you join us, Lady Vanbridge?"

"How kind. Do let me know when you settle on a date, and I'll see if I'm available."

"How is your husband's museum?" Sterling asked. The marquess, a fellow member of the Society, though he rarely attended meetings, had opened a museum with the artifacts his uncle had collected.

"Fabulous," Bernie answered for her. "You simply must go, Sterling. It contains the Oak Island exhibit. Remember me telling you about it?"

"Oh, yes." He vaguely remembered, though his sister tended to wax poetic about each and every discovery she made about the island. It all blended in his mind. "The display gives one the chance to step into the shoes of a treasure hunter if I remember correctly."

Bernie patted her chest, sending a twinge of alarm through Sterling. But it took only a moment to realize it was from excitement, not from the irregular heart rhythm that occasionally plagued her. "It is positively brilliant. I intend to go again soon, though Aunt Edith didn't find it quite as stimulating as I did."

Lady Vanbridge smiled. "I am thrilled to hear you enjoyed it. Vanbridge will be happy to learn it as well." The lady leaned closer to Bernie as if to impart a secret. "It is remarkably similar to an actual shaft. The exhibit gave me chills when I first saw it."

"You were in one of the shafts?" The awe in Bernie's tone nearly had Sterling smiling.

She showed more excitement over a dirt shaft than a new gown. Was it any wonder she had so few friends?

Miss Wright smiled. "Norah and I both were, along with our sister. Many times. Once they were deep, Mother wouldn't permit us to go with Father any longer, as it was too dangerous."

Bernie rubbed her upper arms as if suddenly chilled. "I simply must hear more about your experiences. Are you available for tea tomorrow?"

To Sterling's surprise, Miss Wright looked at him before answering. As if his reaction to his sister's invitation mattered. No doubt she would prefer to avoid agreeing because she wanted to avoid him. He clenched his jaw. That simply wouldn't do. It was important to him that Bernie was happy. If that meant having Miss Wright over for tea, then so be it.

"I do hope you can join Bernie," he said. "Though I must warn you." He paused for dramatic effect.

"Warn me?" Miss Wright's blue eyes narrowed with suspicion.

"Sterling!" Bernie protested and swatted his arm. "You are a tease."

Miss Wright's eyes widened at that claim, and one brow lifted in surprise. Did she think him incapable of teasing?

"I must warn you that my sister's questions about Oak Island will be endless."

The lady's gaze shifted to Bernie. Her genuine smile caused the oddest sensation in Sterling's chest. He suddenly wanted her to look at him and offer that same smile. The unexpected wish had him frowning. Perhaps he shouldn't encourage her to be friends with his sister. Not until he knew more about her and what her motive might be.

But his sister's delight as they confirmed a time for tea made him realize it was too late. His best hope was to make certain he was at the tea as well.

Chapter Two

LENA STUDIED THE impressive façade of Renwick House, uncertain why she felt so hesitant to step out of the carriage. She supposed it was because she knew furthering her association with Lady Bernice meant seeing Renwick again. Obviously, somewhere deep inside, she wasn't certain that was wise.

When she'd mentioned the invitation for tea to her grandfather that morning at breakfast after they'd returned from an early morning ride, he'd been surprised.

"Renwick's sister? I'd nearly forgotten he had one."

"It sounds as if this is her first Season. Do you know Renwick well? I don't recall you mentioning him." Lena didn't know what possessed her to ask him when her grandfather never indulged in gossip. But she couldn't help herself. Renwick might be gruff, but he also caught her interest. She was only curious, she told herself. His concern for his sister suggested he might have a softer side even if he kept it hidden.

"I knew his father, of course. Not a friendly man. Quite serious and consumed with duty. From what little I know of the current duke, he's much like him."

Though tempted to share her nickname for Renwick, His Grumpiness, she refrained, uncertain whether her grandfather would find it amusing. Unfortunately, he didn't have much else to say about the man.

Would she see the duke this afternoon?

"Miss?" James, the footman who had seen her and her sisters through more than a few difficult times, held the carriage door, clearly perplexed as to why she hadn't moved.

No doubt Nancy, her maid, had the same puzzled expression.

With a sigh, Lena took his offered hand and descended to the pavement, followed by Nancy. The day was cool and overcast with no hint of the sun in sight. Tea and conversation would be a pleasant way to spend an hour. At least, that was her hope.

She liked Lady Bernice thus far, which was more than she could say for some of the young ladies she'd met since arriving in London. Many treated her as competition rather than a potential friend. Lena wanted to tell them the likelihood of her marrying was nil. Not with her gift. Therefore, she was no threat to their marriage prospects, though she certainly couldn't share any of that.

Lady Bernice seemed different—unique in a pleasant way. Her lack of artifice and love of books were endearing. The fascination she had with Oak Island made Lena curious if uncomfortable. If only Norah or Ella was joining her, Lena would feel more at ease.

As for His Grumpiness, Lena didn't care for the way he stared at her with suspicion in his dark eyes. Then again, he seemed to look at everyone that way, so perhaps she shouldn't take offense. Surely, the duke wouldn't join them for tea. He would have other, more important duties that took his time.

Reassured, Lena climbed the stairs to the three-story sandstone townhome with its tall, white pillars and black door. Why was it that the color of the door felt like some sort of dour warning, practically shouting, *enter at your own peril?*

She gave herself a mental shake at the ridiculous notion. And here she'd always thought Norah the dramatic sister.

Before James could lift the polished brass lion door knocker, the door swung open to reveal an impeccably dressed butler in a fine black suit. His hooked nose and thin lips made him look far from welcoming. Not so different from her first impression of Davies, her grandfather's butler. The imposing servant glanced at her card, then gestured for them to enter.

The house's entrance hall was more welcoming than she expected, with white marble, touches of pink and gold, and beautiful floral bouquets scenting the air.

In short order, she was shown upstairs to what she guessed was Lady Bernice's sitting room as it was smaller and more intimate than a drawing room. Soft shades of more pink tempered by accents of wood made it a restful space.

The butler announced her, and Lady Bernice rose from a settee placed before the cheerfully burning fire and hurried forward. "Miss Wright, I'm so pleased you could come."

Lena curtsied before drawing closer. "Thank you for inviting me, my lady."

"Please, have a seat." Lady Bernice gestured toward the settee and joined her. Her pale blue gown was simple yet elegant with narrow pleats and white ribbon stitched into the bodice. Tiny white embroidered flowers embellished the neckline. "Aunt Edith will be joining us shortly."

"How nice." Lena held back the urge to ask if her brother would as well.

"From what I understand, you've only been in London a few years. Is that right?" the lady asked after they'd settled on the rose-colored cushions.

"Yes. Three years now. Have you lived in England all your life?"

"I recently returned from a year in Switzerland where I attended finishing school. But otherwise, England has always been home."

"Switzerland? That must've been exciting." Lena had seen pictures of the Alps but couldn't quite imagine living near the sharp, snow-capped peaks.

"At times it was, though I missed home terribly. The air in Switzerland is so crisp and clear. Much different from London.

Better for the lungs, you know."

Her comment made Lena wonder if health issues were one of the reasons she'd chosen Switzerland.

The conversation continued, and soon the lady's aunt, Mrs. Easton, joined them. After visiting with them briefly, she settled in a chair near the window to do some needlework.

With a cautious look at her aunt, Lady Bernice leaned forward. "Forgive me for being curious, but would you share what it was like to live on Oak Island?"

The mention of the place Lena's family had called home for so long was bittersweet. While many of their years there had been wonderful, the loss of her mother and father shaded her memories with grief.

"It is a remote place. Rather wild and rugged with many trees and few people. We had a small cabin." She glanced around the richly appointed if cozy room. "Quite different from this, of course."

"It sounds romantic."

Lena smiled. "I wouldn't call it that. Life was both simpler and more difficult than in London. We spent a small portion of most winters in Montreal, so we weren't completely isolated. But Oak Island was lonely at times."

"Your mother passed away?"

"Yes, she died of smallpox eight years ago. Her death was a blow to us all, though my eldest sister did her best to take her place."

"My mother died giving birth to me, so I never knew her." The lady's expression dimmed, suggesting how deeply the loss had affected her. "It must be lovely to have sisters."

"It is. We are quite close." Lena held back from saying how much Norah and Ella meant to her. She didn't want Lady Bernice to feel worse than she already seemed to.

"I love my brother dearly, of course. I don't know what I'd do without Sterling."

That was one thing Lena admired about His Grumpiness—

his obvious love for Lady Bernice. His attractiveness couldn't be denied either. She just wished he didn't watch her as if expecting her to try to pick his pockets or the like.

"And your father?" Lady Bernice asked.

Lena hesitated, not wanting to share too much. After all, she didn't really know Lady Bernice. She seemed nice enough, but for all Lena knew, she might be prone to gossip. However, sharing what was commonly known couldn't hurt. "He was killed three and a half years ago when the shaft he was digging in collapsed."

"Oh, how terrible." Lady Bernice pressed a hand to her heart, her brown eyes filled with sympathy.

"It was. Simply awful." Lena closed her eyes briefly as a well of grief and guilt flooded her. "It took his partner and others a few days to recover his body. My sisters and I were devastated."

Not a day went by that Lena didn't think of her father and her role in his death. If only her gift had aided her that day. But those details were her secret to keep.

"I can't imagine." The lady's gaze settled on something in the distance, and her expression tightened. "I'm sorry to say I don't miss my father."

Mrs. Easton cleared her throat, sending a frown of disapproval in Lady Bernice's direction.

"I know I shouldn't speak ill of the dead," Lady Bernice whispered, though there was no doubt that her aunt could still hear her. "But he wasn't a nice person. Never happy."

"A bit like your brother then." Lena regretted the comment as soon as it left her lips.

"Sterling?" Lady Bernice appeared shocked by her remark. "Not at all. If it weren't for him, I don't know what I would've done. My father was impatient with my poor health when I was a child. I was nothing but a disappointment to him."

An image formed in Lena's mind of a young version of the duke protecting his sister from their father, his expression fierce. She didn't like the empathy that washed through her or having another reason to admire him.

Mrs. Easton cast another look of disapproval toward her niece, but Bernice lifted one shoulder in a partial shrug, suggesting she didn't care who knew how she felt or whether it was inappropriate to share the information.

In truth, Lena would rather Lady Bernice didn't share such personal details. Especially when she had no intention of doing the same. It would be best to change the subject.

"I would love to hear why you've become interested in Oak Island," Lena said. "How did you happen to learn about it?" The island had few inhabitants, and travelers rarely had a reason to visit.

Her and her sisters' ties to Oak Island were lessening with each day that passed. Six months ago, they had received a letter from Mr. Johnson, their father's long-time partner, stating he'd decided to sell the property. He'd explained that since their father's death, along with his own wife's several years earlier, he no longer had the heart to continue the search. Soon afterward, he'd sent their father's journals, which they'd left behind with the hope the detailed notes would aid his search.

Lena had looked through them once or twice but reading her father's handwriting brought grief. Perhaps in time, she'd be able to look through them more thoroughly.

Mr. Johnson had told them a company had bought the property with the intent of continuing to look for treasure. Though not unexpected, the idea of someone else digging where their father had for so long—perhaps even in the shaft he'd died in—was unsettling.

Lena was torn. She wanted someone to find the treasure to prove her father right, yet it was inconceivable to think of anyone else discovering it. Not after her father had looked so long and sacrificed so much in his attempts.

She and her sisters had often felt he placed the search above them. To be truthful, some days he had. But not always. Still, Lena had never needed protection from her father. Lady Bernice might be a duke's daughter, but that didn't mean her life was easier or better than anyone else's.

To Lena's surprise, Lady Bernice hesitated as if uncertain what she wanted to tell her. That made Lena even more curious.

"As I mentioned, I thoroughly enjoyed *Rambles among the Blue-noses*, though I wish the author would've shared more about the search on Oak Island."

Lena nodded but held her silence, waiting to see what else she might add.

"Upon my return home for the Christmas holiday, I was in the attic, sorting through the decorations, and found some letters in an old trunk." Lady Bernice leaned forward, the glitter in her eyes speaking of her excitement.

"Oh?" Lena didn't understand what that could have to do with Oak Island.

"The letters were written by a privateer who worked on Captain Kidd's ship on several voyages."

"Truly?" Lena's full attention was captured now. Many people, including her father, believed Captain Kidd had buried a sizeable treasure in a pit on the island. However, it was said to have been rigged with a series of tunnels that flooded the pit if not excavated properly. Only those who knew how to circumvent the flood tunnels could reach the treasure.

Numerous shafts had been dug on the island before her father's arrival. So many that the true location of the pit was no longer known. Most of the shafts her father dug had filled with seawater once they were deep enough to raise his hopes that he was nearing the treasure.

"A great aunt of ours died a spinster," Lady Bernice continued. "Little did the family know that was because her heart belonged to a privateer." She sighed, her expression making it clear how romantic she thought the story.

"The letters mention Oak Island?" Lena wanted her to get on with the story. If she'd discovered any details that revealed the exact location of the pit or specific instructions about how to excavate the treasure, that would be remarkable.

"Yes. They're a delight to read."

"What do they say?" Lena knew her tone was short, but she was beyond anxious to know what the lady had found.

"Well, nothing specific. Not yet anyway. After all, they're love letters. I have more of them to read. Just a few at Christmas, and I've started reading them again since my return a few weeks ago."

Lena released the breath she hadn't realized she'd been holding. For a moment, she'd thought Lady Bernice had stumbled upon the secret her father had looked so hard for—the location of the Money Pit.

"Bernie, you're not going on about those letters again, are you?" The deep, masculine tone had Lena rising to her feet as the Duke of Renwick entered the room.

Her body flushed at the sight of his tall, imposing form, especially when those cool brown eyes that seemed to see everything caught on her. What was it about this man that caused her to feel so unsettled?

"Good afternoon, Your Grace." She curtsied, willing away the uncomfortable feeling. He was only a man. Yet her heartbeat quickened along with her breath. If only she could determine the cause.

"GOOD AFTERNOON." STERLING dipped his head, still uncertain why he'd felt compelled to join Bernie and her guest. He told himself it was because he was protective of his sister.

But that wasn't the only reason.

Lena Wright intrigued him. He had the distinct impression she wasn't awed by his title, not that he cared if anyone was. Perhaps it was because she was the granddaughter of a duke or hadn't been raised in England where nobility seemed to carry more weight.

Miss Wright's lavender silk gown was simple but elegant, allowing her natural beauty and grace to shine. So many of the ladies in the *ton* used every possible weapon in their arsenal to make themselves stand out. Miss Wright didn't seem to be trying to do any of that.

He wondered why, when most women considered the need to marry well their singular purpose in life and used every arrow in their quiver to take aim at their quarry.

That didn't mean Sterling enjoyed being their target as he so often was.

"Are you regaling Miss Wright about your discoveries?" he asked. He gestured for her to sit, but he remained standing, undecided whether to stay.

"She asked what I had found," Bernie began, her cheeks coloring slightly at his teasing.

"Do not feel you have to feign interest," he told their guest with an indulgent smile at Bernie.

"I am truly curious, otherwise I wouldn't have asked." The chilly look Miss Wright gave him suggested she didn't appreciate his remark.

Then she looked at Bernie with concern as if worried whether her feelings had been hurt. The realization had him further reconsidering his opinion of Lena Wright.

He tended to assume that anyone who spent time with his somewhat awkward sister had an ulterior motive. He'd experienced it far too often in the past, from mothers who'd wanted their daughters to befriend Bernie when she was younger to ladies attempting to catch his notice in the past few years. Luckily, he'd become adept at seeing through their ruses.

Miss Wright looked back at him, then lifted a brow as if to suggest he should reconsider before further teasing Bernie.

Bernie smiled, seemingly unaware of the silent communication he and Miss Wright were having. "I do believe some of the letters were written to hide the true meaning of what was being said."

"They're in code?" Miss Wright asked with astonishment.

"Not exactly." Bernie tapped a finger on her chin, her eyes narrowing. "However, I can't help but think a hidden message is included in some of the passages."

"How interesting. Are you familiar with the story of Captain Kidd possibly burying treasure on the island prior to his death?" Miss Wright posed the question in a gentle tone.

"Only what I learned during my visit to the museum when I viewed your father's exhibit. I hope to find a book on the topic to explain more but have yet to locate one."

"I'd be happy to share some of what my father thought. Though of course, there are other theories as to who might have buried treasure on the island."

Bernie bit her lip then sent her brother a worried look, suggesting she didn't think he'd like what she was about to say. That look was practically a guarantee he wouldn't. He held back the urge to shake his head to keep her from saying more. He wouldn't always be there to guide her, and she needed to become more adept at sensing what she should and shouldn't say to others.

"Such as treasure from the Knights Templar?" Bernie asked.

He nearly groaned. How could she speak of that theory when it seemed so unlikely?

Lena smiled, causing Sterling to catch his breath. It lit her blue eyes and made her look even more beautiful. "Yes. Among others."

Bernie's eyes rounded with excitement. "Others?"

Sterling decided they had forgotten his presence for the moment. Rather bemused, he sank into the chair he had stood behind, interested in whatever Miss Wright shared.

"One story suggests the French hid gold there. Another insists it was the Spanish."

"I had no idea there were so many." Bernie leaned forward, her gaze fixed on Miss Wright.

Sterling smothered a smile. Her enthusiasm knew no bounds

when it came to the supposed treasure on Oak Island. Would she tell their guest that they had begun a search of their own?

"What did your father believe?" Bernie asked.

A shadow passed over Miss Wright's face, a vivid reminder that he had died searching for the treasure. It had only been a few years ago, and she and her sisters surely still grieved his loss. Especially when it was clear she'd loved him.

The thought had Sterling shifting in his chair. Love was not a word he associated with his own father. Duty. Respect, if begrudging. But not love. Such emotions made one weak, or so their father often told them. And Renwicks were never weak.

Sterling wondered if their father had felt any sort of tenderness toward them. He had certainly never shown it.

"My father," Miss Wright finally began, "thought Captain Kidd was the most likely one to have buried treasure there." She told them how the privateer had taken a ship loaded with riches only to be accused of piracy. He'd hidden the treasure in case he needed to use it to barter his freedom.

"That didn't work well," Sterling remarked.

Those blue eyes shifted to his in surprise as if she had forgotten he was sitting nearby. He couldn't remember the last time that had happened.

"No, it didn't," Miss Wright agreed. "He was found guilty and hanged soon after. But what he said before his death has people dreaming about finding riches to this day. He insisted there was another, larger treasure. If the authorities would allow him, he would show them where he'd hidden it."

"And?" Bernie asked.

"They chose not to believe him. However, my father said that if one considered the various amounts Kidd took while acting as a privateer, which is documented, a massive amount remains unaccounted for."

"Fascinating." Bernie shared a look with Sterling, making him wonder at her thoughts. Did the information make her even more hopeful there was treasure to be found on the island?

"There is also the story of strange lights said to appear on the island." Miss Wright smiled, seeming to dare them to question the story.

"Oh, yes. That is supposedly what drew the original searcher to the island, wasn't it?" Bernie asked.

Miss Wright nodded. "In 1795, a young man of sixteen years, who lived on a nearby island with his parents, swore he saw lights on Oak Island one night. He convinced two friends to join him to row across to the island to see what caused them. They found a strange depression in the ground and carvings on a nearby tree. Some accounts state they also discovered a block and tackle hanging on one of its branches. Would that have been enough to convince you to dig?"

Bernie considered the question as if she thought Miss Wright expected her to follow through on her answer. "I would certainly be curious. Curious enough to investigate."

Suddenly, Miss Wright's focus shifted to Sterling, causing his pulse to leap. "What of you, Your Grace? Would you have dug?"

To Sterling's surprise, he found himself nodding. "What young lad doesn't dream of finding buried treasure?"

"Truly, Sterling?" Bernie asked, obviously surprised.

"Of course." Not that he would've been allowed to pursue such a nonsensical dream. "Those few clues would be enough to make one wonder."

"My father would've agreed." Miss Wright's smile faded. "Though there were days when he swore he wouldn't dig come the spring, he always did."

"From the details in the museum exhibit, he only found a few items," Bernie said.

"Enough to convince him something happened on the island. Wooden timbers aren't found ninety feet below ground unless someone put them there."

"And no one would put them so deep without a reason," Sterling added.

"Exactly. But the work is difficult and dangerous."

"As is most treasure hunting." Sterling had heard enough lectures at the Royal Geological Society meetings to know that.

"Not all digs include traps to prevent searchers from finding what they seek."

"That certainly adds another layer of difficulty." Sterling had considered the risks before buying the land, and he had set a limit to how much he was willing to spend. After all, the treasure hunt was more of a lark to please Bernie than an investment. She'd had few pleasures in her life and asked for nothing. It seemed the least he could do.

He hadn't announced that he was the one who owned the newly formed Oak Island Company. Not even his fellow members of the Society knew. Soon, perhaps.

First, he wanted the dig to be well underway.

The man he'd hired to manage the search, Walter Clarke, was a seasoned treasure hunter with several successful missions to his credit. Whether he'd manage to find anything when David Wright hadn't remained to be seen. However, Sterling was convinced that new technology would yield results of some sort. He also had more funds at his disposal than Wright had.

How would the lovely Miss Wright react when she learned the news? Would she sever her budding friendship with Bernie?

"Could I see the letters?" Miss Wright asked.

"Of course." Bernie popped up as if on a spring. "I'll return with them directly."

Sterling watched her hurry from the room. "Forgive my sister's enthusiasm. You are the first person other than me to express interest in the topic."

He watched Miss Wright's gaze shift toward where Aunt Edith had sat, but she had left soon after he arrived. "My aunt doesn't approve of Bernie's interest in Oak Island. She doesn't think it's ladylike."

He rose and joined Miss Wright on the settee, noting the slight widening of her eyes at his nearness. But he didn't want Bernie to hear when he made it clear that neither he nor his sister were to be toyed with. "Are you truly interested in seeing the letters, or was that a ploy to have a moment alone with me?"

Her mouth gaped at his question, her shock clear. "You cannot be serious." She jerked to her feet, so he stood as well. "Why on earth would I want to be alone with you?"

He took a step closer, though her reaction seemed to confirm she wasn't trying to catch his attention. Or if she was, she wasn't doing a very good job of it. There had been no blatant flattery. No fluttering of lashes or attempt at shyness.

In place of any of that was outrage. The emotion lit her eyes and tinted her cheeks a lovely pink. Her chest heaved with pent-up anger. All of that was incredibly appealing.

"Thus far," he began, watching Miss Wright intently, "the ladies who profess to like Bernie have one thing on their mind."

"Marrying a duke?" Miss Wright's chin lifted. "You have no cause to believe that of me."

"Perhaps not. But past experiences suggest that is the reason you're here." He drew closer still, noting the quickening of his own senses at their proximity with surprise. He dismissed the reaction. Surely it was only a result of the game he played.

"I can assure you that is not *my* purpose." She took a step nearer and glared at him with defiance shining in her eyes.

Damn if he didn't find that incredibly appealing. He dropped his gaze to her mouth, only to realize his mistake. Her rosy, full lips begged to be kissed. Desire sprang forth, much like a fountain gurgling to life.

Unable to resist, he leaned close to test them both. The gurgle became a gusher, surprising him with its strength.

"Here they are," Bernie declared from the doorway.

Sterling stepped back and blew out a breath, whether in relief or disappointment, he couldn't say. But one thing he did know— he intended to kiss Miss Wright if given the chance. She was too tempting to resist.

Chapter Three

LENA SCOWLED AS she marched into Norah's drawing room the following morning. The close encounter with His Grumpiness had made her prone to muttering to herself about the impossible man ever since.

What had he been thinking? Had he been taunting her? Pushing to see what she'd do? Was he attempting to convince her to abandon her acquaintance with Lady Bernice?

"What has you in such a stir?" Norah asked from where she sat at her desk.

Sunlight streamed in from the nearby window, creating a warm golden glow in the room. Norah had added a few feminine touches to the townhouse where she and Vanbridge lived, subtle accents that made it a welcoming, restful place. It was one more reason the two were perfect for one another, each complementing the other, much like Ella and Marbury. Norah brought Vanbridge out of his lair on occasion, and he gave her a reason to enjoy the quiet of home.

"His Grumpiness." Lena knew she'd feel better as soon as she could express her upset. The one disadvantage to living with her grandfather was that she couldn't talk to him about things like this. Only one of her sisters would do.

Since Norah already knew part of the story, Lena had chosen her to share her woes.

"Renwick? Do tell." Norah set aside her pen and paper and stood, gesturing toward the settee, her eyes glittering with interest.

Lena joined her. "Where's your handsome husband this morning?"

"In his study. A new stone carving arrived that he's anxious to examine."

"How exciting." Lena admired her brother-in-law's interest in carvings and his ability to decipher them. But she knew he put Norah ahead of both his interest in history and his museum. That was something she admired even more.

"Yes, it is." Norah smiled with affection. "I can't wait to hear what he discovers. Now tell me what happened with Renwick."

"I had tea with his sister yesterday."

"And His Grace was there?"

"For part of it."

Norah lifted a brow, clearly eager to hear the part that had upset her.

"First of all, Lady Bernice found some old letters from a privateer who visited Oak Island."

"How did she come upon those?"

"It seems the man was romantically involved with her great-aunt and wrote to her on several occasions. Lady Bernice found them in an old trunk in the attic."

"Interesting. What are the chances of that?"

"I thought the same."

"What do the letters say?" Norah asked.

"Nothing specific, according to Lady Bernice, though I intend to read them closely."

"You have them?"

"Yes."

Norah's eyes widened with excitement. "Tell me you brought them."

"Well, no." Lena blinked, realizing her error. "I didn't think to." That showed just how upset she was about the moment with

Renwick.

Norah scowled. "I assume you will rectify that as quickly as possible."

"Certainly. But back to the issue I came to discuss."

"Right. His Grumpiness." Norah stilled. "You weren't alone with him, were you?" She looked appalled at the thought, which was ironic when Lena knew for a fact that Norah had been alone with Vanbridge numerous times prior to their betrothal.

"Lady Bernice and their aunt were there. But both stepped out of the room for a moment. During which Renwick practically accused me of befriending his sister to get close to him."

"The nerve." Her sister's indignation on her behalf was quite satisfying.

"Can you believe it? The arrogance of the man." Fresh outrage filled Lena as the memory played through her mind again.

For one breathless moment, she'd thought he intended to kiss her. That moment had filled her with longing, much to her dismay.

Was her outrage because he hadn't kissed her? Surely not.

She couldn't bring herself to share the full details with Norah. Not when her sister might realize just how affected she'd been. He'd stood so close that she could see the various shades of brown in his wonderful eyes.

Then there was his cologne, an appealing scent that brought to mind walking in the forest on a rainy day. The thought of it was enough to make her knees weak.

When his gaze had dropped to her lips, it had taken all her will to avoid licking them in preparation for a kiss. How ridiculous was that? She wasn't even sure if she liked Renwick.

Not that she would be opposed to kissing him.

She'd tried kissing several times and understood the appeal but hadn't met anyone who tempted her to repeat the experience. The best part about a kiss was the moment just before. The lovely breathless feeling, the dip in her stomach followed closely by flutters. When one's mind was filled with possibilities.

In all honesty, she'd felt all of that and more with Renwick. How unfortunate.

She'd found the actual kisses themselves to be less enjoyable, with scrunched noses, awkward positions, and lips either too wet or too dry. Perhaps she was doing something wrong, or maybe it had been her partners. Despite that, kissing might be worth additional experimentation.

But not with His Grumpiness.

"Do you intend to visit Lady Bernice again?" Norah asked.

"I suppose I have no choice since I'll have to return the letters. It would be rude to send them with a servant."

"Agreed." Norah studied her a moment. "Are you sure the letters don't say anything interesting about a treasure on Oak Island?"

"Not at first glance. Though Lady Bernice suggested there might be some sort of hidden message in them. She found another book about Oak Island's history and is scouring that for information." Lena pondered the matter further. "Do you know that Renwick calls her Bernie? I think it rather sweet."

The puzzled look that came over Norah's face reminded Lena that she'd veered off the topic, but she couldn't help herself.

"He seems to hold her in high regard," Norah said.

"Apparently, their father was not an especially pleasant person. Lady Bernice said her brother often defended her against him."

"That's terrible." Norah looked aghast.

"Indeed." Lena scowled. "I didn't intend to be friends with her, but after learning that, how could I not? My sympathies are now engaged." Lena preferred to keep others at arm's length. It was too difficult to have close friendships without revealing her intuition.

"What of your affections?" Norah asked. "She seems a pleasant person."

"I do like her. She's several years younger than me, of course. I suppose it's a bit of a novelty to feel like an older sister for a change."

Norah laughed. "I never thought you might feel that way. You're wise for your years and often give me advice."

Lena shook her head. "That doesn't exactly sound like a compliment."

"It is. Absolutely." Norah reached to touch her hand. "I am blessed to be your sister."

"Despite my oddity?" Lena pressed a finger to her lips, hardly able to believe the question had escaped. She hadn't meant to allow it out.

"Your intuition is not an oddity. It's a gift. Think of all the good you've done."

"Think of all the good I haven't." Lena swallowed against the sudden lump in her throat. That was what bothered her the most—the times she hadn't understood the feeling or worse, ignored it. The worst had been the day their father died. "If only—"

"Allow me to stop you right there." Norah squeezed Lena's arm as if to emphasize her point. "You helped to find him much earlier than we would've otherwise."

"But it didn't save him." Her breath caught, emotion choking her. "I didn't save him."

"Nor did I." Norah's gaze fell. "If I hadn't argued with him that morning..."

"Norah." Lena waited until her sister met her eyes. "You are not to blame. Ella and I have told you that several times."

"Nor are you. Yet it seems we both need to hear that regularly." Norah sniffed, and Lena leaned forward to hug her, holding tight for a long moment.

"Just when I think I've overcome the concern, it creeps back," Lena confessed in a whisper.

"I know. I feel much the same." Norah drew back to hold her gaze. "I wish we had that day to live over again."

"Only if we knew then what we know now."

Norah frowned. "Though that would make it terrible,

wouldn't it?"

"And I'm not sure it would've changed the outcome. If only I could remember that."

Norah drew a deep breath. "Do you really find Renwick upsetting?"

"Unsettling might be a better word." She dismissed the concern with a wave of her hand. "Pay me no mind. I also find Lady Bernice's interest in Oak Island unsettling. She finds the whole thing romantic."

"Hmm. If she lived it for a few years, she might not." Norah seemed to consider the issue further. "I need only to think of Simon to understand the curiosity that drives her. Perhaps having a purpose is part of its appeal for her. So few ladies have one."

"I suppose I should mention this to Ella," Lena said.

"That might be best in case something comes of it." Norah bit her lower lip. "Do be careful though."

"How do you mean?"

"She's having a few contractions. The doctor has suggested she take care and get plenty of rest."

Lena's heart thumped painfully. "Is there more? Are you telling me everything?"

"Of course, I am. I called on her yesterday, and she mentioned that Marbury is hovering over her to make certain she doesn't overdo things. It's driving her mad."

Lena prodded her thoughts as she considered the news but felt nothing out of the ordinary. Unfortunately, that didn't mean there wasn't anything to worry about. "Shall I mention Lady Bernice's interest in passing? Without all the details."

"Exactly." Norah nodded. "Besides, what could come of Lady Bernice's research? I'm sure she'll only pursue it until something more interesting comes along."

Lena nodded but worried that it wouldn't be so simple.

STERLING FINISHED READING the latest letter from Walter Clarke and smiled, pleased with the man's progress. He certainly seemed to know what he was about. He was already settled on Oak Island and was conducting a thorough survey of the area. His letter stated that more shafts had been dug than expected by previous searchers, including David Wright.

Clarke had included a map of what he'd found thus far, proposed three suggested areas of focus, and prioritized them. The first was the shaft nearest a tree carving, though Clarke wasn't convinced the indecipherable markings had anything to do with the location of the buried treasure.

Sterling thought it interesting that Miss Wright had said a block and tackle had been found hanging from the tree. What sort of pirate would bother to bury a treasure and leave such an obvious sign behind for others to find? He jotted a note to remind him to mention the block and tackle to Clarke. Those sorts of details might change the priority of the shafts the man was going to search.

Though Sterling had been tempted to ask Miss Wright how many shafts her father had dug, he'd held back. He wanted Clarke to form his own opinion after having a chance to thoroughly examine the area.

Sterling wasn't ready to disclose the treasure hunt. He rather liked sharing the secret with Bernie. Once the information became public, he would face numerous questions and comments—and criticism—from fellow Society members.

He wondered how Miss Wright would take the news. Not well, if he were to guess. Perhaps she'd be willing to share insights once the surprise wore off. He'd heard rumors of her father's journals that detailed his search. Would she be willing to share them? While the idea was intriguing, he doubted she would.

A knock sounded on his study door, interrupting his musings. "Enter."

Bernie peeked her head around the door. "Are you busy?"

"Not at all. Join me." He detested how timid Bernie could be at times. That was his father's fault for always barking at her. "What are you doing today?"

"Aunt Edith and I are going to a museum later."

"Oh? Which one?"

"Miss Wright recommended one called the Museum of Olden Things. Apparently, the owner is a friend of her brother-in-law."

"Vanbridge or Marbury?" He knew both as they were members of the Royal Geological Society.

"Vanbridge. I suppose it makes sense to ask since the marquess also owns a museum." Bernie settled into the chair in front of his desk. "I hope I have the chance to meet Miss Wright's other sister. Aunt Edith says she's heard nothing but good things about the Countess of Marbury."

"I have no doubt you will. It seems as if you and Miss Wright are well on your way to becoming friends."

"We shall see." Bernie stared in the distance, her brow puckered.

"Why do you say that?"

She shifted her gaze to meet his and heaved a sigh. "Aunt Edith worries she might be much like the others."

He waited, not following her thought.

"More interested in you than me."

"Bernie." He detested that she had to think twice about meeting new people and whether they were truly becoming friends. Unfortunately, it had happened more than once. "I'm certain you don't have anything to worry about. In fact, I almost think Miss Wright doesn't care for me."

That got her attention. She stiffened in her chair with outrage. "What? I don't believe that for a moment."

Sterling had to smile at her upset on his behalf. He might be overly protective of her, but she was with him, too. "She looks at me with something less than admiration." Though there had been that moment when Bernie had stepped out of the room. Had she felt the same spark he had?

The problem was that he wanted to explore the feeling. He'd had his share of women and knew such chemistry didn't come along often. But dallying with innocents was not something he did. Ever. And he had no doubt Lena Wright was innocent. Nor did he want to become involved with a friend of Bernie's. That would end the friendship growing between them. Bernie didn't have enough friends for him to permit such a result.

"At any rate, I am certain you'll hear from her soon about her thoughts on the letters."

"I had hoped to by now. The delay makes me wonder if she, too, has sensed an underlying conversation in them."

Sterling had read the letters. While he agreed a few sentences were oddly worded, he wouldn't go so far as to say they said anything more than what was written. There were certainly no specifics about where to find the treasure on Oak Island. But he was no expert in love letters or hidden messages, so kept his opinion to himself.

If Bernie wanted to believe they did, he would let her. He almost hoped she was right, and she discovered a potential clue.

"Miss Wright seems intelligent and kind," Bernie continued. "Though I do hope she doesn't truly have an aversion to you."

"Isn't that preferable to liking me too much?" he asked in a teasing tone.

Bernie shook her head. "You are incorrigible. The world does not revolve around you."

"No, it does not."

Another knock sounded on the door.

"Enter," Sterling said.

Foster entered and paused in the doorway. "A message has arrived for Lady Bernice, Your Grace."

"Oh?" Bernie jumped to her feet and hurried toward the butler, leaving Sterling shaking his head.

"I would have happily delivered the message to you, Lady Bernice," the butler stated, a not-so-subtle reminder that decorum was important at all times.

"I'm sorry, Foster. It's just that I am anxious to see who sent it." Bernie took the envelope and quickly opened it. "It's from Miss Wright." Her beaming smile remained as she read the message. She swung her gaze to Sterling. "I'm invited to tea tomorrow afternoon. Aunt Edith is invited, too. Isn't that delightful?"

Sterling nodded. He only wished he was going as well. He wanted to hear what Lena Wright had to say about the letters. Then again, he just wanted to see her, regardless of the reason. He wanted a kiss. Surely Bernie's friendship with her couldn't be ruined over just one.

Chapter Four

"WHAT DO YOU think?" Lena asked as she studied her sisters, both of whom had just finished reading the letters that Lady Bernice had found. Lena had only showed them the ones she thought might hold a clue about the location of the treasure on Oak Island.

The trio sat in the drawing room at Rothwood House as they had so many afternoons over the past three years since their arrival in London. Lena liked to think she was becoming better adjusted to her sisters no longer living there. She should be after this long. Ella had married two years ago and Norah four months later. That made times like this more precious since they weren't a regular occurrence.

If only the topic of their conversation was a more lighthearted one.

Ella, who glowed with good health despite the concerning subject, cast a worried glance at Norah as if wondering about her reaction before she shared her own. No doubt that was because Norah had spent so much time and effort protecting their father's work over the past year. "I'm not certain," Ella began. "It's difficult to say definitively that they are written in any sort of code."

"I would have to agree." Norah stared at the letter she held. "Some of the passages are oddly worded, which makes one wonder. Like here, where he says, 'I miss you so deeply that I feel as if I'm in a shaft where no light can be seen.'" She shook her head. "Is it a poor analogy or a reference to digging on the island?"

"That's not the only one." Ella ran a finger over the sheet she held. "'Your love is a sign that few will understand.' What is that supposed to mean?"

Lena sighed. She'd hoped her sisters would see something she hadn't. Something that might point her in the right direction and allow her to move forward. The idea of finding a clue in the carefully written phrases that would lead to a development as to the location of the treasure was more appealing than she could've guessed.

Perhaps she was more like her father than she'd realized—a treasure hunter at heart who looked for evidence in the smallest details that might reveal a hidden chest of gold.

How silly of her. Especially when nothing but memories tied them to Oak Island now. Even if she found anything meaningful, what would she do with it? She and her sisters had no idea who was involved in the company that had purchased the plot of land that her father and Mr. Johnson had owned and explored for decades.

But she couldn't let it go.

"Would you at least agree that further study of the letters is warranted?" Lena asked. Then again, she had already decided she would proceed, regardless of what her sisters said.

"Certainly." Ella nodded.

Relief filled Lena. She supposed she wanted justification to pursue this. Protecting their father's memory was just as important to her as it was to her sisters. If more clues existed that proved David Wright had been close to finding the treasure before his death, Lena wanted to find them. It seemed the least she could do since she hadn't been able to save him the day he'd died.

Ella skimmed the letter again. "The part where Ebenezer

Jenkins wrote, 'You will find my love near the marked tree. The same mark I mentioned before.' Is it referenced in the other letters?"

"Only once, but it's just as vague," Lena said. "Still, it's so odd that he refers to a marked tree when Father was so enamored with the clue that it started him on the path to Oak Island."

"Enamored is a good word." Norah offered a rueful smile. "The streaks on that tree might have been a result of anything. Bless Father and his optimism, but his insistence that they'd been carved by whoever dug the Money Pit was questionable at best."

"I think those were carvings," Lena argued, despite being uncertain when they'd lived on the island. "We all saw them. None of the other trees looked like that one."

"True." Ella had always been the diplomat of the family. She never discredited anyone's opinion but still managed to bring reason and logic into the discussion. At times, that had been a necessity to counter their father's hopefulness, especially after their mother had died. "While not proof, they could be a clue connected to the carvings found elsewhere on the island."

Norah scowled. "But none of the carvings on the island matched. Nor do we know what any of the carvings mean."

Lena heaved a sigh, wishing she had a valid argument. "The letters are still intriguing."

"Very much so," Ella agreed. "I, for one, would agree that it's worth taking the time to note the oddly worded passages and compare them to see if there's a pattern."

"Oh!" Norah straightened, her eyes widening with excitement. "Excellent idea. Do you want me to ask Simon to look at them?"

"Would you mind if I made an attempt first?" Lena asked. She couldn't explain why she felt compelled to try when she was no expert. Whether the urge came from a knowing feeling or stubbornness, she didn't know.

"Of course not." Norah studied her. "Did Lady Bernice say something more? Anything that is making you wonder if she's discovered a clue?"

"I confess that the same question crossed my mind," Ella said, her head tilted to the side as she watched Lena.

Suddenly the image of Sterling filled her mind. His interest in his sister's opinion of the letters had struck her as curious. He seemed like the last person to indulge in a fantasy such as Oak Island, regardless of how much he cared for his sister.

"Renwick seems to take Lady Bernice's opinions to heart," Lena said at last. "I suppose that lends extra weight to them."

"What are your thoughts on the duke?" Ella asked. "He is a rather stern man, don't you think?"

"Except for when he looks at his sister," Norah added. "The tenderness he showed for Lady Bernice at the garden party was endearing." Her gaze took in both her sisters. "The duke is certainly handsome, wouldn't you agree?"

Ella blinked as if surprised by the question. "I suppose so."

Norah shook her head and shifted her attention back to Lena. "Forgive our sister. She is so enamored with her husband that I don't think she notices other men."

"Why would I when I already married the best of them all?" Ella grinned.

Norah gave her a mock glare. "It's clear that I did. However, we shall argue the point at another time. For now, allow us to agree Renwick is handsome."

Lena's lips twisted as she considered the statement. "His Grumpiness might be handsome, but his manners leave something to be desired."

"His Grumpiness?" Ella erupted into laughter. "Wait until I share that with Leo."

"You can't tell me you don't agree." Lena sniffed. "He doesn't go out of his way to be kind to anyone other than Lady Bernice."

"I don't know him well, but from what I've seen, I wouldn't argue," Ella said.

"To be fair, I'm not certain it's his fault." Lena had only to remember the conversation about the late duke. "Their father was a harsh man, even to his children, from what Lady Bernice said. He was very impatient with her illnesses when she was a child."

"A child?" Ella's mouth gaped in shock. "Who could hold a child responsible for illness?"

"The late duke, apparently. Is it any wonder that Renwick is indulgent toward his sister?" Lena rather wished he wasn't. Then it would be easier to dismiss him from her thoughts.

"That's terrible." Ella still seemed to be absorbing what Lena had shared. "I shall take care to be especially nice to Lady Bernice when I meet her."

"Do you think there could be more to the letters?" Norah asked with one brow lifted as she looked at Lena. "Something she's not telling you?"

Lena considered the question. "Perhaps. She does seem convinced that they say something, but I have yet to see it."

"What if she's holding some back?" Norah glanced between them.

Ella nodded slowly. "That would make sense."

"It's certainly worth further investigation," Norah suggested.

Lena glanced at the letters stacked on the table at her elbow. "If she hasn't already given me the entire collection, what could I possibly say that would convince her to do so?"

"Not so much what you say," Ella suggested. "But what you do."

Lena frowned at her sister. "I don't understand."

"Surely befriending Lady Bernice and her brother wouldn't be so difficult." Norah lifted one shoulder in a half-shrug.

"Exactly." Ella gave a single nod.

"You mean deceive them?" Lena was shocked at the suggestion.

"It's not a deception since you like Lady Bernice," Norah countered. "I would guess that she's in need of a friend."

"Do be careful though," Ella warned. "Her brother might see through any attempts at artifice. Be your normal friendly self and see what happens. If she has been holding anything back, she might eventually be inclined to share it with you once she comes to know you better."

"True." Norah's pleased smile suggested she thought it was the perfect plan. "There's no rush to discover the full truth."

"Perhaps you'll sense something as you continue to read the letters." Ella raised a brow as she watched Lena, obviously wondering how she felt about the idea.

"Perhaps." That was as much as Lena wanted to say.

Her thoughts held on Renwick. Putting herself in close proximity to him seemed a terrible idea. Even the thought of doing so caused her heart to speed. For some reason, she didn't think it had anything to do with treasure or Oak Island.

No. It had to do with the man himself, along with her unfortunate reaction to him.

But the expectant expressions on her sisters' faces left her little choice. "I will see what I can do."

⇒⇒⇒◈⇐⇐⇐

TWO DAYS LATER, Sterling settled into his chair at the breakfast table after an early morning ride. He reached for the cup of coffee Foster had just poured with one hand and *The Times* with the other.

His morning routine rarely varied as he had found soon after his father died that taking time for himself before his day began in earnest had many positive effects.

He prepared to take his first sip as he scanned the headlines, only to abruptly set the coffee down as he stared at the newssheet in shock.

Famous treasure hunter launches a new quest, the headline declared. An uncomfortable feeling lodged in the pit of his stomach. It came as no surprise to see Walter Clarke's name in the first paragraph of the story that followed the headline.

Walter Clarke announced he is now digging for treasure on Oak

Island in Nova Scotia and has already made significant progress.

"While previous treasure hunters made one failed attempt after another," the legendary treasure hunter declared, "I intend to bring new insights and modern methods to the mystery of where the Money Pit is and what is buried in it. The Duke of Renwick formed Oak Island Company and has chosen me to apply my knowledge and skills to the project."

The story went on to explain the history of the treasure hunt on Oak Island. The reporter briefly mentioned David Wright and his partner and the decades of work they had performed with few results. That alone was enough to cause Sterling to groan. While the reporter was respectful of their efforts, another quote from Clarke seemed to dismiss them.

"Significant damage has already been done to the original clues, making this a difficult endeavor. But I have no doubt that with my expertise and the ability to bring new methods to the site, we will soon see success where others did not."

Sterling tossed aside the paper in disgust. He'd requested Clarke not to speak publicly about the project without Sterling's consent before the man had left for Oak Island. Obviously, Sterling should've put that in writing.

"Is something amiss, Your Grace?" Foster asked as he took a second look at the coffee he'd just poured.

"Only with the morning headline," Sterling replied. He looked up at the servant. "Can you please advise me if Lady Bernice is awake?"

"Of course, Your Grace." Foster stepped out of the room.

"Damn," Sterling muttered. Clarke was going to ruin everything. While Sterling had known he wouldn't be able to keep the dig a secret for long, he'd wanted to announce it on his own terms and without fanfare. This was a treasure hunt after all, and there was no guarantee of success.

There was also his sister's new friendship with Lena Wright to consider. The last thing he needed was Rothwood, Marbury, and Vanbridge to be displeased with him. He had wanted the news to come from him, not a reporter, and certainly not from

Clarke. However, the damage had been done.

He could only move forward and see if he could smooth any ruffled feathers. Yet he knew it wouldn't be a simple task to advise Lena Wright of the situation. He had the distinct impression she would suspect the worst. And she had every right to. He had deceived her and drawn Bernie along with him into the mess.

First, he'd speak with Bernie to warn her of this complication.

LENA LOOKED UP from the harp she'd been playing that morning to see her grandfather standing in the doorway. It took only one look at his face to determine he hadn't simply come to listen as he so often did.

His furrowed brow suggested something else was on his mind. And it wasn't good news.

She plucked the last chord and then held her hands against the strings to silence the instrument. "Good morning, Grandfather." She rose, drawing a deep breath to ease the sudden knot in her stomach.

"Lena." He glanced down, bringing her attention to the paper he held. "There's something you should know."

"What is it?" She braced herself. As long as nothing had happened to her sisters or the men they loved, she knew she could endure it. Since he stared at the paper he held, he must've learned the bad news within its pages. Therefore, she assumed their family was safe. What could the newssheet have said that so upset her grandfather?

The answer came in a rush—it had to do with her father.

"As we already knew," he began, "the property your father owned on Oak Island has been sold."

She nodded. "To Oak Island Company." While Mr. Johnson had written to tell them he intended to sell it, their grandfather was the one who'd uncovered further details of the sale.

"Yes. They've started digging. Walter Clarke is leading the search."

The name was familiar. "He's been successful elsewhere, hasn't he?" That alone made her stomach tighten further. As odd as it was, she worried that someone would come along and immediately locate what her father had searched for her entire life. That would make him look like a fool and be difficult for her and her sisters to endure. They'd tried so hard to make certain he and his work weren't forgotten. Could one article erase all that?

"Yes." Her grandfather moved farther into the room until he stood before her.

She didn't want to hear more. Not when what he'd said was bad enough. But ignoring it wouldn't make it go away. "There's more," she suggested, though she already knew.

"Renwick is funding the search." His bushy brows furrowed, stating just how displeased he was.

Shock had Lena taking a step back, trying to catch her balance as she processed what he'd said. "I don't understand."

As often as the topic of Oak Island had arisen, why wouldn't Renwick have told her the truth? Why encourage his sister to ask Lena questions about life on the island? Had it all been some sort of ruse? If so, to what purpose?

"He owns the majority of shares of Oak Island Company."

She shook her head. That hadn't been her question. How could she explain to her grandfather that she felt betrayed by Lady Bernice and her brother? Clearly, their attempt at friendship had been a farce. A scheme.

To what end? They couldn't think she'd tell them any deep secrets, even if she kept any. She hardly knew them.

And what of that moment in the drawing room when Renwick had stepped so close and made her think of a kiss? Had that only been an attempt to seduce her into trusting him?

The notion seemed farfetched. Yet what else could she believe?

Anger took over her shock. She didn't know what his purpose

was, but she intended to find out.

"What exactly does it say?" she asked.

Her grandfather reluctantly held out the newssheet. "Supposedly, progress is already being made."

Lena scoffed. She was the daughter of a treasure hunter, not a naïve young lady. Progress could mean anything from a new shaft being dug to an ox shoe found in the ground.

Treasure hunters tended to put an encouraging twist to any discovery, regardless of the size or importance, with the hope more people would believe and support their quest. Her father had been guilty of that on numerous occasions.

It was as if the more people who believed, the more it allowed the searcher to move forward, despite the cost financially and emotionally.

She took the offered paper and read the story, her anger building.

"Just because it's in print doesn't make it true," her grandfather said, his quiet tone reassuring.

Lena appreciated that he seemed to understand how upsetting the news was. "Do you know much about Walter Clarke?"

"He's spoken at the Royal Geological Society on occasion. He can be charismatic at times, though I would tend to think his ego outweighs his actual accomplishments."

Lena managed a smile and leaned into the one-armed hug he offered. "We shall soon discover if this is his ego talking. Oak Island tends to guard its secrets as closely as the Crown Jewels."

Grandfather held her gaze. "He will certainly gain attention for this. I am surprised Renwick didn't mention it when I saw him at the Royal Geological Society meeting last week."

Lena took some comfort in knowing she wasn't the only one he hadn't told. Then again, he surely knew their grandfather would tell Lena and her sisters.

"I, too, am disappointed that his sister didn't mention it when we had tea the other day." She didn't want to mention that Renwick had been there as well.

"Perhaps she doesn't know."

Lena considered that for a moment before quickly dismissing it. "I think she does. In fact, I think the duke might've decided to start the search with her in mind. The two seem quite close."

"Oh? I suppose they were united against their father. The late duke was a difficult person."

"Lady Bernice mentioned that." While Lena had sympathy for the lady, that didn't mean she appreciated being used. She glanced at the newssheet. "I suppose my sisters now know about this as well."

"I would guess that to be the case. I believe both Marbury and Vanbridge read the paper each morning."

Lena held his gaze. "Do you think they're coming here, or should we go to them?"

Her grandfather smiled and hugged her tighter. "I have to believe they're already on their way here."

She took his arm. "Then perhaps we should ask Davies to prepare tea." Once again, she couldn't imagine life without her sisters. Lena might not be sure what to do or how to approach the situation, but she had no doubt her sisters would have a few suggestions.

Chapter Five

L ENA'S SISTERS AND their husbands arrived soon after her grandfather had shared the news with Lena, much to her relief.

Norah paced the drawing room. "This is unbelievable. Clarke and Renwick working together? What exactly do they hope to accomplish?"

"Why don't you sit down and take a breath, Norah?" Ella requested. "Let us discuss this together." She appeared troubled as well, but as usual, she reined in her feelings.

Norah sat with a huff beside her husband. Only after Vanbridge took her hand did she seem to calm down.

"According to what Clarke said in *The Times*, he expects his search to soon yield results," Norah said in a more composed vein.

"Yes, but how many times did Father say something similar?" Lena asked. "It must be in a treasure hunter's nature to see the possibilities and remain optimistic. That doesn't mean he'll find anything." Her words didn't dismiss the knot in her stomach.

"What new technology do you think he intends to use?" Norah asked.

None of them had an answer. Not even Marbury, Vanbridge, and their grandfather had a guess as to what equipment Clarke could use that David Wright hadn't already tried.

Marbury turned from where he'd stood staring out the window to face them. "I must say I don't know what our response would've been if Renwick had come to us before the article in the newssheet. It's not as if we could stop him from digging."

His gaze met Ella's, the tenderness palpable between them, pinching Lena's heart. She was so pleased they'd found each other.

"True," her grandfather agreed. "But I, for one, am not fond of surprises."

Lena shared an amused look with her sisters. Their arrival in London had proven that to be true. His Grace had been less than pleased to find them on his doorstep when he hadn't been aware of their existence. Only their persistence had worn down his defenses.

"I can't believe that His Grumpiness and his sister were willing to ask me questions about Oak Island, all while they were already having work done on the island." Lena scowled at the thought.

"His Grumpiness?" Vanbridge laughed, along with Marbury. "Is that what you call Renwick?"

Lena pressed a hand to her mouth, surprised the term had slipped out. "My apologies." She glanced at her grandfather, hoping he wasn't offended. To her surprise, he chuckled.

"Renwick is a rather dour man," he agreed. "He seems to find little that pleases him."

It was true, Lena realized. What had happened to make Renwick that way? And what would he look like when he smiled?

"I think the important thing is for us to show a united front on the topic," her grandfather continued. "Do we show outrage at his efforts?"

"Or do we act as if we don't care?" Ella asked. "Though I don't think either will change the circumstances."

"I don't want them to find anything," Norah confessed with a glance at her husband. "It seems like it would shed a poor light on Father's efforts."

"I think we can all agree it's unlikely they will," Vanbridge said. "But it might not hurt to have a plan in place in case they do."

"You mean an idea of what we might say?" Marbury asked.

"Exactly." Vanbridge nodded. "A response of some sort we've prepared so we're not taken by surprise again."

"It's inconceivable to think they'll actually find the Money Pit." Lena shook her head, unable to imagine how she'd feel at that news. "But they might find a few artifacts." She looked at each of her sisters in turn. "That could prove helpful as it would show Father was on the right path."

"It would," Ella agreed. "We will be certain to mention that if asked."

"Have no doubt that we'll be asked," their grandfather said. "And if the Money Pit is found?"

Lena stared at him in surprise. She would've sworn that he would never use the term, given his feelings toward David Wright. The fact that he had was a testament to how quickly life could change, a lesson she should've learned by now.

"I think we'll have to consider that particular possibility for a time before we can say for certain." Ella bit her lower lip. "As Lena said, it's inconceivable."

Lena nodded, her heart heavy with worry. But what if Clarke did? Their father's name would be bandied about as a joke. He'd be remembered for failing where someone else had succeeded with ease. She couldn't bear the thought, and neither would her sisters be able to.

⟫⟫⟪⟪

THERE WAS LITTLE Sterling could do to mitigate any potential damage, which irritated him to no end. He sent a stern telegram to Clarke with an order to refrain from conducting any additional interviews with the press and advising that all future statements were to be run through Sterling. Whether the man would listen when he hadn't the first time remained to be seen.

Though he received several requests from the press for interviews, including one from the reporter who wrote the article featuring Clarke, he ignored them, not wanting to add more fuel to the fire.

He refused all callers so he could spend the morning with Bernie to make certain she wasn't overly distressed. Her upset at the turn of events was understandable, as was her concern about what Miss Wright and her sisters must think.

That was his worry as well, though he knew there were others who would be displeased with him. The Duke of Rothwood was at the top of the list, followed closely by the Earl of Marbury and the Marquess of Vanbridge. Then came the majority of the members of the Royal Geological Society.

The situation was a tangle. He didn't appreciate Clarke sharing the information publicly when he'd ordered him not to. Though he knew Clarke was considered a rebel by many, Sterling had thought they had an understanding.

"I'm going to call on Rothwood now rather than wait until calling hours this afternoon," he told Bernie. Better to have what could be an unpleasant discussion over and done. Face the consequences and move forward.

While Sterling hadn't done anything wrong, advising those who would be affected by the project would've been a courtesy he'd appreciate in their position. He should've told them in advance about his intentions. Now, that ship had sailed from the dock and taken the opportunity along with it.

Damn Clarke and his ego. Sterling was left to manage the situation as best he could.

"Excellent idea," Bernie agreed. "I'm going with you."

"Do you think that wise?"

"I owe Miss Wright an apology." She lifted her chin. "In fact, I believe you do, too."

"Do you?" Never mind that he thought the same.

"We both failed to tell her the truth."

"It wasn't as if we lied." Why he felt compelled to argue was beyond him.

"An omission is a lie, Sterling." She waited with an expectant look, practically daring him to disagree.

"None of this would be necessary if Clarke had followed my orders." He couldn't help but mention the point.

"True, but we must play the hand we've been dealt. Allow me to change." She hurried from the room, leaving him to consider how much his sister had matured while she'd been away at finishing school.

What could he tell not only Rothwood, but Miss Wright, that might lessen their upset? He knew the duke hadn't been an admirer of David Wright or his treasure-hunting endeavors. But he also knew Rothwood wouldn't appreciate the unexpected news, especially since it would most likely upset his granddaughters.

Their carriage arrived at Rothwood House with Sterling still uncertain what to say. He requested a private word with the duke, while Bernie asked to see Miss Wright.

To Sterling's surprise, he was directed to the small reception room to wait, and Bernie was escorted to the drawing room.

As he pondered the reason he hadn't been shown directly to Rothwood's study, the sound of heels clicking on the marble floor of the corridor had him turning toward the open doorway to see Lena Wright walking past.

She paused at the sight of him, then came directly toward him.

"Your Grace." She curtsied, her eyes positively chilly. Her pale blue gown, along with her cool expression, brought to mind an ice princess—a beautiful one.

"Good afternoon, Miss Wright. I hope the day finds you well." He clenched his jaw, realizing he must sound like an ass for bothering with pleasantries. He should've led with an apology.

"It does, indeed. And you?" The glare she gave him suggested she didn't care in the least how he answered.

"Well, thank you." He tried to tamp down the guilt rising within him by clearing his throat to no avail. "I would like to offer my apologies for the unfortunate article in *The Times*."

One elegant brow lifted. "For the article, but not for withholding the truth?"

Too late, he realized the wording of his apology was not what he meant. "I had thought to advise you and your family of the dig once the project was well underway."

"It sounds as if it already is. I don't appreciate being used to gain information on Oak Island by either you or your sister, Your Grace."

Damn if he didn't admire her spirit. So often, ladies he met were so overwhelmed by his title that they barely met his gaze, let alone disagreed with him. Not Lena. She met his gaze and shared her poor opinion of him. That intrigued him more than it should. "That was never our intention," he said with true remorse.

She was too polite to scoff, but her expression told him she wanted to. Bernie was going to be devastated if she lost the chance to have a friend in Lena. He needed to do what he could to make certain that didn't happen. His sister had few true ones, and she already liked and admired Miss Wright.

He took a step closer, surprised at how much he wanted her forgiveness. "Miss Wright, please accept my apologies for not being forthcoming."

Lena watched him, her silence suggesting that she had yet to decide whether to forgive him. He didn't question the urge to explain further but, instead, followed it.

"Clarke wasn't supposed to share the information publicly so soon. But that doesn't excuse the fact that I failed to disclose our intent to dig on Oak Island."

"No, it doesn't." She held his gaze without hesitation, obviously waiting for him to say more.

"Bernie wanted to tell you, but I suggested we wait until our efforts progressed. For that, I am also sorry. I hope my mistakes haven't caused you undue distress." To his dismay, her expression suggested she still hadn't forgiven him. He couldn't blame her. Not when he found it difficult to forgive others, as well.

"Clarke will find Oak Island more difficult than he expects. As will you." She drew back, her gaze lingering on his face, which made him wonder what she saw.

He wanted her to see a man of honor. Someone she respected and possibly admired. That was odd when he normally didn't care what anyone thought. What could he do to change her mind?

She turned away without another word, leaving him to watch the swinging of her skirts as she strode from view. Her reaction made him even more concerned about how his conversation with Rothwood would go. Hopefully, better than the one with his granddaughter.

LENA STEWED AS she climbed the stairs to the drawing room where Lady Bernice waited. Renwick was infuriating. His first lame apology had tempted her to turn her back on him and leave before listening to anything more he had to say.

Such arrogance. As if he could do no wrong. Though she supposed it was to be expected of someone groomed to be a duke from a young age, that didn't make it less irritating. No doubt she would hear from her grandfather that Renwick had been offended by her behavior. The thought had her scowling. She had been tempted to completely ignore proper manners and speak her mind but was pleased she'd somewhat restrained herself.

If he knew it would've been a courtesy for him to advise her, or at least her grandfather, of his intention to dig on Oak Island, then why hadn't he acted on it?

It was also interesting to hear that Clarke hadn't complied

with Renwick's wishes to keep quiet about the treasure hunt. What else might the man decide to share without the duke's approval?

As Lena approached the drawing room to see Lady Bernice, she considered again how she might feel if they discovered the Money Pit and the treasure. But it was still impossible to know how she'd feel if they did.

Nor did she know what to say to Lady Bernice about the entire situation.

She paused in the doorway to find the lady pacing the room. Lady Bernice must've seen her out of the corner of her eye for she whirled to face her.

"Miss Wright." To Lena's dismay, her brown eyes were filled with tears. "I am so terribly sorry." Her gloved hands were gripped tightly together.

"Lady Bernice." Lena curtsied before slowly moving forward.

The woman didn't wait but hurried forward with both hands outstretched. "Truly. I am so sorry." She took Lena's hands in hers, her expression sincere. "I should've told you straight away. There's no excuse to explain my behavior. Especially not when we discussed Oak Island."

Lena was surprised she didn't say that it had been her brother's idea to keep their plan a secret. That would've been an easy excuse.

"I knew the search would soon begin, and I didn't tell you. Can you possibly forgive me?"

Lena's heart softened at the quiet, heartfelt plea. She knew it wasn't completely Lady Bernice's fault. If Renwick told her not to say anything, she would've been compelled to follow his wishes. Still, Lena felt as if she'd been tricked, and she didn't care for it. "It's an unfortunate situation."

Lady Bernice released Lena's hand to press her gloved fingers to her mouth as if to hold back tears. "When Sterling first mentioned the land was for sale, I was excited. I had been studying the letters and was enamored with the idea of searching for treasure. I was also thrilled that Sterling and I could do something together."

Lena gestured toward the settee, her thoughts whirling. Lady Bernice had to have come across something more to convince Renwick to undertake such a massive project. "Are there more letters than what you shared with me?"

Lady Bernice's eyes widened as she sank onto the cushions, and a hint of color tinted her cheeks. "What makes you ask?"

"Because the few mentions of Oak Island in those you allowed me to read aren't enough to suggest digging would be worthwhile." Lena leveled her a look. "It seems to me that you only sought my company to see what I can tell you about Oak Island."

"No. Nothing of the sort." She shook her head. "I'm not very adept at…making friends. The few times I've trusted others with personal information, I've been deceived, as has Sterling. We thought it best not to show you all the letters until I knew you better."

"I see." Lena still felt the lady could've found a better way to engage her. One that didn't require subterfuge. Apparently, Lady Bernice was more like her brother than Lena realized and was slow to trust.

"So few are honest in Society." The lady released a troubled sigh. "Those who act friendly are more interested in my brother than me. They visit with me and smile politely, but their eyes are anything but friendly even as they offer compliments. The moment they have a chance, they ask me about Sterling. It's difficult to know who to trust."

Lena sympathized with the young woman. She and her sisters had found the same to be true since their arrival in London. Lena knew only a handful of ladies other than her sisters whom she called friends. Lady Bernice must feel very much alone without sisters to rely on.

"I do hope that with time, you'll find it in your heart to forgive me." Lady Bernice held Lena's gaze, worry lingering in the depths of her eyes.

Deciding it best to change the subject until she had some time to work through her upset, Lena searched for another topic.

"Do you intend to visit Oak Island while the dig is underway?" she asked.

"That would be doubtful as I don't think Sterling intends to do so."

They had only visited a few more awkward minutes when Renwick appeared in the doorway, apparently having finished with his conversation with her grandfather. As usual, his expression was unreadable.

Lady Bernice stood, as did Lena. "Thank you for seeing me, Miss Wright. I do hope you can forgive me. Goodbye." Then she joined her brother, who gestured for her to precede him.

Lena said nothing as Renwick drew closer. "I would consider it a personal favor if you could see beyond this. Bernie could use a friend."

Lena's upset had already lessened. The fact that both of them had called to apologize impressed her and spoke of sincerity. But she wanted to see what her grandfather thought before she said too much. She didn't trust her own feelings. Not in this matter. And not with Renwick.

"I will try." That was the best she could offer for now.

To her surprise, his gaze continued to hold hers. "And what of me? Is there a chance you'll forgive me as well?"

His quiet words brought awareness prickling along her spine. "Perhaps," she said at last, confused by her reaction to him.

His expression softened. Not quite a smile, but rather a hint of one. He truly was an attractive man.

"I shall make it my mission to convince you to." He bowed low. "Good day, Miss Wright."

Lena released a relieved breath as he departed. What an odd moment that had been. The connection she felt with the handsome duke was puzzling and unsettling. But not nearly as unsettling as the idea of Renwick attempting to convince her to forgive him.

Chapter Six

STERLING WAITED TWO days before venturing into the Royal Geological Society offices on Saville Row for the weekly meeting. He hoped that by now, news of his involvement in the dig on Oak Island had calmed.

The gathering held today was a discussion on South American exploration. Surely that meant his project would no longer be on everyone's minds.

He was pleased he'd called on Rothwood and spoken with him privately. The duke had made his displeasure clear that Sterling hadn't advised him of his plans for digging on the island.

Sterling had apologized and offered the same explanation he'd told Lena, though he wasn't certain whether either of them found it acceptable. The duke's upset on behalf of his granddaughters was understandable and something Sterling could appreciate. He felt much the same way about Bernie.

Rothwood was a man he admired more than he had his father. Sterling had been taught not to show emotion, not to trust anyone, and that caring for others was a sign of weakness. While Rothwood was certainly reserved, that was where the similarities ended between the two men. Sterling was doing his best to show his affection for his sister, in part to repair the damage their father had done as well as to protect her. The way he comported himself set an example for Bernie and made it even more important to do the right thing in this instance.

Rothwood had asked him to share updates as they became available. Sterling hadn't made any promises and was certain the duke realized that. Rothwood had also expressed concern as to whether Clarke was the right person to work on the project.

While aware of Clarke's tendency to forge his own path wherever he went, Sterling felt the man's experience outweighed the concern. Once he received a favorable reply to his telegram, he would feel reassured. Whether that would happen remained to be seen.

He nodded at several acquaintances as he entered the offices, then made his way toward Marbury, who stood visiting across the room.

"Your Grace." The earl gave a stiff bow, his expression somber, eyes flashing with temper.

To Sterling's relief, the other man he'd been speaking with moved away. "Allow me to offer an apology to you, Marbury."

A long moment of silence followed before Marbury at last nodded. "I appreciate that."

"Would you please extend my apology to your wife as well?"

At that, the earl's expression lightened significantly. "I will, Your Grace." He paused, then cocked a brow. "Or should I say Your Grumpiness?"

Sterling frowned. "Grumpiness?"

Marbury's eyes widened in alarm, and his face tightened with remorse. "Now I owe you an apology. I assumed Miss Wright had told you of her nickname for you."

He considered the term for a moment. Was he so stern all the time? He supposed it was apt as he tended to find little to smile about.

But more importantly, he liked the idea that Miss Wright thought of him often enough to come up with a nickname. That alone nearly made him smile. Damn if she wasn't clever, not to mention bold. More than that, he liked that about her. There was more to Lena than he'd thought, and he looked forward to discovering what other secrets she kept hidden.

"I will have to have a word with her about that," Sterling said, his tone light with amusement.

Marbury was obviously relieved he wasn't angry. "Lena might be the youngest of the three sisters, but she is not afraid to speak her mind."

And that was one more reason Sterling admired her. He did not know her well but couldn't imagine her acting a certain way simply to gain his attention.

Marbury seemed protective of her. The earl was older than him by several years, and Sterling respected him for numerous reasons. Perhaps Marbury wouldn't hold the news article against him if he was teasing him about the nickname. However, he still wanted to explain.

"I truly am sorry if recent events caused you and your countess concern," Sterling began.

"They did, actually. My wife was quite upset by the news."

"She knew the land had been sold though, didn't she?"

"Yes, but learning that a new search is underway was still a shock to all three of the sisters."

"Again, my apologies for not advising you in advance." When Marbury said nothing more, Sterling asked, "What are your thoughts on finding treasure on the island? It seems as if your opinion has changed on more than one occasion."

Marbury smiled grimly. "I don't think Captain Kidd's treasure is there. But that doesn't mean someone didn't bury something on the island. It is well documented that the location was used many times throughout the past century by more than one country. However, I certainly don't envy you the task of trying to find treasure when others have failed."

"I hope we're able to bring a few new ideas to the search."

"Clarke mentioned new technology in the story. Is there something specific to which he's referring?"

Sterling hesitated but decided sharing a few details of their plan wouldn't cause harm. The information would soon be public knowledge. "Based on what we know from previous digs, the flooding of the shafts is one of the biggest problems. We will be utilizing new pumps that should solve the problem."

"Wright and Johnson used improved pumps without success." Marbury looked askance, but Sterling didn't offer any additional information.

No purpose would be served in arguing with Marbury or claiming he knew more than previous searchers did. Their results should prove that soon enough. "Hopefully, ours will work better."

"Good afternoon," Viscount Dyke, another member of the Society, greeted them before turning to Sterling. "I understand you have a new endeavor, Your Grace."

"Yes, our efforts are now underway." Sterling waited, certain the man had something to say about it, or he wouldn't have raised the topic. As always, his appearance was tidy, with his brown hair neatly combed to one side and his attire simple but impeccable.

"Wagers are being placed by members as to the outcome." Dyke's brown eyes twinkled with mirth. "Unfortunately, the odds are not in your favor."

Wagers? Sterling nearly groaned. "Surely the members have something more important to keep their attention than another dig in Nova Scotia."

Dyke chuckled as he shared a look with Marbury. "Everyone is following your project closely. When will you have more news?"

"Difficult to say." Sterling didn't intend to share anything about Clarke's possible reply. Not when doing so would stir interest even more.

The viscount stepped closer. "Care to share your thoughts on the dig? I wouldn't want to place the wrong wager. Do you expect results before year's end?"

"I have no intention of sharing any details with you or anyone else, and I don't appreciate you asking." Sterling kept his tone haughty, anger filling him once again that Clarke had placed him in this position. To learn the members were betting on the outcome annoyed him even more. "Surely you have something better with which to fill your time."

"My apologies, Your Grace." Dyke dipped his head and then moved on to speak with someone else, leaving Sterling alone with Marbury again.

Sterling was relieved when Marbury didn't remark on his retort. Perhaps Lena's name for him was more correct than he realized.

"I hope Miss Wright's upset with my sister and me has eased," Sterling said, wondering if the earl would share how Lena was feeling about the situation. He'd sent flowers, signing the card with both his and Bernie's names, not wanting Lena to get the wrong impression. After all, he wanted her forgiveness, but he wasn't courting her.

He didn't want Lena to remain upset with his sister. At least, that was what he kept telling himself. Whether she was still angry with him didn't—shouldn't—matter. Yet it surprised him that it did, an unusual occurrence since he never cared what others thought. Certainly not women, other than Bernie.

Lena was on his mind far too often. Surely once he resolved the situation and she and Bernie were on good terms again, he could put her from his thoughts.

"I'm not sure I would say that." Marbury shook his head. "She seems to be under the impression that your sister only pretended to befriend her to learn more about Oak Island."

"Nothing of the sort. Bernie is beside herself with that worry. Do you have any suggestions as to how I could convince Miss Wright that isn't the case?"

"Lena is slow to trust others and not easily swayed. You'll have to prove it to her. Not so different than you, actually." Marbury grinned. "All I can say is good luck, Your Grumpiness."

Sterling scowled. He was beginning to detest the nickname. Being known as stern had never bothered him before, but having

Lena think of him as such was upsetting. The temptation to try to change surprised him. Convincing her to change her poor opinion of him was a challenge he couldn't ignore.

⟫⟪

LENA TAPPED HER toe in time to the music at the Bancroft ball the next evening, having already danced several times. Her mood was slowly improving after the unsettling news about Renwick's treasure hunt, though hurt lingered, causing her to briefly press her gloved fingers against her chest. The beautiful bouquet from the duke and his sister had been a surprise, though she still had to decide if she was willing to truly forgive or trust them.

Norah was not. Even now, she stood nearby, visiting with Lady Havenby, a family friend. From the bits of conversation Lena could overhear, the topic was the treasure hunt and how displeased Norah was about it.

Ella and Marbury had remained home this evening so Ella could rest. Per her message, the baby was interrupting her sleep schedule before it had even arrived.

Lena glanced at Norah, certain her sister wouldn't be happy until Clarke and Renwick admitted defeat and quit the island. Norah seemed adamant about it.

Lena had mixed feelings. She rather liked the idea of someone continuing to search for treasure. It meant their father's work hadn't been in vain. That he had been right to dig for so many years since others suspected what he had—that a significant treasure was buried on the island.

She just didn't want them to find it too quickly.

As for Lady Bernice, Lena supposed she had mostly forgiven her, though she would guard what she said from now on. It wasn't as if the lady had acted with malicious intent. Instead, the issue was trust. That was something Lena understood since she was slow to trust others as well. Her gift demanded she keep people at a distance. She never knew when it would surface or how others would react if they discovered it. Her life might be lonely, but it was safer this way.

The other complication was that Lena wanted a look at the rest of the letters the lady had. She'd been through the first set several times and found a few passages that might have a hidden meaning. With more information, she might be able to determine if that was true, and if so, what the letters truly said.

Vanbridge had offered to have a look since he was considered an expert at finding patterns and deciphering the meaning of carvings. But Lena still wanted to try on her own first. The quest had become personal. Her father's reputation was at stake.

Lena wrinkled her nose at the worry that she could be using Lady Bernice just as much as the lady had been using her. She brushed aside the concern, reminding herself that she had several things in common with Lady Beatrice and had been beginning to like her before the news story had appeared.

Marbury had mentioned a Professor Lindquist whom he'd come across while searching for their father's stolen journal. The professor had letters from sailors similar to the ones Lady Beatrice had found that he'd compiled, along with a ship's log.

Lena was intrigued and asked if Marbury could arrange a visit with the man soon to see if he knew anything that might help provide additional information on the possible location of buried treasure on Oak Island.

She was relieved to see Vanbridge approaching. Norah sorely needed a distraction. Though her brother-in-law didn't care for balls or people in general, he frequently made exceptions for Norah's sake. A dance with her husband was just what her sister needed to take her mind off the renewed treasure hunt.

Norah halted mid-sentence, and her expression immediately softened at the sight of her handsome husband with his slim build, dark, wavy hair, and green eyes. He greeted Lady Havenby warmly, smiled at Lena, and after a brief conversation, escorted his wife to the dance floor. The love and admiration they felt for each other was palpable.

Lena sighed, unable to suppress the longing that filled her as she watched them. She adored both of her sisters' husbands, but the couples' closeness made her feel a little lonely at times.

"Good evening, Miss Wright."

The deep voice had her turning even as a shiver ran along her skin. She dipped into a curtsy at the sight of Renwick standing before her, attractive in his formal evening attire. The waves of his honey-colored blond hair were smoothed down, making him look even more austere than usual. And of course, no smile eased his somber expression. "Your Grace."

To her surprise, a trace of amusement curved his lips. The sight had her catching her breath. If only he'd smile. Then again, perhaps it was a good thing he didn't since even the suggestion of one made her heartbeat speed.

"Don't you mean, Your Grumpiness?"

She gasped, uncertain what to say even as heat filled her cheeks. Should she apologize? Pretend she didn't know what he meant? She didn't believe he was truly offended but didn't want him to think she was being disrespectful. "I'm sorry."

"Sorry I heard it?" His brown eyes warmed as they held on her.

"Definitely," she muttered, fairly certain Marbury was to blame.

Renwick chuckled, and she could only stare in wonder at the sight of his face transformed. The stern lines eased into something approachable and oh, so handsome. Breathtakingly so. My goodness. If he did that on a regular basis, he'd have an even longer line of ladies following him. Even now, several women edged closer, as if hoping to catch his notice.

"Apology accepted. That is, if you'll honor me with a dance." He offered his hand.

With a glance at a thrilled Lady Havenby, who positively beamed with delight, Lena placed her hand in his, all too aware of the attention they were receiving.

Renwick rarely attended balls and never danced when he did. Which brought to mind the question of why he was there. And why he'd chosen to dance with her.

"Thank you." Her stomach fluttered as he escorted her to the dance floor. It was only because of the people watching them, she told herself. Somehow, that didn't ring true. "Is Lady Bernice here?"

"She is coming with our Aunt Edith shortly. I have no doubt she hopes to speak with you." He glanced at her as they waited for the other couples to clear the floor from the dance that had just ended. "Have you decided?"

"Decided what?"

"Whether you're willing to forgive us?"

She knew she should say yes to be polite. But she didn't know if she had. She couldn't lie when that was the very reason she wasn't happy with them. "For the most part."

His gaze narrowed as he continued to watch her.

"What is it?" she asked at length, aware of the warmth of him where her hand was tucked against his side.

"I suppose I find your honesty refreshing."

She had to laugh. "Ella wouldn't agree." How many times had her eldest sister told her that decorum was more important than honesty in social situations? "You don't sound certain."

"I am." He nodded. "Few people speak their minds these days. Especially to me."

"No doubt they prefer to agree with whatever you say to stay in your good graces. That is a safer way to converse with you."

"Safe can be tiring." He drew her onto the dance floor, ignoring the looks sent their way, his focus solely on her.

The realization only made the flutters in her stomach stronger. She felt breathless and off balance and struggled for something to say before he noticed how oddly she was acting.

"Do you speak from experience? Do you always live life safely?" she asked. She had tended to think of dukes as men near her grandfather's age until the past few days. Curiosity took hold when she considered what it must have been like to grow up under the scrutiny a duke must receive.

"I suppose you could say that. My father didn't appreciate any opinions different from his own. Rebellion wasn't an option."

Her sympathy tugged, for she thought there was more to the story than he was saying. "He sounds like a difficult man."

"A demanding one, for certain. He focused on duty and responsibility above all else."

"That must've made for a challenging childhood." One look at Renwick's expression suggested the topic—or perhaps it was the memories—wasn't welcome. She couldn't help but add, "My father had a singular focus as well. I rarely appreciated it."

Renwick didn't respond, and she wondered if he'd even been listening.

The dance began, making conversation difficult. Rather than trying to talk, Lena focused on the dance. Renwick was an excellent partner, if somewhat stiff. Was that because he didn't enjoy dancing or because he was uncomfortable for some other reason?

He was tall, and though she was as well, the top of her head just reached his chin. As they turned, she caught his scent. The subtle cologne swirled around her, tugging at her senses.

Heat filled her, and not only because of the movements of the dance. The colors of the ladies' gowns swirled around her as they turned. Was it her imagination or was he holding her closer? So close that their bodies brushed against each other.

As she met his gaze, all else fell away. She didn't pretend to understand her attraction to this man when she wasn't even sure if she liked him. He was interesting and a bit of a puzzle. Perhaps that was part of the reason he intrigued her. She'd always enjoyed puzzles.

At last, the music swelled, then ended. How she wished it had lasted a little bit longer. A ridiculous thought when she had no intention of allowing her interest in Renwick to grow. She curtsied while he bowed, which gave her a moment to collect her thoughts.

"Have you received word from Clarke?" she asked, though it seemed unlikely he would tell her if he had.

"Not as of yet." His brow furrowed, making her think he might be concerned about it. He offered his arm, and they slowly made their way toward Lady Havenby. "I find it interesting that our fathers were more than likely very different men but had such a singular focus in common."

Lena looked at him in surprise. She hadn't even been sure he'd heard her earlier. "While the trait helps to make strides toward a goal, its narrowness often keeps others out."

"I like to think I have a broader outlook." His gaze settled on something in the distance.

Lena followed his gaze to see Lady Bernice across the room. His regard for his sister was commendable. The problem was that it wasn't the only thing she admired about the duke.

"Would you accompany me to greet my sister?"

"Of course." Lena wanted the chance to ask if she could see the other letters, despite the guilt that once again threatened.

They made their way across the room until they'd nearly reached Lady Bernice and Mrs. Easton.

"I do wish you wouldn't insist on wearing those," Mrs. Easton whispered with a glare at her charge's spectacles, seemingly unaware of their arrival.

"I don't care if I appear unattractive." Lady Bernice responded with a defiant lift of her chin. "I would rather see."

"I'm pleased you wore them," Renwick said as they joined them.

"I think you look nice in them," Lena added as she studied her. The small spectacles with their gold rims weren't that noticeable and lent her an intelligent air.

Lady Bernice adjusted them, clearly self-conscious. "Thank you. I find it terribly disconcerting not to be able to see what everyone else does."

"Social events are awkward enough without being at a disadvantage," Lena said, ignoring the displeased look Mrs. Easton gave her.

After the near miss with the fountain when she'd first met Lady Bernice, she was surprised Mrs. Easton still disapproved of the spectacles.

"If a potential suitor turns away because of them, I am not to be blamed," the older woman said with a disapproving sniff.

"Duly noted." Renwick shared an approving look with Lena, the moment of connection causing her to draw a slow breath.

Her world tilted as she held his warm gaze. The light of interest in his brown eyes made her stomach dance. The urge to turn away nearly overwhelmed her. There was no need for such an extreme reaction. Renwick wasn't interested in her in a romantic way. Nor was she interested in him.

The connection had lasted only a moment. Much like the flash of a falling star in the night sky. Over and done before one was even certain what had been seen.

Even if she became close friends with Lady Bernice, that didn't mean she'd have further interactions with Renwick. His suspicious nature and lack of trust in others made him far too prickly as far as she was concerned.

Lena could imagine too well his reaction if he ever discovered her secret. All secrets had a cost. The thought was enough to cause her to shiver.

She forced herself to smile at Lady Bernice. "Thank you for allowing me to read the letters. They were certainly interesting."

The lady's eyes lit with pleasure. "I'm pleased you thought so. Why don't I send the remaining letters over so you can read those as well? Then perhaps we can discuss them and compare ideas."

Lena's pulse jumped. "I'd like that." Whether it was her sense of knowing or simply hope, she was certain the other letters contained helpful information about the possible treasure.

"Who knows what the two of you might find?" Renwick asked.

She didn't know what she'd do if they did. She couldn't imagine handing any discoveries over to Renwick so Clarke could take the credit. While she didn't know why she was so determined to find out more, she couldn't let this rest until she did.

Chapter Seven

TWO DAYS LATER, Lena settled in the drawing room at her desk to read the additional letters Lady Bernice had sent over. Then she read them again, only to sit back in the chair with a sigh of impatience. Why was nothing ever as easy as she wished it to be?

Her gaze shifted to the beautiful bouquet sitting on a nearby table as she pondered the additional odd lines the privateer had written. The flowers were still lovely despite the days that had passed since their arrival. Yet looking at them frustrated her as the bright blooms brought Renwick to the forefront of her thoughts. As if she needed a reminder of the man. He was already in her mind far too often.

The dance they'd shared at the ball had stolen into her dreams. They'd been waltzing alone in a ballroom, spinning as they danced, only a breath apart. The lilting music filled her entire being—until passion grew and took its place. Sterling had held her so close. So gently.

Then he'd smiled.

Ha! As if that would ever happen. She dismissed the image with a sweep of her hand through the air. If only she could so easily dispel it from her thoughts. She didn't understand why she'd dreamed of him when she'd danced often without that ever happening.

Renwick unsettled her. She might not be able to name the reason, but he did. Was it only because of the link to Oak Island and her father?

She deliberately turned her back on the bouquet and focused on one of the letters. The privateer was remarkably prolific. He'd written to his love, the great-aunt of Sterling and Bernie, in amazing detail and with surprising regularity.

These were much like the others, full of news of Ebenezer Jenkins's fellow shipmates, questions to the lady about her family, and of course, descriptions of the weather as he sailed about the world. The notes on Oak Island were achingly familiar. The frequent rain, especially in the autumn. The snow and cold in winter. The worst of the heat came in August, and December brought both rain and snow.

From what she could discern, Jenkins had visited the island on more than one occasion, though he never said why.

However, it was the strangely worded passages and vague references that had her rereading. The lack of specifics was maddening.

She'd had high hopes for the additional letters, partly because Lady Bernice had held them back and partly because of a feeling. But perhaps that had been optimism and nothing more.

What did she hope to accomplish anyway? Any details she discovered would be for naught. Mr. Johnson had left the island months ago. Lena had no intention of helping Clarke find treasure, though she dearly wanted to know how he was faring. She studied the last page of the letter again, unable to escape the nagging thought that she was missing something.

But analyzing it revealed nothing. If there was a reference to the location of the Money Pit on Oak Island somewhere in these letters, she didn't see it. There had to be something else. Something she hadn't noticed. A more subtle hint.

Did one of the words serve as a code for the island or a treasure? Rereading it with that in mind didn't work. Besides, why would he be so careful when writing to her? Who did he think might read these and use the information he shared?

Lena opened the drawer and pulled out the notes she'd made earlier in the week while reading the first set of letters. With as much patience as she could muster, she looked over her observations again, hoping to see a connection but nothing struck her.

Her thoughts drifted as she puzzled over the phrases, and her gaze moved to the window where sunshine streamed in, the letter still in hand. She lifted it to reread a paragraph only to have an oddly familiar shape indented in the paper catch her notice. The figure visible through the writing was about the size of her hand and had been made with pressure rather than ink.

Her breath caught. It was a rough map of Oak Island.

Ebenezer Jenkins was more than familiar with the island if he'd drawn a map. Now she need only see if he'd placed any other hidden messages in his letters.

⇻⇻⇺⇺

Making excellent progress. Pumps working well. Thirty feet down already.

STERLING FROWNED AT the telegraph message from Clarke the following morning. It was as if the man hadn't received Sterling's message, as he didn't acknowledge it at all. Blast him.

That didn't sit well with Sterling. He'd expected Clarke to agree to his order to not release information without his approval. He would heed Sterling's request, else Renwick would cut off funding for the dig. He didn't want to work with someone who didn't follow orders.

Thirty feet sounded like progress, but Sterling wanted to know more. Where was he digging? One of the previous shafts or a new one?

He pulled out his map of the island where he'd noted the places Clarke thought the Money Pit would most likely be.

Which one had he decided to dig first?

Sterling would've liked to read Wright's journals to see at what depth his tunnels had flooded. Surely it was deeper than thirty feet. Chances were the pumps wouldn't be necessary until they dug deeper. So why had Clarke mentioned them?

Suspicion rose within him. Was Clarke exaggerating his progress? If so, did he do so to try to distract Sterling from his failure to follow his orders or something else?

He heaved a sigh, remembering how often Bernie reminded him of his lack of trust. Perhaps he needed to give Clarke a chance before assuming the worst.

If only he could discover some helpful information about the island. While he appreciated Bernie's enthusiasm for the privateer's letters she'd found in the attic, he wasn't particularly hopeful that they held any clues. He'd read most of them himself and had been less than impressed. What would Lena think?

Asking her if he could look at her father's journals was out of the question. The man's tragic death while searching for treasure was surely a source of continued pain for her and her sisters.

He was surprised to realize he didn't want to risk hurting her by raising the topic. Her reluctant apology for the nickname she'd given him had amused him. Perhaps he *was* too serious. Dancing with her at the ball hadn't been his intention. Yet how could he have resisted when she'd looked so lovely with a mix of defiance and regret in her expression?

"Sterling?"

He looked up to see Bernie in the doorway. "Good morning. Join me. I've just received a telegram from Clarke."

"Oh?" Her eyes lit up as if he'd promised her the moon, and she hurried forward. "What does he say?"

"All is progressing. He's down to thirty feet in a shaft."

"Does he mention where he's digging first?" She leaned over his shoulder to read it for herself.

"Unfortunately, no. He isn't very specific."

"Perhaps he'll send a more detailed account in a letter." Her frown suggested she wasn't particularly pleased with the response either. "I wanted to advise you that Miss Wright is coming for tea this afternoon."

"Oh?" He was taken aback by the shimmer of excitement that filled him at the thought.

"Yes, we're comparing ideas on the letters. I am most anxious to hear what she thinks."

"As am I. I wonder if you should refrain from sharing the specifics of Clarke's progress for now."

"If you insist. But why?"

"The fewer people who know specific details, the better. I know people will make comparisons between David Wright's work and Clarke's, but I don't want to stir the talk by constantly sharing Clarke's progress. Also, there's a chance Clarke won't find anything. We don't want to act overconfident."

A scowl twisted Bernie's lips. "Clarke is certainly that."

"True. We will wait for him to find something before we release the details. I don't want you to be disappointed if he doesn't find anything. We can't forget that David Wright and his partner dug for years with few results."

Bernie sank into the chair before his desk. "I would hate it if our news hurts Lena, and I'll try to manage my expectations. At the very least, I've enjoyed doing something with you."

"As have I. If you truly want to continue a friendship with Miss Wright, perhaps you should discuss other topics as well. I wouldn't want Oak Island to be the only subject you have in common."

"Nor would I."

Bernie soon departed, and Sterling set aside the information on Oak Island to work on other matters that required his attention. The morning passed quickly, but he kept an eye on the clock, wondering if Lena was already here.

He considered asking Foster but couldn't bring himself to do so. Not when the older servant who'd known him all his life might realize his attraction to Miss Wright. He wasn't prepared to admit it to anyone when he was still adjusting to it himself.

Despite telling himself that he should leave the ladies to themselves, he climbed the stairs to the drawing room later that afternoon. The reassurance that he only wanted to make certain Bernie was well rung hollow. His desire to see Lena was overwhelming.

Perhaps it was because she looked at him differently than others as if she saw him as a man rather than a title. It was refreshing. That was all. Nothing more. He refused to read too much into it.

Then he entered the doorway and saw her standing near the window that overlooked the garden.

Alone. It seemed his sister had yet to join her. Could his timing be any more perfect?

Lena's striped lavender gown accentuated her narrow waist. A small black hat adorned her head with matching lavender ribbons that trailed down the back.

He walked slowly forward, listening for the sound of his sister's arrival, certain she'd be there any moment. He dearly hoped she wasn't.

"Good afternoon, Miss Wright."

She spun in surprise, her lavender skirts flaring slightly as she turned. "Your Grace." She dipped into a graceful curtsy, then smiled.

"I will forever think of Your Grumpiness when you address me as such."

Her blue eyes widened in alarm. "I wish you wouldn't. My eldest sister would be appalled. In fact, both my sisters would be."

"Then perhaps it would be best if you called me Sterling. At least when we're alone."

"Sterling." She said his name slowly as if to become accustomed to it.

Why her saying his given name caused his chest to tighten, he didn't know. What was this link he felt to her? A delicate thread easily broken that bound them all the same.

"You may use mine as well," she added, almost like a second thought.

"Lena." It felt odd to say it out loud after he'd used it so often in his thoughts.

Her small smile suggested she liked their new agreement. He did, too. His feet moved him closer. Then closer still. Until he stood before her, looking into those blue eyes that reminded him of the sky on a rare sunny day, so clear they took his breath away.

A hint of roses fragranced the air, beckoning him. Or perhaps it was simply her. Though the neckline of her gown was modest, a hint of the fullness of her breasts was just visible. Her smooth skin held a pink undertone. Did his presence cause the flush?

Good, he thought, as she certainly caused him to heat. "May I say you look especially lovely today?"

She blinked as if surprised and glanced down at her gown before meeting his eyes again. "Thank you."

"I'm certain Bernie will be here any moment. She was quite excited that you were coming when she mentioned it earlier." He had no idea what was keeping his sister, but dare he hope it lasted a little longer?

"I enjoy speaking with her. Her enthusiasm is refreshing."

"What of me?" he asked.

"I'm sorry?" Her brow puckered, and he clenched his hand to keep from smoothing a finger along it.

"I rather hoped you might like talking with me as well."

"Of course." She licked her lips as she considered him, her eyes narrowing. "But I wonder if I could ask a favor."

"What might that be?" His gaze dropped to her damp, rosy lips and desire leapt through him.

"Would you make an effort to smile at least once each time we meet?"

Sterling chuckled, surprised by the boldness of her request.

"Thank you," she said with an answering smile as her gaze held steady on him. "In a short while, I will no longer think of you as grumpy."

He relaxed his hand and gave into the urge to touch her. He drew a finger along her jaw, thrilled when her eyes darkened at his touch. Even more thrilled when her eyes held on his mouth. Was it possible that she was wondering what it might be like if they kissed?

He certainly was.

"Lena?" He kept his voice quiet, still listening for Bernie.

"Yes?" Did she sound breathless, or was that hopeful thinking on his part?

"May I kiss you?"

Her mouth parted, then closed as if she was uncertain how to answer. Then she said, "Yes."

The single word was the answer to his wish.

He cupped her cheek, part of him in a terrible rush while another part insisted he slow down to savor the moment. He leaned close, their breath mingling.

At last, he pressed his lips to hers, realizing immediately how perfect she was. Her lips were soft and so sweet. Firm beneath his and responding to the kiss, seeming determined to get the most out of it.

Perfect. That was exactly what he wanted.

Sterling eased closer still, loving the way her heat and scent wrapped around him. Just as he considered deepening the kiss, of sliding his tongue between those lips so he might taste her, the sound of his sister's voice coming from the corridor, along with his aunt's, had him jerking back.

He muttered a curse under his breath at the untimely interruption, then dropped his hand and stepped away, his gaze still on Lena.

She looked confused at first until the voices penetrated her thoughts as well. She, too, drew back and turned partially away as if uncertain where she should go or what she should do.

He shifted to shield her from view, so she would have another moment or two to regain her composure. In truth, he needed a moment as well. When they next kissed, he promised himself they would have all the time they needed to explore whatever this was between them.

And after tasting her, he was determined there would be another kiss.

He forced himself to turn toward the doorway and act as if nothing was amiss.

As if his heart wasn't threatening to hammer out of his chest.

As if passion hadn't taken a firm hold of him and refused to let go.

"Sterling." Bernie looked between him and Lena with a beaming smile. "Are you keeping our guest company?"

"Yes," he said, glancing at Lena. "How kind of Miss Wright to call on us again."

"Isn't it though?" Bernie's bright smile left no doubt that she agreed. Then she subtly elbowed their aunt as they continued forward.

"Yes, indeed," Aunt Edith agreed at last, though the lack of enthusiasm in her tone made him wonder.

Pleasantries were exchanged as the ladies took a seat.

Sterling tried his best to keep his gaze from Lena. He would rather Bernie didn't guess at his attraction. She wouldn't be pleased if she did.

He shouldn't be pleased either. He didn't need a complication in his life, and marriage was not yet on his agenda. Then he dismissed the worry. Another kiss or two and Lena would be out of his system.

His aunt moved to her favorite chair by the window to embroider, leaving Bernie and Lena to visit on the settee. Sterling told himself to leave, that he had other matters to attend to. Important matters. Still, he sank into a chair, promising himself to only listen for a few minutes.

"I so enjoyed the Bancroft ball," Bernie said with a glance at him as if wanting him to take note that she was talking about something other than Oak Island.

"It was lovely," Lena agreed. Her gaze also moved to him,

making him wonder if she was remembering their dance.

Ridiculous. Lena was a beautiful young lady with a sizable dowry, and her grandfather was a duke. She most likely had a wonderful time and numerous partners at every event she attended. What he really wanted to know was what function she was going to next and was there a chance Bernie wanted to attend as well?

If he knew when he might see her again, then he could leave the ladies to visit.

The conversation shifted to a few other ladies they were both acquainted with, then on to a new gown Bernie had ordered, and he smothered a smile. He liked that his sister was having a conversation about mundane things with a friend but knew she wouldn't appreciate him saying anything of the sort.

"I must ask, what did you think of the letters?" Bernie asked, shifting to the edge of her chair in anticipation.

Lena reached down to open her reticule and pulled out the bundle of letters neatly tied with a ribbon. "They were interesting to read, weren't they? Though I wished they shared more details on the possible buried treasure on Oak Island."

Bernie's shoulders dropped. "I had hoped that what Ebenezer Jenkins wrote might have more meaning for you since you're familiar with the area."

"Wouldn't that have been intriguing?"

Sterling stared at Lena, sensing all was not as it seemed. Whether it was her tight smile or the way she seemed to be avoiding his gaze, he didn't know. Perhaps she acted that way because of the kiss they'd shared.

"Do you intend to find out more about Mr. Jenkins?" Lena asked.

"I wish I knew a way to do so." Bernie frowned, then turned to Sterling. "Do you have any suggestions?"

Sterling shook his head. "Unless we can locate a descendant of his."

"The name seems fairly common," Lena added. "But I suppose it's possible."

"At the very least, I will submit an inquiry to members of the Royal Geological Society and see if anyone is familiar with the man or the name," Sterling offered.

"Thank you." Bernie's smile was all the thanks he needed.

Sterling couldn't dismiss the idea that Lena was acting oddly. Bernie didn't seem to notice, so perhaps his suspicions were getting the better of him. The intriguing Lena was certainly worthy of further investigation.

Chapter Eight

LENA PACED NORAH'S drawing room later that afternoon, all too aware of her sister's watchful gaze. "I wasn't sure what to say," she said again, though she knew she was repeating herself.

"It sounds as if you didn't say much of anything, which should be perfect."

Lena paused to look at Norah while her sister studied Lena's notes about the letters. "Do you think I'm wrong?" she asked.

"How could you be?" Norah tapped the map of the island that Lena had copied from the letter. "This Jenkins was obviously sending details about Oak Island even if he doesn't specifically mention treasure. But why send those to his love? What did he expect her to do?"

"Unless he was afraid he'd forget the information, and this was a way to document it." Lena pressed a hand to her temple where a headache brewed. "The way Sterling stared at me, I am certain he is suspicious."

"Sterling?"

Lena realized her lapse too late. But now wasn't the time for Norah to worry about the fact that she was on a first-name basis with the duke. "Renwick, I mean." She turned away when she felt her face heat. Her sister knew her too well and might guess what had happened.

The kiss had been unlike anything she'd experienced. For a moment, she'd forgotten where she was. That Lady Bernice could walk in on them at any moment. Instead, all that had mattered was Sterling.

Was part of her attraction because she knew nothing could come of it? As suspicious as he already was, she feared he might discover her intuitive sense if they were together much, and she had no doubt he would consider the ability appalling. Though it wasn't something she experienced every day, the first time she knew something that no one else did, she could imagine the disbelieving look he'd give her. There were times when a feeling came so strongly that it blocked out all else, even those beside her. The gift was impossible to hide in those moments. If it happened when she was with Sterling…

She nearly shivered at the thought.

She shouldn't have allowed that kiss and certainly couldn't allow another. Whether she'd find the strength to ignore the temptation remained to be seen. How hard could it be? It wasn't as if they would have the chance to be alone often, if at all.

"Lena?" Norah's voice came from what sounded like another room.

Lena blinked to clear her thoughts and turned to look at Norah, who had an expectant look on her face. "I'm sorry. What were you saying?"

Norah grinned, a knowing look in her eyes. "You think *Sterling* knew you weren't fully telling the truth?"

"I'm afraid so. But it's not as if I really know anything. The few possible clues I found hidden in those letters aren't enough to act on. Perhaps Lady Bernice noted the map as well and chose not to tell me about it."

"I have a difficult time believing that. Surely, she would've pointed it out to you and asked your opinion."

"If there aren't any specifics in the letters, then why did they hire Clarke?" Lena returned to her pacing. "They have to know something more. Some new information that convinced Clarke to embark on a treasure hunt that everyone knows won't be easy."

"True. But these few references to Oak Island aren't exactly an X on a map." Norah shook her head as she stared at Lena's notes. "Are you sure there wasn't a location marked on the map you found?"

"I'm quite sure." Still, Lena wondered if she'd overlooked something. That was easy to believe since she'd nearly missed the entire map. "I wish I hadn't returned the letters."

"Holding onto them longer might've raised questions. Besides, maybe we need to shift our focus to another source."

"Marbury, Ella, and I are visiting Professor Lindquist as soon as Marbury can make the arrangements. He's the one who has studied letters from various ships' crews to learn more about the whereabouts of the treasure. I'll ask the professor if he's heard of Ebenezer Jenkins."

"I'll be interested to hear what you discover."

"Sterling—I mean, Renwick—is going to ask fellow Society members if they've ever heard of Jenkins." Lena waited for Norah to latch onto her slip, but much to her relief, Norah didn't remark on it.

"Did you mention what you found in the letters to Grandfather?" Norah asked.

"No. I haven't seen him since my discovery. But I will make a point of doing so."

"I wish I could do more to help," Norah said as she set aside the notes. "If you see Marbury before I do, you might ask how much of this we should share with Ella. I know the renewed treasure hunt upset her. I don't want to hide anything from her, but since she's been experiencing contractions, we need to take care. Telling her more might make it worse or it might ease her mind to know you're doing what you can to learn more."

"Yes, we should proceed carefully with Ella. I'll be sure to ask Marbury's opinion." While her sister was healthy, the contractions were certainly a concern. Lena didn't want anything to jeopardize her sister's health or the baby's.

Norah sighed. "None of us seem to be able to think clearly about Father or Oak Island."

How true that was. They each carried guilt for different reasons because of their father's death. For Lena, she didn't think she'd ever come to grips with what had happened that day. If she hadn't been so set on denying her ability, she might've realized her father was in danger. Could she have saved him? That was something she'd never know.

Logic didn't always have a place when it came to love.

STERLING ENTERED HIS club five days later. The day had been productive, and as it shifted toward evening, he was ready to relax, have a drink, and enjoy some conversation. Brooks's was the perfect place to experience all of that.

Living with two females gave him an appreciation for male companionship. Between Bernie and Aunt Edith, he had his fill of talk of fashion and the like.

Things were currently progressing with the treasure hunt to his satisfaction. A letter from Clarke had arrived, detailing his plans for digging. The man had included an updated hand-drawn map with the most likely areas to search for the Money Pit if the shaft he was currently excavating didn't produce results. Each location had been prioritized with the reasons clearly noted as to why he thought it viable. Sterling couldn't have asked for a more thorough report.

The fact that Clarke still hadn't acknowledged Sterling's request to withhold from giving interviews to the press didn't bother Sterling nearly as much, though he certainly hadn't forgotten about it. He had to think Clarke understood and accepted the order since he hadn't argued.

Talk of the wagers among Society members had eased as

well. It had only been mentioned once when he'd been at the Society offices earlier that afternoon. He took that as a good sign.

Bernie had been thrilled with Clarke's letter and the updated map. She'd read it so many times that he was certain she'd memorized it by now. Clarke's confidence was compelling. Sterling was beginning to wonder if they might actually find something.

Now if he could convince Bernie to expand her social engagements so that she might gain a few more friends and feel more at ease at events, he would be quite pleased with life. Thus far, with each invitation they received, she countered with the question of whether he thought Lena might be attending.

How unsettling to know he had the same question. He dearly wanted to see her again. She'd been on his mind since that delightful kiss. He found himself far too frequently wondering how he could have another.

Though he was pleased Bernie had at least one friend, he looked forward to her having more. Surely Lena would introduce her to other ladies if she hadn't already.

As if thoughts of her somehow conjured her relatives, he saw Rothwood, Marbury, and Vanbridge sitting at a table together with drinks before them. He approached slowly, not wanting to interrupt.

"Good evening, Your Grace." Marbury nodded as he and Vanbridge stood to bow. "Care to join us?"

"Certainly. Thank you." He drew back an empty chair and sat as a waiter hurried forward. After ordering a whiskey, he glanced at the three men. "Is this a family meeting?"

Rothwood smiled. "Of sorts." He looked at the men who had married two of his granddaughters with obvious pride and satisfaction. "We have discussed a few family concerns and have since moved on to other topics."

"Glad to know I'm not interrupting."

They visited a few minutes before Marbury caught Sterling's gaze. "Have you heard from Clarke as to progress on Oak

Island?"

"Only basics." He wasn't ready to share specifics when he assumed the other men wouldn't support his efforts. Not for the first time, he wished he'd told them earlier. He'd approached the situation wrong from the start. Now it felt as if the opportunity had been lost, and he didn't know how to get it back.

"No chests of gold?" Vanbridge raised a brow, an amused look on his face.

"You don't think there's treasure on the island?" Sterling asked.

"I have no idea if there is," the marquess answered. "But I do know the island won't give up its secrets easily."

Sterling didn't care for the reminder. He realized he'd allowed Clarke's confidence to make him hopeful. Hope too often led to disappointment. At least, it had every time he'd experienced the emotion.

How often had he thought someone was a friend, only to learn they had pretended to like him because he was heir to a dukedom? His father had proved that to him time and again, making a lesson of each occasion. School had been a lonely place. Then there'd been a young lady who'd professed her love for him during his university days until his father convinced her to show her true colors. The woman had eagerly taken the money his father offered instead of Sterling's affection. Those painful memories were ones he'd never forget.

Hope wasn't to be trusted. Nor were people, except for family.

Was it any wonder that he looked at others with suspicion?

Now, he considered himself a realist. And the past had taught him that people couldn't be trusted. Many wanted something, whether it was an introduction, a favor, or money. As long as he remembered that, he got along fine. He was careful that any relationship allowed him to gain as much as the other person.

But the three men sitting at the table with him didn't need anything from him. He didn't know quite how to act around them.

He didn't want people to make comparisons between Clarke and David Wright's efforts. That would surely hurt Lena. He didn't want her upset because of him. But neither did he want to appear as if he didn't believe in the search.

"Perhaps that's true," Sterling admitted at last. "Clarke seems to think he has a few ideas that could prove helpful. A fresh perspective could provide results."

He glanced at Rothwood to see his reaction. It was well known that the duke had cut off all ties to his only child and her treasure-hunting husband. It had taken the arrival of his grand-daughters on his doorstep to change him. However, Sterling didn't think their presence had truly changed how he felt about David Wright.

"I suppose there's something to be said for a new outlook," Rothwood said. "But whether it outweighs experience hasn't been determined."

Sterling studied the older man, wondering if he spoke about the treasure hunt or himself.

"I'm sure you'll be relieved to know that Marbury and I have refrained from placing a wager on the outcome of your search," Vanbridge said.

Sterling shook his head, still frustrated about it. "The Society members should have better things to occupy their time than betting on treasure hunts."

"It's not just our fellow Society members." Marbury's grin made Sterling frown. "Members of Brooks's are now doing it as well. Do you want to hear the odds?"

"No, I do not." Sterling reached for the whiskey the waiter set before him and took a deep sip. He didn't like being the subject of people's speculation. That was something he hadn't anticipated when he'd started the dig, though he supposed he should've.

"Then you won't be offended to learn they aren't in your favor here either." Vanbridge idly turned his glass on the table.

"What of your wives?" Sterling asked, much to his surprise

and certainly against his better judgment. "Do they think Clarke will be successful?"

Marbury and Vanbridge shared a look before glancing at the duke.

"I believe we will refrain from discussing my granddaughters' opinions since they're not here to share them." Rothwood seemed to find something that caught his interest across the room, suggesting the subject was closed.

Sterling thought it wise of them not to speak on their behalf. Besides, he was fairly certain he already knew the answer. If the ladies' father hadn't found treasure, they most likely thought he and Clarke wouldn't either. Time would tell.

What had started simply as a way to make his sister happy and to fulfill a wish of his own had become far more complicated than he'd ever expected. He need only think of Lena to know that.

Chapter Nine

LENA WATCHED ELLA with concern as she and Norah settled into Ella's drawing room three days later. A new story had appeared in *The Times* that morning detailing the latest on Clarke's efforts. He'd declared he'd found the Money Pit shaft and had commenced excavating it. He also claimed the only challenge that remained was to navigate the flood tunnels.

Lena had been shocked when her grandfather had shown her the article since it had only been two weeks since the previous one. She was certain her sisters felt the same way. It was impossible to believe he'd found that particular shaft so quickly.

All three of them were stunned by the report, but it was Ella's pale face that concerned Lena.

"Surely Clarke is exaggerating his progress," Norah suggested.

"Beyond a doubt," Ella said, her brow furrowed. "He couldn't have found the Money Pit already."

Lena had warned Norah on the way to Ella's to mask the extent of her anger at the situation. It would only upset Ella more. According to Marbury, she was still having mild contractions and suffering from an unsettled stomach, both of which concerned him and the doctor.

While they didn't want to disturb her further, no purpose would be served in ignoring the news from Oak Island. Ella would find out eventually, and the realization that they'd kept it from her would only distress her more.

Lena thought it best if the three of them discussed it. Keeping their worries to themselves wouldn't help any of them, especially Ella.

"With so many holes dug on the island, even Father didn't know which one it was, despite all the years he searched." Norah lifted her chin as if to defy them to disagree. They didn't. "Besides, Clarke can't have dug deep enough to know this quickly."

Legend claimed that once a certain depth was reached in the Money Pit, an airlock would be triggered, which would then fill the pit with seawater.

While their father and Mr. Johnson had kept notes and drawings of their efforts as to where they'd searched, previous treasure hunters' shafts were more of a mystery. In addition to looking for the Money Pit, those searchers had dug shafts with the hope of circumventing the flood tunnels.

"I agree," Lena said. "And even if he did find it, the flood tunnels will be difficult to manage. One can't bail out the ocean."

"Clarke will most likely encounter water even if he's not in the Money Pit. Digging on an island brings water, even if it's just groundwater." Ella's tone was confident, but her blue eyes remained dark with worry.

"I hate to think what people are saying about Father and his efforts on the island." Norah shook her head. "Especially when we've tried to make certain his work won't be forgotten."

David Wright's decades of looking for treasure on the island with so little to show for it were difficult to explain to those who didn't realize the complexity of the search. The weather provided only a narrow window to dig each year. The remote island made obtaining equipment and supplies a challenge. Considering their father didn't have significant resources at his disposal, he had done well to accomplish as much as he had.

"It concerns me as well, but we can't worry about what's out of our control," Ella advised.

"You're right," Norah quickly agreed. "Those special pumps Clarke claims to have can't possibly be any more effective than the ones Father had."

While their points were logical and drawn from experience, Lena couldn't halt her worry. She stilled as a familiar shiver crawled along her scalp and down her spine. She closed her eyes, almost hoping she would sense something helpful about this issue.

"Lena?" Ella's voice sounded as if it came from a great distance. "Are you all right?"

An image filled her mind, and it was almost as if she were back on the island, looking over the meadow where her father had dug several shafts. Her eyes flew open, and she gasped as a sense of knowing filled her. "Clarke's digging in the wrong place. It's not the Money Pit."

Lena blinked, then looked between Ella and Norah, wondering if they believed her. How could they when she didn't always believe herself? The feelings weren't necessarily accurate. This one might be nothing more than wishful thinking.

And yet…she felt it all the same.

"Are you certain?" The doubt coloring Ella's tone sent a wash of uncertainty through Lena.

She jerked to her feet, unable to sit still. "No, I'm not sure. I'm never sure." She strode toward the window to gaze out, trying to hold back her frustration and examine the feeling with objectivity. "It's difficult to say when it happens to be what I want to believe." She spun back to face them. "But this time, I saw something. The meadow near Smith's Cove."

It was a place they knew well. But Lena wondered if what she'd seen was simply a memory. The Money Pit could be in that area. However, the feeling remained strong.

"I hope you're right." Norah rose and joined her to place a comforting hand on her arm. "Clarke will look like a fool when he finds nothing after making these claims."

Lena followed Norah's gaze to where Ella sat deep in thought. Was Ella's concern lessened by what Lena had just said? Lena hoped so.

"That could be months from now." Ella's lips tightened with displeasure. "Maybe even next summer." Her gaze lifted to meet theirs as she placed a hand on her stomach. "That's not good enough. If Clarke continues with these ridiculous reports, Father's reputation, as well as Mr. Johnson's, will be left in tatters. It won't matter whether he finds anything. The damage to Father's memory will be done. It will also harm Grandfather's reputation."

"Surely we can do something to keep people from thinking Father was a fool and Mother one for following him." Norah shook her head. "I don't want us, or Grandfather, to be the center of attention everywhere we go. To face questions as to our opinion on Clarke's efforts. That will be maddening."

"If only there was a way to prove he's wrong." Ella studied Lena. "Did you see anything specific? Anything that could help us?"

"No." The word escaped Lena, leaving her filled with despair. "It's not as if I know where the Money Pit is." How many times had she wished for a feeling that would've helped her father find it? If only the outline of the map she'd found in Lady Bernice's letters had been marked with the location of the treasure. But despite searching, she hadn't found anything.

"Do we know where it's not?" Ella rose, placing a hand on the bump just visible beneath her loose gown, something she seemed to do frequently, and drew closer.

Lena hoped she held a hand there to comfort the baby rather than to ease any pain she felt.

"Is there a difference?" Norah asked.

"Possibly," Lena answered, wanting to give Ella some reassurance to ease her worry. "I'll see if Lady Bernice will share where Clarke is digging and then check Father's journals to see if he has notes on it. I can also look at Lady Bernice's letters again.

Maybe there was something in them I missed. Viewing them with this question in mind could make a difference. Perhaps Vanbridge would help."

"Excellent idea," Norah agreed. "I'm certain he'd be happy to. I'll read Father's journals while you focus on the letters."

Lena nodded and forced a bright smile, wishing she felt more optimistic about finding a way to prove what she suspected.

"I can help, too," Ella protested.

"Your attention needs to remain on feeling well." Norah drew Ella toward the settee and sat beside her. "You and the baby are far more important than the location of the Money Pit."

Lena joined them. "I agree. We'll share anything of interest we find. Now then, let us speak of something more pleasant. Have you given more thought to the updates you want to do for the nursery?" she asked Ella.

Ella's entire demeanor changed, a smile coming to her face along with a hint of color, making Lena certain she'd asked the right question.

Ella shared her plans, and they visited for a little longer before Lena sent Norah a pointed look, not wanting to tire Ella. "We should be going."

Norah quickly stood, seeming to understand the message. "Yes, we should." She moved to hug Ella. "Why don't you rest?"

"That seems to be all I do of late," Ella said as she embraced Lena.

"Yes, well, it takes a lot of energy to grow a baby," Norah said. "Remember, when Mother was expecting Lena, you said she rested often."

Ella grinned. "And she ate frequently as well. Hopefully, I will soon feel more like eating."

Lena hugged her again, this time for an extra moment, wishing she could share some of her own strength with her sister. Ella had always been their rock, and Lena wanted to be the same for her now. "Do not worry about any of this," she ordered as she held her gaze.

"I will do my best." Ella nodded, but her eyes held shadows that Lena didn't like.

"She looks so pale," Lena told Norah as they walked down the front steps toward the carriage they'd shared. "I don't like it."

"Nor do I. Did you notice how often she held her stomach? Do you think she's having contractions?"

"I hope not." Lena shook her head as they stepped into the carriage. "If only we could find a way to silence Clarke. To prove he's wrong now rather than later. That would help Ella tremendously. Reviewing Father's journals and Lady Bernice's letters seems like our best hope."

"You mean our only hope. I'll speak to Simon and see when he could look at the letters and ask if he has any other ideas on what we could do."

Lena nodded. "As good as he is at solving puzzles, he might think of something. Marbury might as well."

"I'll send him a message to call so we can discuss it," Norah offered. "I'd also like to know how he thinks Ella truly is."

"As would I." Lena's frustration grew. Darn Clarke and his confidence. If only she could tell Sterling how much his search was upsetting her family. But she didn't know him well enough to even hope that would change his plans.

Did he believe Clarke's claim of finding the Money Pit? Then again, he didn't have any reason not to. But she did. "Should I say something to Renwick?" she asked Norah.

Norah stared at her in surprise. "Such as what? That you have a feeling Clarke is wrong? I hardly think that would serve a purpose other than make him suspicious of you. From what Simon said, Renwick is short on trusting others as it is."

"You're right. I won't say anything until we can find proof."

"Anything to make people wonder if Clarke is making false claims would help. That would shift the attention to him rather than Father." Norah smiled. "Surely we can manage that."

Though she didn't see how, Lena returned her sister's smile.

STERLING RUBBED A hand over the back of his neck as he exited his study and walked down the corridor toward the front stairs. He'd been reading reports from his steward until his eyes were nearly crossed, and he was more than ready for a break. Looking in on Bernie would be the perfect diversion.

He took his duties seriously, just as his father had taught him. Not that his efforts would've been good enough. Sterling had been strong enough to ignore his father for the most part, except for when the duke harangued Bernie. That was something Sterling had refused to allow.

No wonder he and his sister were so close. It had often been the two of them against their father.

However, the sight of Lena standing near the front entrance slowed his pace and sent his pulse scrambling.

"Good afternoon, Lena."

She spun to face him and gave a quick curtsy. "Oh. Your Grace. How nice to see you." A hint of color stole across her cheeks, and her gaze darted away, then back.

Did his presence cause her unease? That he could understand as hers did the same for him.

"I didn't realize you were here." Sterling glanced about the entrance hall, wondering where Foster had gotten to and why Lena was standing alone.

"I was just visiting with Lady Bernice." Lena gestured toward the stairs as if he didn't know where the visit had taken place.

How odd. "Oh?"

She patted her reticule. "She allowed me to borrow the letters again." Her bright smile seemed out of place for the topic. "Norah, my sister, wishes to see them."

"I see." But he didn't. She was overexplaining herself, which made him curious.

"I hope you don't mind," she added, then patted her reticule again. "About the letters, I mean."

"Not at all."

Her gaze shifted around the area before returning to him. "Foster was kind enough to fetch my maid from the kitchen."

"I see." That explained why she was temporarily alone in his entrance hall. But not the uncomfortable look on her face. If he didn't know better, he'd think she felt guilty about something.

"You are well?" she asked. Her pale blue silk gown made her eyes even more beautiful than normal. A tiny matching hat with short ecru plumes perched on her head.

"I am. And you?"

He didn't want to exchange pleasantries. He wanted a true conversation. And perhaps another kiss. Both would be preferable.

"Fine. Thank you."

He glanced over his shoulder, pleased there was no sign of Foster or her maid. He took the opportunity to draw nearer, appreciating the way her eyes widened and her lips parted.

"Lady Bernice mentioned she might attend the Stanhope ball tomorrow evening," she said in a rush.

Sterling nodded with a smile. "She told me the same, though she didn't want to unless you were attending."

"I will be there." She looked at him from beneath her lashes, the long sweep of them incredibly appealing. "It always helps to have friends at such events."

"Thank you for being her friend. I appreciate it." More than he could say.

"I enjoy her company."

He wanted to ask if she enjoyed his as well. But he wasn't ready to test the waters. Not yet. "Perhaps I shall see you tomorrow evening, as well."

"Perhaps." She seemed to finally relax as her gaze held steady on him. "However, I do believe you're forgetting something."

"Oh? What might that be?"

To his surprise, she moved closer and tapped a gloved finger on his lapel. Right over his heart, causing it to lurch, then pivot. He watched her closely, unable to decide what she intended.

The corner of her mouth curved. "A smile, Sterling. Remember?"

She'd said his name in a slightly breathless tone. Damn if he didn't like it. He grasped at his thoughts, trying to focus on the conversation. "Ah, yes. Our agreement." Just the mention of it was enough to make him smile.

"There it is." Her approving gaze swept over his features much like a caress, warming him from the inside out. Her lower lip caught in her teeth, which sent desire spearing through him.

He forced himself to remove the smile, watching her own dim. "There is a way you can have another," he offered, hoping she knew he was teasing.

"How?"

His gaze lowered to her lips. "A kiss would certainly make me smile even more."

"Would it?" Her eyes glinted with amusement.

"Most certainly."

"Well then." She eased closer and placed her hand over his heart. "I would like to see that."

The simple touch sent need shooting through his entire body. Or perhaps it was her smile. Maybe her lovely scent. Or just her. "Just" wasn't the right word. Not when it came to Lena.

She was a quiet force that could erode a man's will with one look. He should know, as she was certainly eroding his.

He bent to take her offered lips, reminding himself to keep it short, even as he reached for her waist. Foster would return with Lena's maid at any moment. Bernie might come down the stairs. Or Aunt Edith.

But the moment their lips touched, those concerns fell away. His focus shifted to her mouth, which responded with fervor to his. He couldn't resist deepening the contact, testing how much she'd allow by pressing the seam of her mouth with his tongue.

She opened for him and then stepped into the circle of his

arms as if she trusted him to treat her with care. He held her tighter, and his tongue swept along hers, sending passion cascading over him, threatening to drown him.

Kissing Lena was like drinking a carefully aged brandy or a fine wine—it created warmth inside him and went straight to his head. He couldn't begin to guess what might happen if they took this further. But he wanted to know. Desperately.

A sound had him drawing back to listen, disappointed to realize someone was coming.

"Until tomorrow evening?" he whispered.

"That depends."

He frowned, confused by what she meant.

"You still owe me a smile."

He had to laugh. He'd never had a woman tease him in his entire life. Not even Bernie. But he kept his composure as best he could. "Do you intend to collect another tomorrow night?"

"Absolutely. I look forward to it. Perhaps even two." She stepped back and looked every inch the proper lady as her maid joined her. "Good day, Your Grace."

With that she was gone, leaving him to draw a deep breath to settle himself, only to breathe in her scent. He had never looked forward to a ball the way he was to the one tomorrow evening. Already, he was plotting ways to claim a few moments alone with her. Surely, he could manage to find a way to have one more kiss. Never mind that he now worried whether it would be enough.

Chapter Ten

LENA ENTERED THE Stanhope ball the following evening with high hopes. She perused those in attendance, only to realize she was looking for Sterling's tall form. How ridiculous when the hour was still early. Even if Lady Bernice was among the guests, it didn't mean Sterling would be.

"Whom are you in search of?" Norah asked as she joined her.

"No one in particular," Lena lied. "Just curious to see who's here."

"Hmm." Based on Norah's narrowed eyes, her sister didn't believe her. "Considering that you looked past me without so much as a blink, despite us planning to meet here, you have someone in particular on your mind."

"I did wonder if Lady Bernice had arrived." Lena hoped that placated her sister.

"Do you mean her brother?" Norah smiled. "How are the two of you getting on? Do you still refer to him as His Grumpiness?"

Lena's entire body heated as the image of Sterling smiling—not only smiling but teasing her—came to mind. He was even more handsome when he relaxed his normally stern expression. "If the occasion warrants the name," she said at last.

"Heaven forbid he finds out." Norah shook her head. "That will make him even grumpier."

"He knows." Not only knew, but the term had become a private jest, much to her surprise. Lena wasn't about to share any of that with her sister. "I think Marbury might have told him."

Norah's blue eyes went wide. "Oh, dear. Was he angry?"

"Irritated, perhaps. But he couldn't deny that it's true."

"Tread carefully, Lena. He is a duke, after all."

"I could hardly forget that." If anything, his title made him less appealing. The scrutiny of being a duke's granddaughter was bad enough. She couldn't imagine being a duchess. Besides, Sterling probably had an understanding with a woman with an impeccable pedigree and a fortune.

Lena was certain that since she had no title, she wouldn't be considered. Not that she wanted to marry Sterling. Not at all. Two kisses and a bit of harmless teasing didn't mean anything.

To her surprise, she found herself scowling at the thought.

"What is it?" Norah asked.

Lena searched for an excuse to explain her sudden change of mood that didn't involve telling her sister about kissing Sterling. With mixed feelings, only a small portion of which was relief, her gaze latched on Lady Clara, a woman neither of them particularly liked as she was abrasive. She was marching toward them with determination. "Lady Clara is coming this way."

Norah groaned but didn't follow Lena's gaze. Rather, she turned in the opposite direction. "I have no desire to hear what she has to say this evening. It's never anything good."

Lady Clara had moved firmly onto the spinster shelf in the eyes of most of polite society. Most, that was, except the lady herself.

Lady Clara seemed to still have hope and no small amount of determination to attract a potential husband. However, she seemed to have the word "desperate" written across her forehead. She tried too hard to gain eligible men's attention, laughing loudly at their jests and flirting at every turn, practically forcing them to ask her to dance. With a tiny dowry and a rather plain appearance, most men avoided her at all costs.

Lena was tempted to advise her to act as if she weren't interested in marrying with the hope it would make her appear more natural. Surely the right man would come along if she stopped trying so hard. But it was clear that Lady Clara wouldn't welcome her advice.

"I don't think she has forgiven you for marrying Vanbridge before she could lay claim to him," Lena whispered, careful to shift her attention away from the lady with the hope she didn't intend to speak with them.

Norah's satisfied smile nearly made Lena snort with laughter.

"It's not my fault that Simon rarely attended balls. Even then, Lady Clara wouldn't take no for an answer. She insisted he dance with her even after we were betrothed. He wasn't interested in her anyway, as she has no appreciation for history. I did them both a favor."

Despite their efforts to pretend they hadn't seen her, Lady Clara planted herself beside them, seemingly unaware of their reluctance to speak with her. "Good evening, ladies. A lovely ball, is it not?"

"Indeed." Lena smiled, feeling a tug of sympathy for her. Marrying well was the one and only job women had in Society's eyes. Failing to achieve that left many feeling useless, relegated to living with relatives, and hoping not to be a burden.

"I must ask your thoughts on the news article about Clarke's success on Oak Island." Lady Clara's brown eyes were wide and glittered with anticipation, much like a cat prepared to pounce on an unwary bird.

At that, Norah turned to face her. "Success? I don't know what you mean."

Lena nearly groaned at Norah's defensive, biting tone.

"It's not as if he's truly found anything," Norah continued.

"He's found the Money Pit. Isn't that what your father searched for without success all those years?"

Lena's sympathy dropped away like a boulder off a cliff, replaced by cold anger. "Just because Clarke *claims* to have found it doesn't mean it's true."

"But it's in writing and in *The Times*, no less," Lady Clara protested. "That must mean it's true."

"Actually, no, it doesn't." Lena wished she could share how certain she was that he was exaggerating his progress. Since that wasn't possible, she had to find another way to silence the talk. "It's not as if he's found buried treasure. Only a shaft in the ground. There are many on Oak Island, which makes it impossible to say whether it's the right one until he finds treasure."

"I'm certain I'm not the only person surprised by his claim." Lady Clara's brow furrowed as if she were puzzled. "Especially given the *decades* your father spent there."

Norah's cheeks turned bright red, her eyes flashing with temper. Lena couldn't blame her when she felt much the same way. It was as if Lady Clara hadn't heard a word she'd said. Nor did she appreciate the emphasis the woman used.

"The shaft he's working in has probably already filled with water," Norah said with a lift of her chin.

"Doesn't that mean he truly is digging in the Money Pit?" Lady Clara asked. She almost seemed to enjoy their upset. "If he encounters the flood tunnels, it will be proof he's in the proper place."

"When you dig on a small island, there's a good chance you'll hit water of some sort," Lena countered.

"Then it's a good thing Clarke has pumps to remove it, isn't it?"

Norah shared a look with Lena that suggested she wouldn't be able to contain her anger for long.

How many other people shared the same thoughts as Lady Clara? Lena wished she had a way to respond that would halt the talk. She struggled for a clever answer only to see Lady Clara's focus shift to something past Lena's shoulder.

Even as the lady's eyes widened with excitement, Lena felt shivers run along her skin. She didn't need her extra sense to know who approached. Though she'd been looking for him earlier, his timing couldn't be worse.

"Your Grace," Lady Clara gushed as she dipped into an alarmingly low curtsy and tipped forward as if to offer a better view of her decolletage. "We were just speaking about your great success. It's terribly exciting, isn't it?" She pressed both gloved hands to her chest as if nearly overcome.

Lena lifted her eyes to the ceiling, wishing she could give the lady a shake to bring her to her senses. Then she turned to face Sterling, hoping he might understand just how upsetting this subject was to both her and Norah.

STERLING RAISED A brow, feeling as if he were stepping into a situation he didn't fully understand. While he'd heard enough to guess the topic was Clarke's claim about Oak Island, he didn't care to discuss it. Not until he knew for certain if Clarke spoke the truth. And not when he continued to be annoyed with the man for sharing details with the press before he shared them with Sterling.

He couldn't say who the lady was in the unfortunate yellow gown that made her skin look as if she suffered from a terrible illness, but he recognized the gleeful look in her eyes. He didn't care for it.

Especially when Lena and her sister both appeared upset.

"Exciting?" he asked with a glance around the crowded room, hoping to pretend he hadn't heard their conversation and therefore, changed the subject. "If you are referring to the ball, I haven't been here long enough to say."

"Not the ball, though it is lovely," the woman said, her gaze holding firmly on him. Apparently, they had been introduced at some point or she wouldn't be speaking to him. "You and your progress on Oak Island, Your Grace."

He bit back a grimace, not wanting to upset Lena and her

sister further. He only wanted to dance with Lena. To watch the sparkle in her eyes as she attempted to coax him to smile. And if his luck held, perhaps they could share another kiss. That was all he'd been thinking about since he'd seen her yesterday.

Speaking of the treasure hunt could easily put those hopes in jeopardy.

He didn't understand what Clarke was trying to accomplish by providing another update to the reporter, but Sterling was not amused. Working with someone so far away who seemed unable to follow orders was proving more difficult than he'd expected.

"There has been some progress with the treasure hunt," he answered reluctantly. "Only time will tell, of course."

"You must be ecstatic to have come so far so quickly compared to…others." The lady glanced at Lena out of the corner of her eye.

"It's too soon to make any claims." That much was true.

"But—"

"Now is not the time to speak of business," he interrupted with a frown. The woman was like a dog with a juicy bone, determined to savor every morsel of the subject. "Rather, we should be enjoying the ball."

He'd had enough of the conversation and intended to whisk Lena away if she'd allow him. Hopefully, Lady Vanbridge would take the opportunity to escape the annoying woman's company, as well. "Miss Wright, may I have the honor of a dance?"

To his surprise, Lena hesitated, causing his mood to plummet. Hadn't she thought of their upcoming dance as often as he had? The realization was highly concerning when his mind had been consumed with it. Or rather, with her.

If he hadn't been watching closely, he might've missed the subtle nudge Lady Vanbridge gave Lena, as if to remind her to answer.

"The pleasure would be mine, Your Grace." The tightness of her expression suggested otherwise, but perhaps he could shift her mood just as she so easily changed his.

"If you ladies will excuse us," he said, offering his arm to Lena.

His entire body relaxed when she took it. He tucked her hand in the crook of his elbow, pressing it firmly against his side, enjoying the contact more than he should. He guided them toward the dance floor, anticipation filling him.

She looked beautiful as always in a pale green silk gown with a square neckline, mauve trim, and a small train. She moved gracefully, her long limbs lending her an elegant look.

"Has Clarke truly found the Money Pit?" Her lips twisted after she asked, making him think she didn't really want to know but couldn't resist.

"So he says." He didn't want to talk about it. Not when he knew the topic upset her. "I would prefer to speak of something else. Anything else. How did you find the weather today?"

The question nearly made her smile, and she met his gaze. "Surely, we haven't resorted to speaking about the weather."

"It was a particularly fine day. One worthy of discussion."

Her genuine smile held him captive as if she were the reason they'd been graced with sunshine earlier in the day. The realization caused an odd ache in his chest. One he couldn't help but rub, hoping to ease it to no avail.

"Is Lady Bernice here?" Lena asked while they waited for the other dancers to clear the floor.

Obviously, Lena hadn't been struck by the feeling he had, or she wouldn't be asking about his sister. He needed to take a firm hold of his ridiculous thoughts.

"She should arrive soon. Aunt Edith didn't like the way Bernie's hair was arranged because it made her spectacles more noticeable." He shook his head. "At times, I wonder if she is the best choice for a chaperone. She is more critical of Bernie than I'd like."

"Does your sister enjoy her company?"

Sterling frowned. "I'm not certain. I suppose I haven't asked." Lena's question made him realize he should. Bernie needed a chaperone, and Sterling wanted a family member to be that person. Though he had to admit that even family couldn't always be trusted. He rewarded Aunt Edith handsomely to watch over Bernie and lend her expertise, but he didn't want the older woman to make Bernie miserable.

"I never imagined wearing spectacles would be such an issue." Sterling shook his head. "Bernie was already a bit self-conscious about them, and I fear Aunt Edith has made it worse."

"It can be difficult to know what personal agendas people have, can't it? When we arrived in London, Grandfather chose Lady Havenby to chaperone us. While we weren't certain about her at first, she has proven to be a friend we all love dearly. She has our best interests at heart, even if her thoughts and opinions don't always mirror our own." She glanced at him. "Perhaps the same is true for Mrs. Easton. Do you think there's a reason she is so concerned about the spectacles?"

"Aunt Edith had a difficult life. I suppose she wants to help Bernie avoid the issues she faced. She firmly believes duty is more important than happiness."

"Do you share that opinion?"

"Of course," he said, surprised she'd asked. "With my title comes the weight of responsibility. Happiness is secondary at best." He reconsidered, wondering if that was even true. He could count on one hand the times he had felt true joy in his lifetime. Satisfaction, certainly. But happiness was a rare and fleeting thing not to be counted on.

Lena's puckered brow suggested she didn't agree.

"What is important to you?" he asked, nodding at an acquaintance who passed by.

"I'm not a man, and certainly not a duke, so I suppose it's different for me."

"That's not an answer," he pressed. He wanted to know what she thought, though he couldn't say why it was so important.

After considering the question for a moment, she smiled. "You'll laugh."

"I'm grumpy, remember? I won't laugh." He hadn't noticed how little he smiled until Lena had pointed it out.

That caused her to laugh, and the sight had him smiling. His mood lifted, causing a warm lightness deep inside him. Maybe there was more to being happy than he'd realized.

They took their place on the dance floor, but his attention held on Lena, still waiting for an answer.

She met his gaze as they stood before each other, her blue eyes filled with an emotion he couldn't interpret. "Love."

His heart tripped at her answer. The term was a foreign concept to him, nearly as unfamiliar as happiness. Of course, he loved and trusted his sister, but that was the extent of his experience. He quickly dismissed her response. Surely, she jested. She had probably said that to tease him.

If that wasn't the case, they had little in common.

The thought was sobering. He didn't expect to experience love. The emotion was fleeting at best, painful at worst, and certainly unreliable. Trust was all that mattered. One didn't have to love in order to trust.

He gave himself a mental shake. The conversation was ridiculous. They would've been better off speaking of the weather, as he'd suggested. It wasn't as if they were planning a future together. What she believed shouldn't—didn't—matter.

He did his best to ignore the quiet voice inside him that argued otherwise.

The music started, and they took their first steps. Seemingly unaware of his swirling thoughts, Lena continued, "Love for family, friends, and life." She smiled again. "The world would be a better place with more love."

"You don't mention love for a husband." He watched her closely as they moved in time to the music. She was a beautiful lady of marriageable age. Her sisters had already found husbands. Surely, she intended to do the same.

"That is a more difficult task." Her gaze fixed on something in the distance, her smile fading. "To be not only accepted and trusted but loved, despite one's imperfections, is much to ask."

Accepted? The word confused him. What did she mean? He didn't know her well enough to ask, nor was this the time for such a serious conversation.

Instead, he'd settle for another smile.

"You couldn't possibly have imperfections," he teased, hoping to coax a smile from her. He much preferred them over the worry that shadowed her face.

To his surprise, the shadow deepened. "We all have a few. Some are easier to overlook than others."

Her remark made him all the more curious. To what could she possibly be referring? Perhaps whatever it was explained the air of reserve that often came over her, the one that kept others at arm's length. As if she had a secret she guarded closely.

He told himself that he didn't want to know. And he didn't. Sharing secrets meant trusting, and he wasn't ready for that. She didn't seem to be either.

"True," he agreed, at last.

Lena was beautiful and intelligent. Any failings she thought she had were surely minimal. She never lacked for dance partners, that much he knew for certain, as Bernie had commented on it with a hint of envy.

They continued the rest of the dance, speaking little. They seemed to agree not to delve any deeper into the topic. Soon, the last strains of the music faded, and the dance ended.

After they curtsied and bowed, Sterling offered his arm, reluctant to return her to her sister's side. He liked spending time with her even in companionable silence.

Lena squeezed his arm as if to gain his attention, and he glanced at her. "You still owe me a smile, Your Grace."

"I believe I smiled several times during our dance," he protested, pretending to scowl just to see her response.

"Those were accidental." She lifted her chin, a teasing glint in her eyes. "I insist you keep your word."

"Hmm." He looked about the room with a frown, seeming to

find little to smile about. "If I am to smile again, I would need a reason." He focused on her and raised a brow. "You will have to provide one."

"Me?" She blinked, clearly surprised by his demand.

A familiar anticipation ran through him as he guided her the long way around the ballroom, which took them past the door to a corridor that held no guests at the moment. If memory served him from his previous visits to Stanhope's house, the passage led to a small receiving room unlikely to be used this evening.

He feigned nonchalance as he eased them just inside the corridor, blocking them from the view of the ballroom. He turned to face her, expectation—or was it desire?—stirring as he studied the lovely woman before him.

Lena's chest rose and fell quickly beneath his interested gaze. Was she looking forward to a moment alone together as much as he was? Was she anticipating what might happen?

"How do you suggest I convince you to smile?" she asked, her voice barely above a whisper in the dim, quiet space.

"It won't be easy." He pretended to ponder her question. "I do have one suggestion." His gaze fell deliberately to her mouth as he reached for her waist.

"What might that be?" She stepped closer until their bodies touched. Her playful boldness was a force he hadn't predicted. Her scent wrapped around him, tempting him further.

"A kiss." He bent his head until their lips were only a breath apart.

"How can you smile if we're kissing?" she murmured.

"I'll smile after." A mix of affection and desire curled through him. He took her mouth with his, need making him more forceful than he'd intended.

Rather than pull back in alarm, she pressed more firmly against him, her hands reaching around his neck, her fingers moving along the back of his head. His senses were immersed in all things Lena, from her scent to her touch to the feel of her soft form against his length.

He couldn't remember being as tempted by a woman as he was at this moment. Given his title, he'd had more than his share of ladies trying to gain his notice. But Lena did it with little effort. It was as if she didn't want anything from him except himself.

The thought had him drawing back to look into her eyes, his heart pounding fiercely. The idea was unsettling. One he didn't understand. Everyone wanted something from him.

Then she lifted onto her toes to kiss him, and the concern fell away. She opened her lips, and a shiver ran along his skin when their tongues met. The thrill of being inside her in this small way was nearly more than he could stand. And it made him long for so much more.

"Lena," he murmured, wondering if she understood what she did to him.

"Sterling." His name on her lips heightened his passion further. She eased back to look into his eyes. The teasing glint had disappeared, replaced with something that looked like surprise mixed with a hint of worry.

Good, he thought. That made two of them. He didn't pretend to understand what this was between them. But he intended to find out. To analyze it until it made sense. Perhaps then, he'd discover what it was she wanted.

"I should go," she whispered.

He nodded but didn't release her. How could he when she felt perfect right where she was?

She released him and stepped back, breaking his loose hold on her. She smoothed her gown. With one last look at him, she was gone, leaving him standing in the dim corridor with the hope his body would calm down so he could return to the ball.

But after a few minutes with only his imagination for company, he realized that was unlikely. With a frustrated oath, he continued down the corridor, away from the ballroom, and turned left, which he knew from previous visits led to a garden door.

He passed Stanhope's study, surprised to see light shining

from the slightly ajar door. He would've thought the lord would be in the ballroom to see to his guests. The murmur of voices reached his ears, and he paused, hoping whoever was inside didn't decide to step into the corridor and catch him wandering about the house.

The conversation was somewhat heated based on the tone of the voices. That would give him the chance he needed to escape before being seen. He took a step forward, listening closely to make certain their voices didn't move in his direction.

"Clarke insists he'll find treasure."

Sterling stilled in surprise at the thought of anyone talking about Clarke and the treasure in a secluded study at a ball. Then he remembered the numerous wagers being placed on the success of the hunt. With a disgusted shake of his head, he prepared to depart when one of the men spoke again.

"He said he'll advise us of his plan once he knows more."

Had the person contacted Clarke with the hope of learning more to win a wager? That hardly seemed sporting. Sterling eased back into the shadows as the voices drew nearer, wanting to see who was speaking.

The first man was unfamiliar, but the second was Viscount Ludham, a man Sterling had little use for. Stanhope was nowhere in sight.

"Renwick might think he has Clarke's loyalty, but he'll soon learn that's not true." Ludham chuckled. "The duke is being played for a fool."

"Clarke is willing to pay well for more information."

"With Renwick's money, I would assume," Ludham suggested.

"More than likely. The longer Renwick is kept in the dark, the better."

"Someone must know more about the island. It's just a matter of discovering who and what. You're going to see Johnson?"

"I'm traveling to see him next week. Let us hope he has something helpful to share."

"I'm not sure how you'll convince him to tell you if he does," Ludham said.

"I'll think of something. Have no worries on that account."

Anger filled Sterling. Once again, he'd been proven right. Clarke couldn't be trusted. It seemed no one could. He drew a slow breath with the hope of cooling his temper to better think. Confronting the pair now would serve little purpose. They'd only refuse to say anything more. Better that he try to discover what Ludham was up to before raising the viscount's suspicions. He'd send a warning to Johnson, as well, with the hope the man would take care.

The hunt for treasure on Oak Island had just gotten more complicated. How annoying to realize he'd been right not to trust Clarke. Who else was keeping secrets from him?

Chapter Eleven

Lena looked about with interest as she and Marbury, with Nancy trailing behind, walked along the pathway that led to Professor Lindquist's residence. Ella had remained home, her unsettled stomach making outings of any sort difficult, according to Marbury.

His concern for Ella increased Lena's own. If she were to guess, he was more worried than he admitted, based on how distracted he was. When they finished this visit, she intended to press him for details. The drive here had taken nearly an hour, so there would be plenty of time.

Lena wasn't certain what she had expected for a professor's residence, but it wasn't the modest two-story home with an unkempt garden and rusty gate in a questionable neighborhood.

Marbury smiled at her wary expression. "The interior was better than the exterior the last time I called."

Lena nodded, hoping that proved true this time as well.

The elderly servant with a hunched back and rheumy eyes, who took Marbury's card, brought to mind a character out of a novel. Why a man who'd taught at Oxford lived in a house on a narrow, crooked street that bordered the East End puzzled her. She'd expected something grander or at least tidier. Had the man fallen on hard times, or did he prefer to live in such surroundings?

As they waited in the dim front entrance for the servant to

advise the professor of their arrival, Marbury leaned close. "Lindquist seems to prefer to spend his time and resources on what he enjoys rather than worrying over appearances."

"I hope his research skills outweigh his housekeeping abilities."

Marbury smiled at her jest, but the shadows that marked his eyes didn't recede.

The servant returned to show them to the study, where Professor Lindquist rose from his desk with a smile, adjusting his smudged spectacles as if to better see his guests. He had a round face and untidy white hair that he attempted to smooth down upon seeing Lena.

"Good afternoon," he greeted them and bowed. "It's been some time since your last visit, my lord."

"Thank you for seeing us," Marbury said. He introduced Lena, and the professor studied her closely.

"It's a pleasure to meet one of David Wright's daughters." He brushed his hair down again then gestured for them to sit. "While my focus isn't Oak Island in particular, but rather pirate-related documents, I have come across numerous mentions about the place."

"How interesting."

"It is. My research started with letters from a member of a ship's crew and expanded to similar ones, in addition to ships' logs. Tracing the various routes has proven fascinating, and I hope it helps locate treasure. In fact, I'm putting together a book to share what I've learned."

"Please keep me apprised of your progress," Marbury said. "I would be happy to recommend it to members of the Royal Geological Society if I find it helpful."

"I appreciate that." Lindquist beamed.

"Have you come across anything new regarding Oak Island?" the earl asked.

"References to it, for certain. I am cross-referencing letters from crew members to ships' logs to paint a better picture of the use of the island over the years. The place was used more than I anticipated."

He shared a few details that Marbury seemed to find interesting, but Lena was anxious to ask the question uppermost in her mind.

When the conversation paused, she took the opportunity presented. "Have you by chance come across any mention of Ebenezer Jenkins in your research? He was a crewmember on Captain Kidd's vessel."

"Jenkins." The professor frowned then pulled out a sheath of papers from a desk drawer. "The name sounds vaguely familiar, though it's fairly common."

Lena shared a hopeful look with Marbury.

Lindquist ran his finger along a list of names. "Jenkins," he repeated as he searched. "Here it is. Ebenezer. Yes, he was listed as one of the crew on two different vessels. May I ask why you want to know?"

"A friend of ours has letters he wrote to one of their relatives. We're interested in learning more, if possible."

He turned several pages, his brow furrowed as he studied his notes. "From what I've found, he was born in Lincolnshire then spent several years working as a blacksmith. He moved to London and lived there for a time before signing on with Kidd on the *Adventure Galley.*"

Lena's thoughts swirled. Lincolnshire was the location of Sterling's country estate. Lady Bernice had mentioned how much she enjoyed their time there. Perhaps that was where Jenkins had met Lady Bernice's great aunt.

"I do believe he has descendants in that region," the professor continued. "Perhaps they could provide additional information."

"Did he serve on other vessels in addition to Captain Kidd's?" Marbury asked. "With another privateer, perhaps?"

"Yes, I believe he did." The professor consulted his list. "He was on board the *Revenge.*" Lindquist listed two other vessels, but they weren't familiar to Lena.

"Have you found that he's connected to the possible treasure on Oak Island in any way?" Lena asked, knowing it was unlikely.

"No, but so often that sort of information isn't documented. They didn't want anyone to know, you see."

"Of course." While it made sense, Lena was still disappointed.

Marbury asked a few more questions then raised a brow at Lena, as if to ask if there was anything else she wanted to know. She shook her head, disappointed they hadn't learned more.

Then again, while she was interested in learning more about Jenkins, that wouldn't solve the problem of deciphering his letters.

She stood, well aware Marbury was anxious to leave based on the way he sat forward in his chair.

The professor bid them a reluctant goodbye and suggested they visit again soon, making Lena wonder if he was lonely. He seemed to only have a few servants and his research to keep him company. While history could be interesting, she thought both Marbury and Vanbridge had realized it wasn't enough. Learning tantalizing details from the past was wonderful but sharing them with others who had an appreciation for them made it even more so.

Once they'd returned to the carriage, Lena studied Marbury, her concern growing. "Care to share what's on your mind? Is it Ella?"

He opened his mouth as if to deny her claim then grimaced. "She didn't want me to tell you or Norah until she has a chance to tell you herself. She's been having more contractions."

"Oh, dear." Worry sent her heart racing. "The baby?"

"Is fine, as far as we know," he quickly reassured her. "The doctor has advised her to remain in bed to rest with the hope they stop."

"Surely, that will help." She studied him. "Do you think concern over the treasure hunt is upsetting her?"

"She insists not, but I know it bothers her. I wish she'd speak of it more." Marbury rubbed a hand over the back of his neck, clearly troubled.

As was Lena. Ella would be devastated if anything happened to the baby. They all would.

Lena looked out the window but didn't see the passing scenery. Instead, with caution, she gently probed her thoughts for a hint of anything that might foretell an outcome for Ella and the baby. She didn't know whether to be relieved or frustrated when nothing came to mind. If only she could provide assistance, but like always, she couldn't.

She turned back to Marbury. "You'll keep us advised of how things progress?"

"Of course. Come and visit her soon. I've told her what little we've learned. While I don't want her thinking we're withholding details, neither do I want to dwell on the topic."

"Agreed." Anger flooded her at the situation. And at Sterling, Clarke, and the supposed treasure on Oak Island. Never had she expected that Ella and the baby could be at risk because of all of this.

But most of all, she was angry with herself for not being able to help.

"Lena," Marbury began, his green eyes dark with worry, "would you tell me if you..."

"If I have any feelings?" she finished for him. She considered the request carefully, reluctant to agree. Her gift couldn't be depended on. Even if she had a feeling, it could be wrong. "You know that any sense I have isn't necessarily right." She lifted her gloved hand only to let it drop to her lap, at a loss as to how to explain. "Even if I experience a sense of foreboding, it doesn't mean it would pertain to Ella."

"I know." He sat forward to touch her arm as if to show support. "But perhaps it's more reliable than you think." She opened her mouth to protest only to have him raise his hand to stop her. "Think of how much you helped Vanbridge."

"It didn't stop him from being hurt." She stared out the window again as the carriage swayed, frustration filling her. "What help is it when it doesn't save those I care about from harm?"

She didn't know if Ella had told him how badly she'd failed when their father died. That terrible day, she'd known something was wrong but hadn't been able to identify the cause. In truth, she'd smothered the feeling, not welcoming its intrusion.

She should've known it had to do with her father. She should've allowed the feeling to come. If only she'd checked on him. Instead, she'd done nothing other than try to ignore the unsettling sensation.

"You don't know that." Marbury's tone was quiet but firm. "Perhaps you and Norah interrupted whoever it was from injuring Vanbridge further. You might've saved his life."

"Doubtful." She knew she was being difficult but couldn't help it.

"But possible." He smiled. "Would you agree with that much?"

She heaved a sigh and considered the idea. "I suppose that's true."

"Some feeling is better than none at all." He leaned back against the carriage seat. "Too many times, people have an instinctive thought or a sense of foreboding but choose to ignore it. Think of the times you have acted and focus on that rather than on the times you couldn't use it at your whim."

Whim was an interesting word choice. But she understood his point. Just because she couldn't control the feeling didn't mean it wasn't helpful at times. On that much, she could agree.

"Thank you, Marbury." She shared a smile with him. "I appreciate your thoughts." If only others were as understanding about her ability as he was.

When she'd been young, perhaps only six or seven, and her mother had been alive, she'd had a terrible feeling during a visit from Mrs. Johnson, her father's partner's wife. Lena had shared the thought—that Norah was hurt—and the woman had stared at her, her expression clearly suggesting Lena had lost her mind.

When Ella brought a limping Norah, who'd twisted her ankle, home a few minutes later, Mrs. Johnson had crossed herself as if to ward off evil, her gaze holding on Lena. Lena would never forget how she felt at that moment—embarrassed and hurt. The incident had shaken her to the core, putting a crack in the foundation of her belief in herself and her sense.

She'd asked her mother about it after Mrs. Johnson had left.

"Perhaps it's best if we keep your ability to ourselves. Not everyone will understand. In fact, most won't. And what people don't understand, they often fear."

There had been other times as well. Times when what she was sensing would slip out, causing any who noticed to stare at her in alarm. Was it any wonder that she had never been comfortable with the ability?

If she didn't have to guard her thoughts so closely and could open herself to what she felt, she might have a better relationship with the gift. But that was a dangerous path when the feeling could come at any given moment, regardless of where she was or who she was with.

What people thought of her affected not only herself, but her sisters and her grandfather, Lady Havenby, Marbury, and Vanbridge. The circle was growing ever wider. Living in London made it much more difficult to hide her ability than the isolation of her childhood home.

"Shall I tell Ella you'll be by soon to visit?" Marbury asked, returning her thoughts to the current problem.

"Yes. I'll call on her in the morning. I'll do my best not to dwell on the treasure hunt." If only Sterling would halt the treasure hunt before something terrible happened. She didn't need a premonition to think it would.

STERLING LOOKED AROUND the Society offices, hoping Viscount Ludham had chosen to attend the monthly meeting. He wanted to speak with the viscount and make certain the conversation moved to the treasure hunt and see how Ludham reacted to discussing it and possibly gain more insight as to what Ludham intended.

Sterling had sent a letter to Mr. Johnson to advise him that he might be asked for information on the treasure hunt. Perhaps even pressed for it and to take care. He didn't know what Ludham and his companion thought they'd learn. Obviously, if Johnson knew anything, he would've found the treasure himself.

Sterling had reviewed the conversation he'd overheard numerous times, wondering if he'd misinterpreted the hint of a threat. Logic said yes, but his instincts said no.

Ludham and his companion might not have truly meant any of it. Perhaps it was all a lark. But the fact that they'd met in private in Stanhope's study suggested they didn't want their conversation overheard. Whoever Ludham had been speaking with had left immediately afterward, making Sterling suspect he hadn't been a guest at the ball. That might explain why he hadn't recognized him—the man wasn't a member of the *ton*.

Sterling walked into the large, nearly full meeting room, noting Marbury, Vanbridge, and Rothwood were all absent. He found that curious since at least one of them usually attended the monthly meetings. He hoped nothing was amiss.

His thoughts turned to Lena as the meeting was called to order. Bernie had hoped to see her at a garden party the previous day, which had nearly been enough for Sterling to consider attending. Other duties had kept him away. That had proven to be a good thing since Bernie reported afterward that Lena hadn't been there.

Concern seeped through him as he considered Lena's absence yesterday added to the three men's absences today. He worried something was wrong, though there was little he could do to discover if anything was amiss. Sending a message to Lena would be too forward. The fact that he'd danced with only her at two different balls had probably already caused talk. He needed to take care, or others, including her grandfather, might gain the wrong impression.

Lord Fremont summarized the Society's activities over the past month and provided updates on several explorations the group helped to fund. Viscount Worley was leading a particularly interesting dig in South America and had sent a report outlining the results which were quite favorable. This was Worley's second search there and much was being accomplished. Sterling looked forward to his return to hear firsthand about his discoveries.

At last, the meeting ended, and Sterling took the time to visit with several others while keeping an eye on Ludham. He made certain the viscount saw him and waited to see if he approached.

Sterling conversed with Viscount Dyke followed by the Duke of Wyndburg, all while watching Ludham. Unfortunately, the man kept his distance, leaving Sterling no choice but to attempt to initiate a casual conversation. He made his way across the room to speak with someone who stood close to Ludham and, after a brief exchange, turned to face Ludham.

"Good afternoon, Your Grace." Ludham bowed after Sterling greeted him.

"Worley's efforts in South America are impressive, wouldn't you agree?" Sterling asked.

"Quite," Ludham agreed. "Does hearing of his success make you more anxious for your own?"

Sterling frowned. "It's not a competition."

"Isn't it?" Ludham raised a brow. "Isn't all exploration and treasure hunting? After all, it only matters if you're the first. Much like other areas in life."

The remark made Sterling realize why he didn't care for the man. "Competition is all well and good when it's used productively. Rushing through difficult tasks is fruitless and often dangerous."

"When it comes to exploring or hunting for treasure, danger is part of the risk." Ludham's sly smile suggested he was hoping to stir Sterling's ire.

And he was, which only annoyed Sterling further. "Do you intend to do some of your own?"

Ludham shrugged. "I don't care to battle the jungle or dig in the dirt." He lifted a hand to study his nails as if pleased no dirt was visible beneath them. "Some of us are better suited for managing projects rather than laboring."

"You make it sound as if you're actively involved in one now." Sterling waited to see how he'd respond, watching his face closely.

"Not as of yet. But like many of our fellow members," he said as his gaze swung around the room, "one is always looking for opportunities."

"Hmm. Are you sure you haven't found something that has caught your interest?"

Ludham smiled. "Time will tell."

Though tempted to press him for details, Sterling held back. Whatever Ludham and his associate were up to would soon be revealed. Nothing remained secret among Society members for long. "I do hope you'll keep us apprised."

"What of your dig on Oak Island?" Ludham asked. "Have any serious discoveries been made?"

"We're still in the early stages." Sterling cocked his head. "Are you fishing for information out of true interest, or have you placed a wager on the outcome?"

Ludham laughed. "Placing a wager on a treasure hunt is much like throwing away money, wouldn't you agree? Then again, you're already throwing money down a shaft or two on Oak Island, aren't you?"

"As you said, time will tell." Sterling refused to allow Ludham to get under his skin. Not unless the viscount showed his hand. Making annoying comments wasn't a crime, though with men like Ludham, Sterling wished it was.

"Did I see you dancing with Lena Wright at the Stanhope Ball?" Ludham frowned as if trying to remember. "Surely you're not interested in her." A sly, knowing look came over his expression. "Of course. I see now. You're attempting to gain information for your treasure hunt from Miss Wright, aren't you? Using a lady for such an ulterior motive seems like poor behavior. Tsk. Tsk."

Sterling clenched his fist, suppressing the urge to plant it in the man's face. "I don't appreciate you suggesting such a thing. Nor do I intend to do anything of the sort."

"Of course not." Ludham clearly didn't believe him, not that Sterling cared. Still, it irritated him. "I would do the same if I were you. Lena Wright is a delectable morsel, isn't she?"

"Mind your manners, Ludham." Sterling refused to listen to him talk about Lena, and the urge to punch him became even stronger. "Do try to remember you're a gentleman. At least, you're supposed to be."

With that, he turned on his heel and strode away. He didn't know what Ludham was up to, but it wasn't good. He certainly didn't like his comments about Lena. Sterling knew he wasn't the only one intrigued by her. According to Bernie, Lena's popularity was ever increasing. She had numerous friends, both men and women. Sterling was pleased to be among them but even happier to be the one she'd kissed.

He shrugged a shoulder to dispel the guilt that threatened. Ludham was wrong. Sterling would never attempt to obtain information about the island from Lena, even if that had been the reason Bernie had befriended her. There was more to their relationship than a treasure hunt. Much more.

A smile threatened to curve his lips at the thought. He was thoroughly enjoying coming to know Lena and looked forward to the next time he'd see her. He hoped it was soon.

Chapter Twelve

"Good morning." For the second day in a row, Lena settled in the chair beside Ella's bed with a bright smile. She kept her visits short—no longer than an hour. The point of Ella being on bed rest was so she could actually rest. A constant stream of visitors wouldn't help, even if it eased her boredom.

Ella gave a less-than-sincere return smile. "You're beginning to make a habit of this. Did Leo request that you visit again?"

"Of course not. You're my sister. I came of my own accord to keep you company." Based on the doubtful look Ella sent her, she didn't believe her. "I *do* enjoy spending time with you."

Ella heaved a sigh and pressed two fingers to her temple. "Forgive me. I enjoy being with you as well. I just don't like being treated like an invalid."

"Understandable since you're not one. You are a strong, healthy woman who will soon have a baby to hold."

"Yes." Ella's entire being softened at the mention of the baby, and she placed a hand on the growing bump visible beneath the bed cover. "Yes, I will. And I will do anything asked to make certain he or she is healthy. But being ordered to remain in bed is more difficult than I could've imagined."

"I'm sure. It gives you too much time to think, doesn't it?" And worry. But Lena didn't add that.

"True." She held Lena's gaze for a moment. "Is there any

news from Renwick about the treasure hunt? Leo refuses to allow me to read the newssheets until I'm feeling better."

"I agree. None of the headlines are good these days. The papers seem to think only bad news sells copies." When Ella continued to watch her, Lena added, "There is no news from Renwick or Lady Bernice or in *The Times* on the topic of the treasure hunt. Does that ease your mind?"

"I suppose. I just keep thinking about how upset Father would be if Clarke found treasure after digging for only a few weeks." Her brow puckered, a testament to her worry.

The concern bothered Lena as well. While she was still certain Clarke was digging in the wrong place, that could soon change. However, it would be nice to discredit him, which would quiet talk of the hunt.

"Yes, he would've been displeased," Lena agreed. "But his efforts might make any progress Clarke has easier."

Ella scoffed. "Do you think he will admit that? I certainly don't."

Lena shifted forward to squeeze Ella's hand, alarmed at her upset. She'd obviously been stewing on the topic. "Why don't we speak of something else? There is nothing we can do to change the outcome of what happens on the island."

"Do you still think he's digging in the wrong place?"

"Yes." For all the good it did.

"If only we could prove that." Ella worried her lower lip, clearly trying to think of a way to do so.

"Ella." Lena waited for her sister to meet her gaze. "Stop. What truly matters is you and the baby. Nothing else." She reached into her reticule and pulled out a tiny white nightgown she'd stitched for the baby, certain it would distract her. "I still need to embroider the neckline, but what do you think?"

"Oh, Lena. It's beautiful." She took the garment with both hands and set it on her lap to smooth the soft fabric. "Each time I see clothing for the baby, it makes it even more real that I will soon be a mother."

Lena's chest tightened with emotion as she imagined Ella tending to a baby. "You are going to make a wonderful mother. I know this time isn't easy, but soon you will be so busy that you'll wish you enjoyed this rest more."

Ella laughed, just as Lena meant her to. "I'm sure you're right." With one last admiring look, she handed the gown back to Lena. "It's beautiful. Thank you for making it. Your stitches are perfect, as always."

"I will have it done soon." Though she hated to mention how many days had passed since she'd last worked on it.

"Leo seems to think I shouldn't even embroider." She shook her head. "Sitting idle only allows my thoughts to churn. I'd much rather stay busy."

"Perhaps you can do a little of both," Lena suggested. "Day-dreaming is something all three of us should do more."

"That sounds better than simply sitting here worrying." Ella smiled. "We've never had much of a chance to do anything of that sort while growing up, did we? There were always chores that needed to be done."

They reminisced for a time, though Lena wasn't certain doing too much of that was a good idea either. Focusing on the past only brought their father more to mind.

Lena shared details from the last few social events, not wanting Ella to feel like she was missing anything. Soon, the end of the hour was drawing near.

"I should go so you can rest." Lena rose and leaned down to hug Ella. "Try not to worry. Hold good thoughts for both you and the baby. I'll visit you again soon." Lena and Norah had already agreed one would call in the morning and the other in the afternoon to help break up the long day. Hopefully, that wouldn't prove to be too much for Ella.

"Thank you, Lena."

"I have a new poetry book that's quite lovely I could bring you," she offered.

"I'd rather have something more interesting. Perhaps a romantic tale or a detective novel. Those might better hold my attention."

"I'll see what I can find." Norah probably had a new book or two. Lena would send her a message to suggest she bring Ella one this afternoon. She bent to kiss her sister's cheek. "Take care. And remember that Leo only wants what's best for you because he loves you dearly."

Ella smiled, the joy in her eyes saying much. "I know. I love him as well." She heaved a sigh. "I look forward to your next visit and promise to be in better spirits."

"I shall hold you to it." Seeing Ella still so upset about Clarke and his dig made Lena more determined to see what she could find to prove him wrong.

The time had come to call on Lady Bernice again to see if she had found any more letters and if she had updates on Clarke's efforts.

⇥⟫⟪⇤

STERLING STRODE INTO the entrance hall. "Foster, do you know where Lady Bernice is?"

"In the drawing room, Your Grace. She's having tea with Miss Wright."

Pleasure curled through Sterling at the news. "Thank you." He started up the stairs.

"Should I have fresh tea and another cup sent up?" Foster asked.

"Yes, please." He wasn't certain if the ladies would appreciate him interrupting, but he couldn't help himself. The temptation of seeing Lena was too much to resist.

He slowed as he neared the doorway, curious as to what the ladies were talking about. He hoped Bernie didn't speak too much about Oak Island. Lena probably didn't want to hear more about the treasure hunt.

"Do you have any news on the treasure hunt?" Lena asked.

Sterling nearly halted in surprise, though he supposed it was only natural that she was curious.

"Progress continues, according to Clarke's most recent correspondence." The happiness in Bernie's tone pleased him.

He'd been concerned that when she returned from Switzerland, she'd find little to occupy her mind or her time. She had few true friends. Those near her age weren't interested in the same things she was. While she enjoyed fashion, she didn't care to spend much time shopping. Her reading was varied but the fact that she'd rather read a book than look at a magazine set her apart as well.

Lena seemed similar to Bernie in many ways, though she was obviously well-liked. She was always visiting with others when he saw her at events. He was pleased the two had found each other.

He nearly scoffed at the thought, willing to admit the truth to himself. He liked that *he* had met Lena. She was an unexpected brightness in his life. Each time he saw her, or even thought he would, his mood lightened. She appealed to him in many ways, some of which he didn't understand.

However, he had yet to determine whether she could be trusted. That was a leap he wasn't ready to take. He moved closer to the doorway and looked inside.

Lena sat on the edge of the settee, hands on her lap, her head tilted to the side as she listened to Bernie. Her gown was a pale pink, much like a swath of spun sugar, a delicate treat he'd once had while in Italy.

She was truly a beautiful woman with a slender frame and long limbs. There was a strength to her body and in her spirit. She was kind and intelligent. But her reserve made him wonder at its cause.

His physical reaction to her was puzzling. Concerning, actually. He couldn't think of the last time a woman had made him feel like this. Each time he saw her, his breath caught, his heartbeat sped, and his entire body tightened. Was this only lust? He didn't think so. While he would enjoy another kiss, he also looked forward to speaking with her.

Then she turned her head and looked directly at him as if sensing the weight of his regard. Her lips curved, and her eyes sparkled, suggesting she was pleased to see him. Good, because he was pleased to see her as well.

"Good afternoon. I hope I'm not interrupting."

Lena rose to curtsy. "Good afternoon, Your Grace." She placed a slight emphasis on the last word. No one else would notice, but he did. He liked that they shared a private jest.

"Sterling, have you come to join us?" Bernie asked with a smile.

"Perhaps for a few minutes, if you don't mind." He bent to kiss his sister's offered cheek then glanced around the room. "Where's Aunt Edith?"

"She has a bit of a headache so is resting in her room."

He nodded then gestured for Lena to sit before he did the same. Their aunt seemed to have an even more delicate constitution than Bernie had in her younger years.

"I hope it's nothing serious," Lena said as she smoothed her skirts.

"As do I." Bernie frowned. "She should find more activities that bring her joy. So few things do."

"You don't think she likes attending events with you?" Sterling asked.

"She says she does, but those don't seem to be enough."

He hid a smile. Bernie was practically describing herself until she'd started on the goal of discovering all she could about Oak Island. Having a purpose could be very satisfying, something he could attest to, as well.

"Speaking of events, which ones are you attending in the coming week?" Lena asked as she reached for her tea and took a sip.

They discussed the possibilities, which included two balls, a garden party, and several musicals, as Foster entered with a tray.

"I took the liberty of requesting fresh tea and another cup," Sterling said.

If he hadn't been watching Lena, he wouldn't have noted her lips tightening, as if she wasn't particularly pleased with his intention to remain for a time. Surely it wasn't because he'd interrupted her questions about Oak Island.

They passed a pleasant half hour before Lena said, "I must be going."

"Already?" Bernie seemed surprised then glanced at the clock on the nearby table. "I didn't realize how quickly time was passing. Are you certain you can't stay?"

"I have another call to make." She stood with a smile.

"Of course." They bid their goodbyes with Sterling adding his.

"It was a pleasure to see you again, Your Grace." Lena curtsied.

"I enjoyed the visit. I hope you call on us again soon." Sterling was disappointed he and Lena hadn't had a moment alone but told himself it was for the best.

If they had, he would've been tempted to kiss her again. He shouldn't allow himself such liberties. Not unless he intended to court her, and he wasn't prepared for that. Marriage was an important duty in his future but not for some time. In truth, he had doubts as to how enjoyable it would be unless he found a lady he not only trusted but cared for. That seemed unlikely thus far.

"Thank you." Lena looked again at Bernie. "I look forward to seeing you at the Evanston ball."

After Lena left, Bernie turned to him. "Miss Wright is such delightful company."

"Indeed." On that, they agreed, yet he couldn't help but wonder. "Did she have any particular reason for calling?"

"Sterling." Bernie's brown eyes, so much like his own, flashed with annoyance. "She doesn't have to have a reason. Couldn't it be that she enjoys my company?"

"Of course." Remorse immediately filled him. The last thing he wanted was for Bernie to doubt herself and her ability to make friends.

"You must learn to set aside your suspicions of people," she admonished. "Not everyone has an ulterior purpose."

"Perhaps." That was the best he could offer. Too often he'd been taught that everyone wanted something.

"Besides, what could Lena possibly want from us? Her grandfather is a duke." Bernie's eyes narrowed as if she were turning over the possibilities.

For that, he was sorry. He should've kept his suspicions to himself. While he didn't want Bernie to be so naïve that people took advantage of her, neither did he want her to guard herself more than she already did.

"I'm sure you're right," he agreed. "I only meant that perhaps she was curious about our progress on Oak Island."

"She did ask, but we didn't discuss it after you joined us. She also wanted to know if I had any more letters, which I don't." Bernie frowned, suggesting his questions had her wondering the same thing.

He dismissed his concern. Lena and her sisters were probably anxious to know what was happening with Clarke's efforts, though he wasn't sure if they supported the dig. Not after seeing their father work so hard for so long.

"Shall I escort you to the Evanston ball?" he asked as he stood, wanting to change the subject.

"I would like that. Thank you." Bernie smiled brightly. "I couldn't ask for a more thoughtful brother."

Guilt threatened at her words. In truth, he'd offered because he looked forward to seeing Lena again. He told himself he wanted the opportunity to make certain she wasn't trying to use his sister to gain information on the treasure hunt. While that was true, it wasn't the only reason he looked forward to seeing Lena. She appealed to him in many ways. He looked forward to seeing where that led. Never mind the odd feeling in his chest each time he saw her. That was a concern for later.

"WHAT HAVE YOU discovered?" Norah asked in a whisper at the Evanston ball.

Lena turned after finishing a conversation with Lady Whitmore to glare at her sister. "Truly? No greeting? No exchange of pleasantries? Just business?"

Norah had the grace to look sheepish as she watched Lady Whitmore step away to speak with someone else. "My apologies. I spent the afternoon with Ella. Some of her angst seems to be spreading to me."

"You're certain it's not the other way around?" Lena knew Norah was more upset than any of them about Clarke's hunt on Oak Island.

"I certainly hope not." She grimaced as she considered her feelings more closely. "I have tried my best to act as if it doesn't matter and change the subject when she brings it up. But you can't tell me the topic doesn't follow you day and night."

Lena sighed then nodded. "True. I've gone through the letters again and again. But I haven't found anything else. Why would Jenkins draw a hidden map of Oak Island if not for a purpose?"

"I don't know. I have wondered the same. I've reread some of Father's journals, but I'm not finding anything helpful there either. Did you have a chance to visit with Lady Bernice again?"

"I called on her yesterday. She doesn't have any other letters. I had just asked what news she had from Clarke when Sterling joined us."

Norah's brow rose and an amused look crossed her expression. "His Grumpiness joined you for tea? How interesting."

"He might not be as grumpy as I thought." Only then did Lena realize he hadn't smiled yesterday. That meant he owed her an extra one. She would be certain to remind him of that if she had the chance to speak with him this evening.

"Seriously, Lena. Renwick never smiles." She tipped her head toward the ballroom entrance.

Lena turned to follow her gaze and saw Sterling and Bernie standing there. Her heart thudded in response.

Sure enough, Sterling wore his usual dour expression while Bernie looked over the crowd with a mix of excitement and nerves. Lena recognized her expression as she'd felt much the same way their first Season in London. Her spectacles flashed in the light. Lena was pleased she was wearing them.

Mrs. Easton stood just behind them, her nose lifted in the air as she surveyed the crowd with curiosity.

Lena returned her attention to Sterling, who looked so handsome in his formal evening attire. His chiseled features and erect posture matched his somber expression. Yet Lena could now see beyond that.

She didn't like to think what his upbringing had been like to forge him into the man he was today. His father must've been harsh indeed.

Then his focus caught on her and his expression immediately softened. A hint of a smile—just a hint—curved his mouth, and Lena smiled in return.

"Except when he looks at you." Norah's voice sounded as if it came from a distance and took a moment to sink in.

"Whatever do you mean?" Lena asked though she hadn't managed to pull her attention from Sterling.

"His Grace is almost smiling at you." The disbelief in Norah's tone would've been amusing under other circumstances or if it pertained to a different topic. "I cannot wait to share this development with Ella."

Sterling turned to his sister, who was speaking to him, breaking the spell that had held Lena in its grasp. She blinked, stunned by her swirling emotions. How could one look across a crowded ballroom cause such turmoil within her?

Norah's remark struck her. "Do not dare to say anything to Ella." The last thing she wanted was her eldest sister, who would like nothing more than to see Lena married, to focus her attention on the possibility of Lena and Sterling marrying.

"So you're admitting there *is* something between you." Norah's blue eyes lit with excitement.

"I'd not admitting anything of the sort." Her ears prickled with the heat of embarrassment. Only one of her sisters could do that so easily.

"This is perfect. Don't you see?" Norah clutched Lena's hand with enthusiasm.

"I have no idea of what you're speaking." Trepidation filled Lena so strongly that she had to resist the urge to jerk her hand away from Norah's.

"We must tell Ella. This is exactly the sort of distraction she needs. Her focus will shift to wondering what might be happening between you and Renwick rather than the treasure hunt. Meanwhile, you'll be able to spend more time proving that Clarke is lying. I'll watch over Ella and tell her you're busy with Renwick."

Lena stared at Norah in disbelief.

"Did I hear mention of my name?" Sterling asked, one brow lifted, as he and Bernie joined them.

Lena wanted to hide behind the nearest potted plant. Her mind was completely blank as she struggled with an explanation. How much of Norah's ridiculous ideas had he heard?

Based on Norah's wide eyes, she wondered the same.

Lena dropped into a curtsy, hoping beyond hope Sterling hadn't heard them.

❦

Chapter Thirteen

STERLING DIDN'T PRETEND to know what was happening, but the guilty look on Lena's face roused his suspicions. It was the same expression she'd had when they first met, and she'd rescued Bernie from toppling into the fountain.

He'd heard Lady Vanbridge mention Oak Island and his name. That wasn't a complete surprise, but Lena's expression caused him to wonder about the nature of their conversation.

"Good evening, Your Grump…er, Grace." Lady Vanbridge curtsied, two bright spots of color on her cheeks.

"Good evening." Sterling wasn't certain whether to be annoyed or amused by the near slip. His gaze returned to Lena, who also seemed to be trying to regain her composure.

"Lady Bernice, what a lovely gown." Lady Vanbridge smiled. "That shade of green is so flattering on you."

"Why, thank you." Bernie glanced down and smoothed the mint green fabric with her white gloves. "It is one of my favorites."

"Forgive me, Your Grace." Lady Vanbridge's charming smile nearly put him at ease. "I was just asking my sister if you'd shared any updates on the dig."

Sterling considered the explanation. Though reasonable, he wondered if there was more to their conversation.

"Nothing new of late," Lady Bernice answered for him. "We

do hope to receive an update next week. Isn't that right, Sterling?"

"Yes."

Apparently, his answer didn't satisfy Bernie as she cast him a warning look. One that suggested his mistrust was showing. At times, he wished he had the same faith in others his sister did. How different his life would be—one filled with friends and laughter.

He gave himself a mental shake at the improbable wish. As he'd told himself before, it would be more suspicious if they didn't ask about the treasure hunt.

"Clarke normally sends updates twice each month," he said at last. "I'm sure we'll know more details soon." Hopefully, it would include more than a glowing report about his progress. Sterling wanted facts, not wishful thinking.

"Indeed." Bernie nodded.

"Good evening." The Marquess of Vanbridge joined them, his attention quickly moving to his wife. The affection between them was palpable and sent a surprising pang of envy through Sterling.

What he saw between them made him consider what sort of relationship he hoped to have with his future wife. His plans hadn't gone much further than his intention to marry a lady with an appropriate title and a sizable dowry to expand the ducal holdings, as his father would've wanted.

Yet having seen Marbury and his wife, along with Vanbridge and his, Sterling reconsidered. What might it be like to have a true partnership built on love, respect, and shared values with one's wife?

Perhaps there was more to happiness than he'd realized. His gaze caught on Lena as she watched her sister and Vanbridge. A small smile played along her lush lips, making him think she appreciated their relationship as well.

Bernie bumped his arm again, making him realize he'd lost track of the conversation. "I'm sorry?"

"I asked what you thought of Worley's efforts in South America," Vanbridge asked.

"It sounds promising from the report given at the last Society meeting."

Vanbridge shared a few additional details that were included in a letter Marbury had received from Worley. The conversation made Sterling hope Clarke would discover something soon, as well.

His attention returned to Lena, and that hope dulled. He didn't want any success Clarke found to hurt her or her sisters. And he knew it would. He'd already heard a few people remark on how ineffective Wright's efforts had been if Clarke was making inroads on locating the treasure already.

No one wanted to hear that about their father, especially when they had obviously loved him.

Lena met his gaze, those clear blue eyes stealing his breath. He'd told himself he wouldn't dance with her this evening. Three balls in a row would cause gossip. If he gave into the urge, he'd have to find one or two other ladies to dance with. Doing so would give everyone the impression that he was seeking a bride, and that was the last thing he wanted to do.

But as he looked into Lena's eyes, he couldn't find it in himself to care. He only wanted to dance with her.

"May I have the honor of a dance?" Too late, he realized he'd interrupted Vanbridge. "My apologies."

A knowing smile crossed the marquess's face, one that had Sterling shifting uncomfortably. It was almost as if Vanbridge knew what Sterling was thinking.

Surely not.

"Of course." Lena looked at the others. "If you'll excuse us." She stepped forward to take his offered arm.

"My apologies," he murmured as they walked toward the dance floor.

"For what?"

"My behavior. I didn't mean to draw attention to…us."

A lovely rose color washed over her face. "Us?"

Us. He turned the word over in his mind, surprised at how much he liked it. "Yes. Us."

She frowned as if uncertain whether she liked it. That caused him to smile. Knowing she was off balance made him want to push further to see her reaction.

"You and I." He watched her closely.

"Hmm."

Her noncommittal response had him chuckling, and she studied him as if wondering if he'd lost his mind.

Perhaps he had.

The fact that most other eligible ladies would've been crowing with delight if he'd said something similar to them, while Lena had yet to decide whether she liked it, was highly amusing.

Her astonished gaze made him ask, "What is it?"

The astonishment slid into a delightful grin and her eyes softened with what almost looked like tenderness and, dare he say, affection. "You laughed. I liked it very much, Sterling. I hope you do that again soon."

With a light heart, he drew her into his arms as the music began, wondering just where this lovely lady was going to lead him.

꙳꙳꙳

LENA SET ASIDE the book she'd been reading as a shiver washed over her. The deep sense of dread had her shrugging with the hope it would go away to no avail.

She'd been enjoying a quiet evening at home—the first in three days—until now.

Grandfather was at his club, having dined with her earlier. He seemed to understand her frequent need for time alone, making her wonder if he felt the same way at times. She'd always appreciated—and needed—time alone. It helped to calm the restlessness that so often came over her, especially after attending events several days in a row.

She also wanted some time away from Sterling with the hope her growing feelings for him would calm. The last dance they'd shared three nights ago lingered in her thoughts far too much.

Now, as unease held her tight, her thoughts flew to Ella, but some probing at the feeling suggested neither of her sisters was in danger. Then who? Grandfather? Marbury or Vanbridge? None of them seemed to worsen the feeling. Who else?

She rose to pace the room, allowing her thoughts to roam. Sterling? No. Then it came to her in a rush—Lady Bernice.

The sense of foreboding grew even stronger, causing her heart to race and chills to crawl along her skin. She tried to remember what event, if any, Bernie had planned to attend this evening. Surely, wherever she was, Sterling was with her to help if anything was wrong.

The thought didn't ease her angst in the least. Something was wrong. Terribly wrong. She rubbed her upper arms but that didn't stop her chills.

She'd send a note to Bernie at home. She hurried to the writing desk to pull out a sheet of paper only to hesitate. What could she possibly say that wouldn't make her sound crazy?

Just wondering if you are well.
I urge you to take care this evening.

She set aside the paper with a shake of her head. A message wouldn't do. She would have to call on her and see for herself that she was safe. An excuse of some sort would come to mind if all was well. Whether she needed to warn Bernie to be careful remained to be seen.

Still, Lena hesitated. Calling on her at this hour was unseemly but what else could she do? Situations like this were not only embarrassing but placed the secret of her gift at risk. Bernie would wonder why Lena had called. She would certainly tell Sterling.

She sighed, wishing a different solution came to mind. He'd

already looked at her on more than one occasion with suspicion in his brown eyes. She would much rather he look at her the way he had just before they'd danced.

When he'd said "us" as if it were a foreign word. "You and I," he'd whispered, looking into her eyes. Then he'd smiled. And laughed. She pressed both hands over her heart as a completely different emotion swelled there.

She'd relived that moment numerous times. While she couldn't claim to know what this was between them, she didn't want it to end. And somehow, she knew in her heart that if he found out about her sense, it would, just as other friendships had, once they realized she was different in an inexplicable way.

Lena closed her eyes, indecision making her thoughts race.

She drew a deep breath and opened her eyes. That didn't matter if Bernie was in danger. The risk was terrible, but one she had to take. With resolve, she hurried down the stairs to request a carriage, along with the request for James and Nancy to accompany her.

James took one look at her worried expression and seemed to know something was amiss. The footman had witnessed her gift on more than one occasion. Rather than question her or stare at her in fear, he assumed whatever she was feeling was the truth and should be acted upon. His belief in her was refreshing.

It didn't take long before they were driving toward Renwick House. Lena wished her sisters were with her so they could help form a plan. Ella would be her practical self and ask what they would do if Bernie wasn't home. Lena considered the question but had no answer.

Norah would ask what excuse they could give for calling so late. Lena didn't have an answer for that either.

She should've brought one of the letters. At the very least, she could say she had a question about it. Though she didn't know why such a question couldn't wait until tomorrow.

"Are you well, miss?" Nancy asked, her worried gaze holding on Lena in the dim carriage light.

"Yes. Quite." The maid's question made her wonder if she'd been talking to herself.

Lena hoped answers came to her once they arrived. Bernie was probably fine and would stare at her as if she were crazy. Then again, knowing Bernie, she would be delighted that Lena had called, regardless of the hour.

The thought was reassuring. Bernie didn't have the same suspicious outlook her brother did.

Soon, the carriage rolled to a halt. James assisted her and Nancy to alight then hurried up the front steps and knocked on the door before they'd joined him.

Nerves struck Lena as she glanced up at the darkened windows of the upper floors. How ridiculous of her to come. A houseful of servants was inside. Foster would not approve of her calling at this hour. Heaven forbid if Sterling was home. She hated to think of what he'd say about her visit.

She turned back to look at the carriage, wondering if she should just go. But even that temptation didn't make her feet move from the front step.

The door swung open to reveal a surprised Foster. His expression tightened with disapproval, but Lena lifted her chin. She was determined to see this through now that she was here.

"I am terribly sorry, but I have an urgent matter to discuss with Lady Bernice. Is she at home?"

The butler hesitated for a long moment, making Lena think he intended to send them away. At last, he gave a single nod. "Allow me to see if she's receiving."

Lena could've hugged the man, despite his dour expression. Bernie must be here, and that alone was a relief.

They were shown to the small reception room that adjoined the entrance hall to wait. Nancy and James both watched her pace the small room. When several minutes passed without Foster's return, Lena moved to the doorway, only to look up to see a maid and a footman hurrying along the upper floor.

A few moments later, Foster rushed down the stairs.

"Is there a problem?" Lena asked, her worry heightening.

The butler frowned. "We are having difficulty locating Lady Bernice, miss."

Lena's heart thudded dully as she met his worried eyes. She looked away, willing the knowing feeling to provide a hint of where Bernie might be. Nothing came to her.

A familiar helplessness threatened to weigh her down like a stone in the river. How many times had she longed for clarity but never received it? Why should she expect anything different now?

She shoved away the doubt and focused on Bernie. She closed her eyes and brought Bernie's image to her thoughts, well aware of the servants watching her closely.

Instead of seeing Bernie, she only saw books.

Shelves of books, to be precise.

Her eyes flew open as anger and frustration took hold. What good was her ability when she couldn't help others?

Then a possible answer came to her—were books somehow connected to Bernie? The idea felt right. More than right, in fact.

"We should look in the study," Lena advised Foster. Surely, Sterling had books in his study.

The servant frowned, seeming to think it highly unlikely they'd find Lady Bernice there. Or perhaps he was confused about why she'd suggested it.

Lena didn't bother to explain as urgency filled her. She hurried past the man and down the corridor, certain Sterling's study was in a similar place as her grandfather's.

"But, miss—" Foster began.

"It's best to see if she's right," James advised the man then followed her.

Lena opened the only door along the corridor, her gaze catching on a lit candle sputtering on a small table near the dark fireplace. "Bernie?"

Disappointment stole through her when she realized the room was empty.

Then a soft moan echoed in the quiet space.

"Bernie, is that you?" Lena rushed forward, scanning the room as she tried to place from where the sound had come. She moved to pick up the candleholder and held it aloft, the sight of a form on the floor near the desk catching her eye.

She hurried forward to see Bernie lying face down, one arm flung to the side and her legs twisted in the opposite direction.

Lena knelt beside her, searching to see what might be wrong. "Bernie?" She touched her shoulder and said her name again.

Bernie moaned once more, the sound reassuring that she still lived.

James joined her and took the candleholder, allowing Lena to brush Bernie's hair from her face. "Bernie."

Voices sounded in the corridor, one of the deep tones achingly familiar. Relief flooded Lena to know Sterling had arrived.

Bernie rolled to her side and raised a hand to the back of her head. "Oh…" The single quiet word didn't sound like her in the least.

"Don't move," Lena ordered, afraid doing so might worsen her injuries. "Can you tell me what happened?"

"My head," she muttered, her eyes fluttering open to rest on Lena in confusion. "Lena? What are you doing here?"

"I am wondering the same thing," Sterling said from directly behind her.

Lena looked up to see Sterling staring down at her, his eyes narrowed, and her heart sank.

⤞⟫⟪⤝

PANIC GRIPPED STERLING at the sight of Bernie lying on the floor, her face pale. He couldn't make sense of what was happening, nor had Foster been able to explain the problem.

The fact that Lena was kneeling beside his sister confused him all the more. What on earth was she doing here at this hour?

But what truly concerned him was Bernie's face, taut with

pain.

"What happened?" he asked as he knelt next to Lena. He didn't care who answered the question. He only wanted an answer.

Bernie hissed as she touched the back of her head where her hair was twisted into its customary chignon.

"Did you fall?" he asked, unable to see much of anything in the light of the single candle flame. He glanced at Foster who dipped his head and rushed toward the wall sconce to light it.

A warm glow filled the room as Bernie lifted onto her elbow, another moan escaping her lips. "No. Someone struck me."

Sterling jerked his gaze to Lena, shocked when her gaze fell away as if she were somehow guilty. He didn't believe for a moment that she'd hit his sister. Yet why did she look so uncomfortable?

Foster brought another candleholder closer, allowing Sterling to better see Bernie. Sterling gently touched the area where she'd pressed her fingers and found a lump. A damp lump. She was bleeding.

He muttered an oath then looked into Bernie's glazed eyes. "Can you sit up?"

"Yes." She eased to a sitting position with his and Lena's assistance.

"Are you hurt anywhere else?" Lena asked. The concern in her voice and expression touched him.

"I-I don't believe so." Bernie started to shake her head only to halt with a grimace. "But my head aches terribly."

"Can we move you to the settee?" Sterling held Bernie's arm, ready to assist her.

She drew a breath, seeming to consider his question before giving the barest of nods.

Lena's footman moved to Bernie's other side and between them, they helped Bernie to her feet then guided her to the settee, where she sank onto the cushions with a grateful sigh.

"Foster, we need some warm water and a cloth to clean Lady

Bernice's injury," Lena said as she set the candleholder on the nearby table and perched on the edge of a cushion beside Bernie.

Relief flooded Sterling to have her help since he certainly wasn't thinking clearly.

"Of course, miss." Foster hurried from the room.

"What happened, Bernie?" Sterling sat on the opposite side of his sister and took her hand in his.

She blinked, looking around the room as if trying to remember. "I came in here to get our notes." The weakness of her grip concerned him. "I wanted to read through them again. I heard something—or rather, someone—behind me and turned. Then everything went black. That's all I remember."

Anger flooded him, white and hot. To think Bernie had been injured in their home, where she should be safe, was inconceivable.

Sterling released her hand and stood to check the garden door, finding it unlocked. Though he knew it was pointless, he stepped outside and glanced about. It seemed doubtful that whoever had broken in would linger, but he had to check.

Feeling a presence behind him, he glanced back to see Lena's footman. The tall man looked around the dark garden as well. "Shall I have a look, Your Grace?" he asked.

"Please. You check the front. I'll check the back." Sterling moved slowly to the rear of the garden.

It took a minute or two for his eyes to adjust to the darkness as he followed the familiar path to the garden gate, which was locked. That didn't mean whoever had been here hadn't jumped over it. Few homes were impenetrable if the intruder was determined to gain entrance.

Finding nothing of interest visible in the dark, Sterling returned to the study door at the same time as Lena's footman, who shook his head to indicate he hadn't found anything either. Sterling nodded. "I'll have a closer look in the morning."

When they returned inside, Lena was tending the lump on Bernie's head with a damp cloth, speaking in a calm and reassuring voice.

"Lady Bernice insists there's no need to send for the doctor," Foster advised, his tone making it clear he disagreed.

Sterling glanced at Lena, who met his gaze. "The cut doesn't look as if it needs stitches, but I am certainly no expert." She gestured to the bump for him to look for himself.

He drew near to study the injury while Lena held Bernie's hair to allow him a better look. "Hmm. Perhaps not. But I would feel better if he examined you." He studied his sister's pale, pinched face, detesting that she was in pain.

"No need." Bernie straightened, seeming determined to show them she wasn't terribly hurt. "It's just a bump."

"Bernie," he began, well aware of her dislike of doctors since she'd seen more than her fair share in her youth.

"Please, Sterling." Her dark eyes begged him not to press her on the issue.

"If you're sure." Sterling watched her closely.

"I am," she insisted, her tone firm.

"The bleeding has stopped." Lena set the cloth in the basin of water. She, too, studied Bernie as if to gauge how she was feeling. "I'd recommend someone stay with you through the night to make certain you rest comfortably. If your headache worsens, the doctor should be sent for."

"Excellent idea," Bernie quickly agreed.

Sterling knew his sister would agree to almost anything if it meant avoiding the doctor. "You didn't see anything else, Bernie?" Sterling knew he shouldn't ask for details when she wasn't feeling herself, but he needed to know what had happened. Who could've been so bold as to hit her in their home? And why? Had someone been looking through his study when Bernie interrupted their search?

"No." Bernie's brow puckered as she considered his question. "The room was dark when I entered, though I held a candleholder. It didn't cross my mind that anyone was near."

"Do you have a sense as to how long you were in here before

it happened?" Lena asked.

"No more than a few minutes. I decided to find a book, as well, and had just started looking when it happened."

Sterling glanced at his desk, wondering if anything was missing. But before he looked, he wanted to see Bernie settled for the night.

"You should try to get some rest," Lena said. "I will check on you in the morning."

"Yes." Bernie stood, her hand touching the bump, suggesting it still hurt terribly. "I do believe I would like to lay down."

Foster moved to hold open the door, watching Bernie closely. "I've already taken the liberty of asking your maid to await you in your chamber, my lady."

"Thank you, Foster."

Sterling took her arm and looked at Lena. "If you'll wait a few minutes, I'll return directly."

Her eyes widened. "I should go. We can speak in the morning."

"Please wait." He was anxious to see Bernie settled but wanted to know why Lena had come.

Lena hesitated then nodded. "Rest well, Bernice. I'm so relieved you're all right."

"Thank you." Bernie offered a weak smile then moved toward the door, the fact that she didn't say more a sign she truly wasn't feeling well.

He escorted his sister to her room, doing his best to offer comfort, hoping she could rest rather than dwell on the events.

"I will return to check on you shortly," he said. He smiled at the maid. "Please send for me if she needs anything."

"Of course, Your Grace."

After kissing Bernie's cheek, he departed and hurried down the stairs.

To his relief, Lena had remained in his study, though she was standing, making it clear she didn't intend to remain long. Her footman and maid stood just outside the door.

"Will you tell me what you know?" he asked her.

"I asked to see Lady Bernice and that was when Foster realized something was amiss." She gestured around the study. "He and the other servants searched for her, and we found her in here."

"Did you and Bernie have plans for this evening?"

"No." Her gaze held on something just past his arm. "I wanted to speak to her about the letters and thought she might be home."

"Thank goodness you did." He ran a hand through his hair. "It might've been much longer before she was discovered." He shook his head. "I can't imagine who did this or what they intended."

"Nor can I. I'm so sorry she was hurt."

His stomach dropped at the idea of something worse happening. This wasn't a simple theft since nothing had been disturbed. "I have to think whoever it was hoped to find something specific."

"Something to do with the treasure hunt," she suggested.

"It has to be." He walked to his desk, relieved to see the drawers still shut. He tried the top right one, a sinking sensation flooding him as he pulled it open. A glance inside showed his notes that had been locked inside were missing. The treasure hunt was proving to be more dangerous than he could've guessed.

Chapter Fourteen

U PON RETURNING HOME, Lena flung herself onto her bed, exhausted from the evening's events. Relief that Bernie hadn't been hurt worse added to the feeling, as did the fact that neither Bernie nor Sterling had questioned her presence despite the late hour.

She thought for certain Sterling would want to know why she happened to be at his home the very night Bernie had been hurt. Instead, he'd acted grateful she was there.

Surely, once he had time to consider the matter further, he would wonder why she'd called so late. Or worse, he might think she had something to do with Bernie's injury.

She dearly hoped he didn't.

Nancy knocked on the door and then entered, casting a sympathetic look at the sight of Lena lying on the bed. "This has been quite the evening, hasn't it, miss?"

"Indeed, it has."

"To think someone broke into the duke's home is terrible, but to harm his sister is another matter entirely." The maid pulled out Lena's nightgown and laid it on the bed as Lena slowly stood. "I can hardly believe it. Thank goodness you called on Lady Bernice when you did."

Nancy's quiet chatter as she helped Lena prepare for bed helped to soothe Lena's frayed nerves. Lena also liked that the maid seemed to have gained an appreciation for Lena's gift.

Soon, Lena was settled beneath the covers for the night with a single candle on her bedside table, sifting through her thoughts. What had been taken from Sterling's desk drawer? He hadn't shared any details, nor had she felt she could ask. Perhaps he didn't want her to worry, but she also wondered if he didn't want her to know.

She didn't need any special intuition to understand that the thief had been after details about the treasure hunt. She pulled the covers tighter as she shivered at what could have happened to Bernie. If whoever had been searching Sterling's desk had struck her harder…

The thought didn't bear consideration.

Lena hoped she hadn't played a role in what had happened this evening. She had told several people who'd asked over the last few days that Clarke was digging in the wrong place. The timing of the incident this evening made her wonder if her comments had struck a chord with someone. The dig had been underway for a few weeks now and nothing like this had occurred before.

She should be prepared to explain why she thought Clarke was digging in the wrong place—a challenge since she had no proof. Only a feeling. Eventually, Sterling would hear of it and ask how she knew. The thought had her releasing a frustrated breath as she rolled to her side.

The whole situation was complicated and far from over. For tonight, she needed to put it from her mind and rest. Tomorrow, she would continue to search for proof that Clarke was lying. It seemed the least she could do to honor her father and his decades of work. No one should be able to erase that in a few short weeks.

She didn't want any further harm to befall Bernie or Sterling. She only wanted to protect her father's reputation. To save his memory since she hadn't been able to save his life. Unfortunately, sleep eluded her for some time.

THE FOLLOWING MORNING, Sterling looked in on his sister, pleased to find her still sleeping. Her maid reported that she'd had a restless night, so he'd told her to let Bernie sleep as long as she could. Once she woke, he'd reconsider whether a visit from the doctor was necessary.

He hadn't slept well either. Knowing someone had broken into their house filled him with anger. Outrage. A desire to strike something or someone. Thoughts of how much worse the situation could've been had circled through his mind all night. The fact that he'd failed to protect Bernie only added to his fury.

The police should arrive momentarily, but Sterling took another look at his desk drawers. As he'd noted last night, only one had been forced open. The others were still locked tight. Perhaps that was because Bernie had interrupted the thief's search of his desk. Why had the person taken his notes on Oak Island but not the map Clarke had sent that showed his plan for digging? That should've been of more interest than Sterling's notes.

Next, he looked around the garden now that there was light to see if the thief had left any clues. They had surely departed in a rush after striking Bernie.

Unfortunately, a thorough search revealed little. The ground was too firm for footprints. A bit of black thread was caught on the top of the wrought-iron gate, which might very well have come from the intruder. But it wouldn't help determine who it might've been or even what they'd been wearing.

Detective Inspector Stephens and Captain Thomason from Scotland Yard arrived before Sterling finished breakfast. Thomason was a burly man with light-colored hair and a military bearing. The inspector was tall with intense brown eyes, a thick moustache, and a sober demeanor. He jotted down notes as Sterling shared what little he knew, including the missing notes.

"Were they of significant value?" Stephens asked.

"Only to someone with interest in the treasure hunt on Oak Island."

The inspector paused to raise a bushy brow that was remarkably similar to his moustache. "Are many interested?"

The numerous wagers being placed on the outcome came to mind, but it was difficult to believe anyone would bother to break into his home simply to try to win a bet.

Viscount Ludham and the stranger's conversation at the ball passed through his thoughts, as well. He decided against sharing what he'd overheard with the police as he didn't want to cast doubt on the viscount until he knew more. What little he'd heard wasn't enough to warrant the inspector speaking with Ludham when he'd only deny involvement.

"Your sister was harmed?" the inspector asked.

Sterling explained how they'd found her unconscious on the floor from a blow to the head.

"Would it be possible for us to speak with her?" Thomason asked.

"She's resting now. However, she knows very little. She hadn't been in my study long before she was struck from behind. She didn't see anyone." Sterling shared the timeline of the events, though he left out Lena's presence. Mentioning her seemed unnecessary.

After answering a few more of their questions, the detective examined the drawer that had been opened. Then a footman escorted the pair to the garden to look over the area where Sterling guessed the thief had both gained entrance and escaped.

Sterling paced his study as he waited for them to finish, though he doubted they'd find anything of significance since Sterling had already looked.

They returned a few minutes later. The inspector still held his notebook.

"As you suggested, there's little to go on, Your Grace," the captain said. "We will make a few inquiries and advise you if we find anything. Please notify us if you experience any further problems."

"Thank you." Sterling scowled as they were shown out. He didn't care for the helpless feeling the break-in caused.

Reminding himself that what truly mattered was Bernie's recovery, he looked in on her again. She was sitting up in bed, her maid adjusting the pillows behind her. Her long, dark hair was bound in a loose braid that hung over her shoulder. Her face was pale, but she offered a smile as he entered the room.

"How are you feeling?" He drew a chair close to her bed, noting that pain dulled her eyes.

Bernie touched the place where he knew the lump to be and sighed. "My head aches, of course, but otherwise well enough."

"I would like the doctor to stop by," he began, wishing he would've pressed harder to have him come last evening.

"It's only a bump, Sterling. Even Lena didn't think a visit from the doctor was necessary."

"Still, it wouldn't hurt for him to have a look."

She shook her head though careful not to move it over much. "No, thank you. I will be fine in a day or two. Did the police come?"

Sterling relayed what the inspector had said, wishing he had better news. "Have you remembered anything else?"

Her brow puckered as she considered the question. "I've been trying to think of whether I heard any sounds before I was hit, but I didn't. Thank goodness Lena came when she did."

"Indeed." Perhaps he should have a word with Lena's driver. He might have witnessed something while waiting outside. There was always the chance Lena remembered additional details, as well. "I'm surprised she called so late."

"As am I. I didn't have the chance to ask if there was something she needed."

Another maid arrived with tea and toast, and Sterling was relieved to see Bernie partake of both. He was also pleased she didn't seem in a rush to rise. Rest would do her good.

They visited for a while longer, then Sterling rose. "I'm going to call on Lena to review the evening's events." He hoped she or her servants might have remembered something that would help catch whoever had hurt Bernie.

"Please give her my thanks again," Bernie said.

"Of course." Sterling kissed her cheek then departed.

Lena's presence still struck him as curious. Why had she come to see Bernie at such a late hour? Was it truly a coincidence that she'd arrived within minutes of Bernie being hurt? Yet he had no doubt her concern for Bernie was genuine. The time had come to gain some answers.

LENA GLANCED UP to see Davies standing in the doorway of the music room, where she'd been idly playing the piano with the hope of settling her thoughts without success. Not when she continued to worry how Bernie fared.

"The Duke of Renwick is calling, miss." Davies's surprised expression surely matched her own. "Are you receiving?"

She jerked to her feet, her stomach tightening with worry. "Of course. Please show him to the drawing room." Had Bernie taken a turn for the worse? Or had he come to question her about the true purpose of her visit last night?

There was no point in wishing it was neither. That he'd only come to advise her that Bernie was recovering and see how she fared.

Lena gave herself a mental shake. Her attraction to him was making her long for what could never be. This was no more than a passing fancy, she told herself with the sternest of thoughts. Despite that, she pressed a hand to her racing heart, hoping to slow its rapid beat.

As Davies departed, she glanced down at her morning gown, wishing she'd worn a prettier one than the serviceable blue muslin. But she wouldn't delay the visit by taking the time to change. Chances were he wouldn't notice her attire when his thoughts were centered on his sister and discovering who had broken into their home.

She'd told her grandfather about the unsettling events this morning when they'd had breakfast and knew Davies had heard as well.

Her grandfather had been alarmed, but to her surprise, he'd been equally concerned for her welfare. His regard touched her, a pleasant reminder of how much he cared. Luckily, he hadn't questioned why she'd chosen to call on Bernie at that hour.

Now, Lena hurried down the stairs to the drawing room, unable to slow her pace despite her uncertainty as to Sterling's purpose. The few minutes she waited before Davies announced Sterling felt like a lifetime with her worry getting the better of her.

"Good morning, Your Grace." She curtsied which Sterling acknowledged with a nod. "How is Lady Bernice this morning?"

"Resting at the moment." He shook his head. "Still refusing to see the doctor." Shadows marked his eyes, a testament that he'd had a sleepless night, as well.

Her heart melted at his obvious concern for Bernie. "Her condition hasn't worsened?"

"No." His lips twisted, his displeasure obvious. "But I would feel better if the doctor examined her injury." His dark gaze settled on her, sending her heart thumping once again. "I hope you're none the worse for the wear after what occurred."

"Not at all," Lena said, noting Nancy's arrival in the doorway. Davies must've requested her presence as a chaperone. The butler was a stickler for such things.

"You're certain?" Sterling asked as he drew closer, the intensity of his regard making her sure he saw more than she wanted him to.

"Yes." Lena hoped she didn't look as tired as she felt. "I am pleased to hear news of Bernie. I've been wondering how she's faring."

"She asked after you, too. The police came by but didn't find any clues."

"How frustrating."

"I wanted to ask if you remembered anything that could be helpful."

She searched her memory, wishing she could be of help. That she might remember a detail that would keep him from asking why she'd chosen to visit Bernie at such an odd hour.

"I'm sorry, but I don't." She'd been so focused on Bernie that she hadn't paid attention to her surroundings.

"Would it be possible to speak with your driver and the footman to see if they remember anything?"

"Of course." She should've thought of that earlier. She directed her attention to Nancy. "Could you send for James and Stephen?"

"Of course, miss." Nancy hurried away, leaving them alone.

"You're certain you're well?" Sterling asked again, moving closer as his warm gaze searched her face.

"Other than not sleeping well, yes. I kept seeing Bernie lying on the floor." She couldn't help a shudder as the image filled her mind once again. She'd been so worried that she had arrived too late. That her premonition had failed her as it so often did.

But she wasn't about to share any of that with Sterling.

"How lucky that you happened to call when you did."

Her face heated at his words, and it was all she could do to act naturally. "You would've arrived soon anyway."

He ran a hand over the back of his neck, his distress obvious. "Yes, but would I have found her? I don't always look in on her at that time of the night. If she'd remained there longer—"

"Sterling." Lena reached out to touch him, wanting to offer comfort. The feel of his muscled forearm beneath the fabric of his suit coat sent a thrill through her. To her surprise, he took her hand, though she wasn't certain he knew he had. "She's going to be fine."

"I don't know how you happened to be there when Bernie

needed you, but I am pleased you were."

"Truly, it was nothing." Lena searched her thoughts, desperate to turn his focus away from her involvement. "Her maid would've looked for her soon."

"I suppose that's true." He ran the pad of his thumb back and forth along her bare hand, his touch both soothing and arousing at the same time. "But thank you."

"Of course. She doesn't remember anything more either?"

"No. My guess is that the person hid when she entered the study then struck her when her back was turned. How unfortunate that they didn't simply wait until she left."

"Perhaps it seemed as if she intended to stay for a time. Did they take something from your desk?" She hid a grimace, annoyed that the question had slipped out.

"My notes about the progress on Oak Island." He frowned, suggesting it troubled him.

Lena bit her lip to keep from saying something she shouldn't. This was not the time to state that she was certain Clarke was deceiving him. Besides, he would only ask why she thought that which was impossible to explain.

"I suppose that narrows the list of possible suspects," she said at last.

"Given that was all they took, it seems a clue in itself." He shook his head. "Taking the notes was bad enough, but hurting Bernie was a step too far. And I don't understand why they left the map. I would've thought that was more important than my notes."

"The map?"

"Clarke sent one that noted the location of the current shaft he's excavating as well as the priority of the next ones."

"That's not what they were in search of," Lena murmured as a chill seeped over her, the sense of knowing narrowing her focus.

"What? How do you know?"

Lena blinked as she tried to process what he'd asked. She

pulled her hand from his grasp, trying to clear her thoughts and dispel the sensation. Why had she allowed that to slip out? Her gift was bad enough, but the urge to speak of what she suddenly knew was even worse.

She shook her head as she stepped back and forced a smile. "I'm only guessing." Her thoughts raced as she tried to think of an explanation that sounded believable. "It seems unlikely that it's important to know where Clarke is working if they believe he already found the Money Pit. Wouldn't it make more sense that they'd be looking for something else? Something that might point to how to access the treasure? To navigate the flood tunnels?"

Sterling's eyes narrowed as he considered what she'd said. "But his map stated where he thinks the treasure is located."

"Not if he's wrong. Not if he's digging in the wrong place."

"Lena, why would you think that? He's said he found the Money Pit." His lips pressed tight. "And if I had anything that clarified how to navigate it to find the treasure, I would've already shared it with Clarke."

Lena only knew Clarke wasn't being completely honest and that he was digging in the wrong location. How that connected to what was taken from Sterling's desk drawer, she didn't know.

For the briefest of moments, she wanted to take his hands in hers and share the truth. But she knew from experience that he would only brush away what she told him or look at her as if she were an oddity. Perhaps even a combination of both. Or worse.

She nearly shuddered. How she wished she didn't have a secret to keep. One that created a vast space between them. Then this handsome man who stood before her might be here for a reason other than concern for his sister or capturing a thief.

But that wasn't the case. She needed to remember that.

"I'm only suggesting you proceed cautiously. I know from experience how difficult it is to find the Money Pit. Father thought many times he'd found it, only to realize that wasn't the case. Take care, Sterling. Things aren't always as they seem." She hoped he didn't realize she wasn't only talking about Clarke and the treasure hunt.

Chapter Fifteen

"A QUESTION HAS crossed my mind," Grandfather said, startling Lena from her thoughts.

They were sharing a quiet meal at home later that evening, something they did several times each week. Lena knew she was poor company, but after all that had transpired, she couldn't think of anything but what ifs.

What if Bernice had been hurt worse?

What if the thief returned?

What if Sterling had been the one hurt?

"Of course." She managed a smile and then took a bite of the salmon with piccalilli sauce. The tartness of the mustard pickle topping was usually one of her favorites. No matter that it tasted like sawdust because of her upset. Heaven forbid if Cook thought she didn't like the way one of her favorite meals had been prepared. With that in mind, she took another bite.

"Why are you so determined to prove Clarke wrong?" The weight of his gaze had her reaching for her wine to take a deep sip with the hope of gathering her thoughts.

How could she explain? It wasn't just her father's reputation at stake, but her mother's too, for she had believed in him. That meant it was tied to the man sitting at the table with her. But all of those things were tangled up with her premonition—the bone-deep knowing she continued to have that Clarke was wrong.

What could she do but be honest? With one exception, of course. She had no intention of sharing her bouts of intuition. Not when she'd been able to hide them thus far. At least, she hoped she had.

"I don't want Father to be thought a fool. Or Mother either." She met his gaze. "Or any of us." Did he understand that she included him, along with her and her sisters?

"I understand that. But surely the truth will prevail eventually. Why create a fuss?" He took a forkful of the salmon as he waited for her answer.

"It could take years for Clarke to be proven wrong. All the while, people could be laughing at David Wright's efforts, wondering what took him so long when the treasure will so easily be found by another." She pushed the herbed potatoes around on her plate. "Then there's Ella to consider and how much this is upsetting her in her delicate state."

"Your sister is stronger than you realize."

She looked up at that and smiled at the confidence in his tone. "You're right. She is. But I still worry."

"As do I." His lips twisted, suggesting he worried more than he was willing to admit. "But why are you so certain? Or should I ask, *how*?"

Heat filled Lena's cheeks as she wondered how to explain yet keep her sense a secret. "Surely you don't think it will be easy to find the Money Pit and its treasure when Father spent so many years searching."

"Agreed. But based on your confidence, that's not what has you convinced."

Lena's breath caught. Her gaze searched her grandfather's face. He couldn't know about her premonitions. Could he?

Her best—only—hope was to act nonchalantly. "Just a feeling. An instinct, I suppose you could say. I'm sure you have those feelings at times." Everyone did. It was just that hers were heightened. She released a quiet sigh at the lie.

He nodded and continued with his meal, though she was

certain he wasn't finished with the subject.

"There's something you should know." He set down his fork and leaned back in his chair. Davies started forward to clear his plate, but Grandfather waved him back with a flick of his fingers.

Unease curled through her. "Oh?"

"Your grandmother, God rest her soul, often had a feeling. A sense, you might say." He smiled even if his expression held a hint of sadness.

Lena held her breath, not wanting to move or say a word in case he changed the subject. He rarely spoke of her grandmother.

"She had a Scottish grandmother. One who'd believed in things that few do. Especially not in these modern times." He frowned as he turned the stem of his wine glass, obviously deciding what and how to tell the story. "She had a gift. The second sight some called it. She had visions that told of the future. She knew things that no one knew. Your grandmother had a touch of it as well. Nothing so clear as what her grandmother had. Perhaps the ability was reduced in the generations that followed her. But a gift, nonetheless."

Tears filled Lena's eyes, and she drew a shuddering breath. To think she wasn't alone. That she wasn't the only one who had these feelings was overwhelming and such a comfort.

The duke lifted his gaze to meet hers, and she knew that somehow, he knew she had that gift as well. "The day I met your grandmother, she told me I would propose to her one day. I dismissed the remark as we were young. Too young. We'd only just met, and it wasn't as if our families were arranging a marriage between us."

"But you did," Lena whispered, loving the story.

"I did. Three years later. I was thrilled when she accepted. Of course, she had to remind me that she'd known all along that we belonged to each other." His smile held the light of fond memories.

Lena pressed a hand to her aching heart, touched by the sweet tale. "Did Mother know?"

Her grandfather heaved a sigh. "No. After your grandmother died giving birth to her, I found it difficult to speak of her. I suppose I left that to the servants to do. That was one more mistake I made with your mother. One of many."

"She never mentioned anything to me. She didn't quite know how to help me with the premonitions I have. But she never dismissed them. I'm sorry to say I'm not like Grandmother. The feelings aren't always right. Nor can I call them on demand." She lifted her hand in the air only to let it fall back to her lap. "They are of little aid." She didn't add that she hadn't managed to save her father the day he died.

Grandfather smiled again. "I wouldn't be so quick to dismiss them. Your grandmother said she had to allow them in. To coax them forth at times and give them room. But the same was true for her—they weren't something she could order about."

"I'm so pleased you told me about her. The ability is often unsettling and…odd. It's lovely to think I have it in common with her."

"After dinner, there's something I want to show you." He glanced at Davies, who waited patiently for them to finish. "Let us have dessert and then I'll meet you in the drawing room."

Lena couldn't imagine what he wanted to show her. He normally retired to his study after their meals together. Having a little additional time with him was a gift. If someone would've told her when she and her sisters first arrived in London that they would share meals and meaningful conversations as often as they did, she would've said they were mad. The gruff, distant man who'd refused to acknowledge them or speak to them was only a memory. Her and her sisters' gradual success in wearing away his defenses was a testament to the power of patience and persistence.

In short order, she waited for him in the drawing room, staring at the cheerfully burning fire. Her thoughts once again returned to the question of who had struck Bernie, but no answer came to mind.

"Here we are." Grandfather walked in, holding a small velvet box as he sat on the settee with her. "This was your grandmother's. I would like you to have it. I think she would, too."

Lena gently took the green velvet box and opened it. "A locket. It's beautiful." The gold oval was filigreed and lovely. Inside was a pressed flower, its purple petals still vibrant. Lena's heart filled with peace as she ran a finger over the delicate chain.

"Consider it a talisman of sorts. One that might help you with your gift. To allow your mind to open when the universe has something it wants you to know."

She fastened it around her neck and held the locket with two fingers. "Thank you. It means so much. More than you can possibly know." She leaned forward to hug him, pleased when he hugged her back.

"I hope we can find some sort of proof that Clarke is, indeed, digging in the wrong place," he said when he eased back to hold her gaze. "His supposed success has come far too quickly. That alone makes it seem unlikely."

A mix of hope and joy filled her at his words, along with determination. "It does, indeed."

STERLING SAT AT the breakfast table the next morning when much to his surprise Bernie entered the room.

"Should you be up and about?" he asked, his hand pausing mid-air from reaching for his coffee.

"My head is a bit better today." She patted his shoulder as she passed by to take the seat Foster held for her. The pat didn't reassure him in the least.

"Only a bit?" That didn't sound like enough improvement to justify her presence at the breakfast table. He would much rather she stayed abed.

"You must not worry so, Sterling." She smiled as Foster

poured her tea. "I will rest later if I feel worse. For now, I would much prefer to have something to occupy my thoughts other than my aching head. And I'm hungry."

He frowned, able to see her point, but hoped she wasn't pushing herself too quickly.

"Did you speak with Lena?" She took a piece of sausage along with some scrambled eggs, which helped to convince him that her appetite hadn't diminished.

He shared a small portion of his conversation with Lena, reluctant to say too much about her insistence that Clarke was digging in the wrong location. He didn't pretend to understand why Lena held that opinion.

"Did her servants see anything helpful?"

"Unfortunately, not. The driver heard a carriage leaving soon after he arrived, which might've been the thief. But he paid it no mind at the time and could offer nothing in the way of a description." He took a sip of his coffee as he watched Bernie spread butter and jam on her toast.

Her face was still pale, and he had the feeling she was doing her best to pretend she felt better than she did. He couldn't blame her. He wouldn't have liked to stay in bed either.

She held his gaze for a long moment before biting her lip, a sure sign of her upset. "Do you feel we need to take extra care when going out?"

He set down his cup, detesting that she was nervous to continue with her normal routine. "I have requested extra footmen to remain on duty for the foreseeable future. An extra one will accompany you everywhere you go, as well."

She nodded. "The police haven't found anything of interest either, I assume."

"No." He didn't want to lie and give her false hope. "Apparently, this treasure hunting business is more dangerous than I initially thought. We may have to take extra precautions while Clarke is working."

Her smile eased the tightness in his chest. "It will be worth it if he finds treasure."

Had David Wright worried about his family while he was searching on the island? Surely, he had. It was impossible to keep such things secret. Most treasure hunters seemed to thrive on the notoriety they often gained. For some, it fueled them as much as the search for riches.

"Can you think of anything, in particular, you've found in your research that might cause interest in the search?" he asked.

"I was wondering the same thing. How can those old letters cause someone to break into our home?" She shook her head but did so slowly as if it still hurt. "Thank goodness Lena had the letters or they might have been stolen, too."

"I think the time has come to make certain Clarke is doing what he claims to be doing."

"How do you intend to do that?" Her eyes widened in alarm. "Surely, you're not going to Oak Island?"

"No." He wouldn't leave Bernie alone after what had happened. "I have an acquaintance in Nova Scotia who should be able to look in on him with some discretion."

"That's an excellent idea. Will you tell Lena?"

He paused, considering the question. "I don't see the point until I have something to report. If all is as it should be, then I won't have any news."

"But recent events have you wondering."

"Yes, they do." He told himself it was wise to protect the investment he was making in the dig, and it was. But Lena's insistence that Clarke was searching in the wrong place combined with the break-in made him uncomfortable.

Something foul was afoot and he was determined to find out what.

He excused himself from Bernie's company and then went to his study to compose a telegram to the man he knew in Nova Scotia, hoping he'd be agreeable to assisting him with this matter. Afterward, he leaned back in his chair, considering what to do next.

He needed to discover the identity of Ludham's companion. A few inquiries with fellow members of the Royal Geological Society would be an excellent place to start. He should've taken action when he'd first overhead Ludham's conversation. By letting the matter go this long, Sterling was partially at fault for what had happened to his sister.

The thought had him ringing the bell for his carriage. A few members were always at the offices and perhaps one could identify who Ludham had been speaking with if Sterling described him.

Sterling was pleased to see Viscount Dyke there, as he always seemed to know what was happening amongst his peers.

Sterling struck up a conversation with him, waiting until Dyke asked about the progress on Oak Island. Sure enough, he did. Sterling shared a few details but decided against telling him about Bernie's injury or the break-in. The fewer who knew, the better.

"Did you place a wager like so many others?" Sterling asked.

"No," Dyke said with a shake of his head. "I prefer to wager on cards. Improves my chances of winning."

"Do you know if Ludham placed a wager?"

"Yes, but he's betting against your success."

"That doesn't surprise me." Ludham had never been friendly, not even in their university years. He seemed to resent Sterling's title and everything it brought. "I saw him with someone at the Stanhope ball. A short man near our age. Brown hair, round face, moustache."

"Sounds like David Winslow. The pair frequently venture to gaming hells together."

"Do you know much about him?" Sterling asked.

"Only that he always seems to have some scheme or other up his sleeve. He tried to talk me into investing in a Brazilian mine not long ago."

"Did you?"

"No. I like to keep my money in England where I can watch

over it." He stilled, regret flashing across his face. "Terribly sorry, Your Grace. I meant no offense."

"None taken. Any idea where I could find Winslow?" Sterling had no idea what he might ask the man if he had the chance to speak with him that wouldn't put both Ludham and him on guard. But it wouldn't hurt to learn more while he had the chance.

"I believe he's a member of the Exploration Club."

Sterling nodded. The club had started over fifty years ago by a group of friends who determined the organization was the best way to be certain they didn't drift apart. While a few of the members had gone on expeditions, most simply enjoyed talking about the trips others had taken. The last Sterling heard the group numbered well over fifty. Several were members of the Royal Geological Society, but not all.

The focus of the club tended to be social in nature rather than scientific. There was nothing wrong with that as far as Sterling was concerned. Any reason men gathered to have an intelligent conversation was fine.

"Do you know if Ludham is a member, as well?" Sterling asked.

"Yes, I'm sure of it." He frowned. "Many of the Royal Geological Society members are."

Sterling nodded. "I'm aware. Just curious about Ludham."

"I believe they meet this evening, so you might find them there at some point," Dyke advised.

It would be simple enough to drop by to see what more he could discover about Winslow. Perhaps he would be there, and Sterling could ask a few direct questions.

After thanking Dyke for his time, Sterling took the carriage to Albemarle Street, which wasn't far. He entered the establishment with the faint hope of finding his quarry but was soon directed by one of the members to a reception room where several familiar faces were enjoying a drink and a lively discussion.

If he didn't know better, he would almost think Winslow

stiffened at the sight of him. How interesting.

Sterling exchanged pleasantries with a few of the men before looking directly at Winslow, who had eased back a few steps as if wishing to avoid him. "Winslow, might I have a word?"

The man glanced at his companions, suggesting he hoped they might provide an acceptable reason for him to refuse. No one said a word.

"Of course, Your Grace." He bowed and gestured toward the opposite side of the room.

Sterling decided to get straight to the point. "I understand you're acquainted with Walter Clarke."

"Clarke?" He frowned as if trying to place the name.

"I'm sure you remember him," Sterling insisted, trying to hold onto his patience. "He's leading the dig on Oak Island at the present time."

"Oh, yes. Right. I have heard of him." Winslow tilted his head. "Do you think it's true? What everyone is saying."

"What might that be?"

"That he's digging in the wrong place."

Sterling did his best to hide his temper. "Where did you hear such nonsense?" How many people had Lena told of her suspicions?

"Several have mentioned it." Winslow's brow rose, and his eyes gleamed with amusement.

Sterling knew the man was simply trying to gain a reaction. Still, it was all he could do to keep from giving him the satisfaction of knowing he'd gotten under his skin.

It was only logical that Lena would share her theory with her brothers-in-law. While annoying that she stated her claim without proof, she was entitled to her opinion. The best he could hope for was that Clarke provided results. Then no one could deny the truth.

However, there was also the chance she was right. He liked to think he would gracefully admit defeat if that happened. He hoped he wouldn't have to as he didn't want to disappoint Bernie.

"Have you been in contact with Clarke?" Sterling asked, returning to the purpose of his visit.

"Me?" His eyes widened in surprise. "Why would I? Have you not heard from him of late?"

"I receive reports on a regular basis." Sterling hated that he was becoming defensive and allowing his distrust of Clarke to color his response. "I would like to know what you know about Clarke."

"Very little." Winslow shrugged. "I've only met the man once."

Sterling nodded reluctantly. He had the feeling that wasn't completely true, but his questions weren't getting him anywhere.

He departed soon afterward. Perhaps he'd be better off speaking with Ludham to see if that brought any information to the surface. He was also going to have another conversation with Lena and discover why she was so convinced Clarke was wrong.

Chapter Sixteen

LENA BLINKED IN surprise at Foster's beaming smile when he opened the door of Renwick House the following day.

"Good afternoon, Miss Wright. What a pleasure to see you." He swept his arm toward the interior of the home in a welcoming gesture, something he'd never done before. "Please come in."

"Thank you." Lena stepped cautiously inside, puzzled at the change in the butler's demeanor. "I was wondering if Lady Bernice was feeling well enough to receive callers."

"I'm certain she'll make an exception for you. If you'd like to wait in the reception room, I'll advise her you're here." His smile turned even brighter, leaving Lena to continue to stare at the servant in disbelief.

"Thank you, Foster."

Much quicker than she'd expected, she was shown into Bernie's sitting room, where her friend was resting on the settee with a woven blanket on her lap and a book by her side. "Lena, how lovely of you to call." She started to rise only to pause when Lena waved her back.

"Please don't move on my account," Lena said then dipped into a brief curtsy. "You look far too comfortable to disturb."

"I confess I haven't regained my strength since the other night." She gestured toward the nearby chair for Lena to sit, then touched her head as if to check to see if the bump was still there.

"I think that is normal. Ella had the same experience when she was struck on the head a few years ago." Lena studied Bernie, noting her pale face and the tightness around her eyes. "How is your head? Still aching?"

Bernie glanced at the doorway. "A little, but please don't tell Sterling or my aunt," she whispered. "They are already driving me mad with their overprotectiveness." She sighed. "My head is improving, but I'm sure it will take another day or two. Sterling acts as if I should be recovered completely or something must be wrong. It reminds me of my youth, and those years are nothing I want to relive."

"You were often ill?" Lena couldn't imagine enduring a lengthy illness, especially with a father less than patient or supportive.

"My heart doesn't always beat at a steady pace. It frightened me when it first happened. The more it scared me, the more often it seemed to occur. Father had doctor after doctor examine me, insisting they should be able to heal me. When that didn't happen, he began to believe the fault was mine." She closed her eyes briefly, which told Lena just how painful the memories were. "I tried very hard to fix it without success."

"I'm sure the strain didn't help your condition." Sympathy filled Lena for the scared little girl with no mother or sisters to comfort her. "Thank goodness you had Sterling."

"Yes." Bernie forced a smile. "But life was difficult when he was gone at school. I found it easier to remain in bed, feigning illness even when I was well just so I wouldn't have to face Father."

"How clever of you."

Bernie frowned. "Clever? I think you mean cowardly."

"Not at all," Lena insisted. "What purpose would be served by enduring your father's unhelpful comments? Better to preserve your strength and mental fortitude."

The younger woman seemed to consider that before slowly nodding. "I suppose I never thought of it quite like that."

"Self-preservation is a skill everyone should learn." Lena knew that from personal experience. How often had she avoided questions, changed the subject of conversations, or outright lied to avoid speaking of her gift? More times than she could count. She didn't like having to do so but felt she had little choice. Not if she wanted to keep her ability a secret.

"How interesting." Bernie stared at her in surprise. "I will have to think upon that. It certainly changes how I've always thought of myself."

"What does?" Sterling asked from the doorway. Then his gaze shifted to Lena, quickening her pulse. "Good afternoon."

Lena stood to curtsy and did her best to hide her reaction. "And to you, Your Grace."

When Sterling's attention returned to his sister, Lena took the opportunity to study him. He truly was handsome, his features refined, giving him an aristocratic look. His honey-colored hair was a variety of shades and made her long to run her fingers through it. The careless tousle of the waves made it look like he had recently done that very thing.

Then those compelling brown eyes that seemed to see right through her latched onto her again, stealing her breath. Was that heat in their depths or was she imagining things? Even so, her body warmed in response.

Her reaction to him remained a puzzle. She wanted to share another kiss with him, yet a small part of her insisted she keep her distance if she wanted to remain safe.

She no longer wanted to be safe.

The realization came as a surprise. A shock even. Especially since she knew any sort of true relationship with him was impossible when she had to keep her ability a secret.

Wasn't it?

When she was near Sterling, she began to wonder. To hope. Was there a chance he might understand? That he wouldn't stare at her with the suspicion so often in his eyes?

Lena tore her gaze away from him, only to realize she'd lost track of the conversation. With a stern reminder to pay attention, she focused on what Bernie was saying.

"Just this morning, the cook told me she had a feeling that evening before dinner that something bad was going to happen," Bernie continued. "If only she'd told me, then perhaps I would've taken more care."

"You can't be serious, Bernie," Sterling said as he walked forward to join his sister on the settee. "You should know by now that Mrs. Roberts is always having those feelings and rarely do they mean anything." He frowned then shook his head. "In fact, I think the only time she happens to be right is when she tells us afterward. You mustn't listen to such nonsense."

A lump of emotion lodged in Lena's throat, threatening to bring tears to her eyes. She'd known that would be his response. After all, it was similar to everyone else's. Few believed intuition could be trusted. How could she blame him when she didn't always trust it either? He was a practical, pragmatic man. He would not be looked upon favorably if he believed in nonsensical things.

Still, his reaction stung.

"I don't know," Bernie countered, her lips twisting to the side as she considered the matter. "I think there is something to it. You have admitted to having a bad feeling on more than one occasion. You are often right."

"That's hardly the same thing. When presented with a set of circumstances, we all have a response to the possible outcome based on our past experiences. An instinct, if you will. You have that as well." His gaze shifted to Lena again. "I'm certain Miss Wright does, too."

"Do you, Lena?" Bernie asked.

Lena couldn't believe she was having this conversation. Yet both Sterling and Bernie watched her with expectant looks. "I suppose I do." Hopefully, the answer was noncommittal enough to satisfy them but hide how uncomfortable she was.

Sterling's eyes narrowed, tightening her stomach. There was

no possibility of him knowing that she wasn't telling the full truth. Was there?

STERLING WATCHED LENA closely as Bernie continued to share several other stories of the cook's supposed ability to foresee trouble. The older woman tended to see trouble in nearly everything. If Bernie would pay more attention, she'd see how often Mrs. Roberts mentioned her feeling after an event had occurred.

Lena shifted in her chair, fidgeting with the tip of her gloved finger, looking anywhere but at him.

Did her opinion differ from his? Was that the reason she looked so uncomfortable? Or was there more to it?

Her gaze shifted to Bernie, and she smiled politely at what his sister was saying. As he continued to watch her, something niggled at the back of his mind. He searched his thoughts to try to understand the feeling, much like he'd forgotten something he'd wanted to remember.

Then he scoffed at himself. Here he was, telling Bernie to ignore Mrs. Roberts's premonitions when he was acting just like the cook. How ridiculous. How often had Bernie accused him of suspecting everyone? He'd promised to work on that, but old habits were difficult to break. He brought his thoughts back to the conversation.

"Are you still reviewing the letters?" Bernie asked Lena.

"Yes. They're rather enjoyable to read, aren't they? A personal account of another time." Lena's polite smile brought the nagging feeling back in a rush.

She wasn't telling the truth. Or at least, was only telling a modified version of it. Why?

Even as the question came to mind, he chided himself for making assumptions. Still, he wanted a moment alone with her to find out what was going on, but how? Bernie was clearly settled in for a visit. He didn't need the ability to predict the future to know Bernie would rather he leave them to talk. The looks she kept throwing his way made that abundantly clear.

He waited for a pause in the conversation then stood to take his leave. As he passed through the entrance hall, he requested Foster to tell him when Lena was departing so he might have a word with her.

Then he paced his study for nearly thirty minutes before Foster showed Lena into the room, advising her that he would fetch her servants.

Sterling watched the butler's friendly behavior with some amusement. Foster practically treated her like a member of the family. His opinion of Lena seemed to have greatly improved since she'd helped to aid Bernie.

"I wanted a word with you before you left," Sterling began as Foster stepped out of the room, leaving the door ajar.

"Oh?"

There it was again—that same uncomfortable look she'd had earlier. What did it mean?

"How do you think Bernie is truly feeling?" he asked, moving forward until he stood before her. He hoped *he* didn't make her feel uneasy.

"She says she is much better."

"Yes, she's told me that as well. But it's not completely true."

Lena smiled, a genuine one that eased some of his tension. "She doesn't want you to worry."

"Is that what she told you?" He couldn't resist running a finger along the length of her jaw, the smooth skin threatening to distract him from his purpose.

Her eyes darkened at his touch, but still she answered his question. "Yes. I do think she's feeling better but not quite herself."

He nodded. "That is what I thought. As long as her headaches aren't worsening."

"I don't believe they are. In my experience, she should feel back to her normal self in another day or two." She licked her lips and desire stirred.

"And you? How are you feeling after what happened?"

"I'm only worried about Bernie. And you." She met his gaze. "It must be quite distressing to know someone broke into your home, let alone attacked your sister."

"It is." Despite the seriousness of the topic, he could only think of the woman standing before him.

Those lush lips drew him in an inexplicable way. He had to have another taste of her. Time was of the essence. Foster would return any moment with her servants. Who knew when this chance would come again?

He cupped her cheek and took her lips with his, his thoughts falling away at the contact. She settled him, giving him an anchor. He wanted more of her and tested the seam of her lips, delighted when she opened for him, allowing him to deepen the kiss. His tongue swept along hers, her scent swamping his senses.

Rather than assuaging his need, he only wanted more. He grasped her narrow waist with both hands to pull her against his length. She rested her gloved hands on his chest, the pressure feeling wonderful despite the layers between them.

Need, hot and heavy, pulsed through him, pulling him under until he couldn't think—could only feel. She tasted sweet. Perfect, in fact. Like an elixir he couldn't resist.

The faint murmur of voices in the corridor penetrated his mind. He broke the kiss, jerking back to stare into her blue eyes— the color of the sky on a spring morning—with no small measure of surprise. Or perhaps it was shock. Whatever this was between them was unique. Special and unsettling. Certainly not easily dismissed.

And he had no idea what to do about it.

Chapter Seventeen

THE FOLLOWING AFTERNOON, Lena bent to kiss Ella's offered cheek, pleased to see her sister looking so well. The delicate bloom of good health lit her face and her eyes sparkled with happiness.

"It seems there's no need for me to ask how you're feeling." Lena smiled as she sat in the chair beside Ella's bed, relieved to see improvement. "Bed rest is obviously suiting you."

Ella gave her a brief mock glare before allowing a smile, her hands settling on the ever-increasing swell of her middle. "Do not say that out loud. And whatever you do, do not tell Leo."

"I'm sworn to secrecy," Lena said with a laugh. "Fewer contractions this week?"

"Yes. The doctor is pleased with my progress but wants me to continue resting for a while longer before he decides if I can return to normal activities."

"I'm pleased to hear that." So pleased that she didn't want to mention recent events. She had no doubt that Marbury knew about the break-in at Renwick House since he was well acquainted with Sterling. Whether he'd told Ella of the situation seemed doubtful. Lena had no intention of being the one to do so.

"Worley is to return today. Leo is meeting him at the dock."

"That's wonderful. He's been gone so long."

Viscount Worley was a long-time friend of Marbury's, who'd

become a dear friend to Lena and her sisters, as well. His expeditions to places all over the world were frequent and always exciting to hear about. He'd made another exploration trip to South America, where he'd found a previously unknown site. His letters to them had been filled with stories of his adventures, from the snakes and spiders he'd seen to an ancient temple he'd uncovered.

"I hope we can see him soon."

"I have no doubt you will." Ella studied her closely. "You haven't come to visit for several days. Norah said you've been busy but didn't share with what."

"Just a few social engagements that took more time than I expected." She leaned forward to squeeze Ella's hand, not wanting her to think she didn't care. "Norah and I don't want to overwhelm you with our visits, so we thought it best to spread them out." Would Ella believe the rather lame excuse?

Lena didn't want to tell her of her lack of success in finding proof that Clarke was digging in the wrong place. That was the true reason she hadn't called, along with Bernie's injury and her upset over her growing feelings for Sterling.

Upset might not be the right word.

Confusion? Yes.

Surprise? Definitely.

Uncertainty? Absolutely.

Especially after that last heated kiss. The one that had nearly buckled her knees. She had no idea what to do about how she felt. How silly when it wasn't as if she could act on her emotions. There was no possibility of a future with Sterling even if she wanted one. He probably wanted a lady with a wonderful title and a fortune to match as his wife, even if nothing formal had been announced.

The thought depressed her spirits more than she could say. Her feelings for Sterling spiraled between joy and despair. Ella would note them immediately if she wasn't careful, which was why Lena had kept her distance the past few days.

Not wanting to worry her sister, she smiled brightly.

"Oh, no." Ella's eyes rounded with worry. "What has happened?"

"Whatever do you mean?" Lena fought to act nonchalant.

"Just tell me the truth. I'll only worry more if you don't."

"The truth about what?" Lena searched her mind desperately for something to say that her far-too-wise and observant sister might believe.

"Tell me." Ella sat up straighter. "Is it Clarke? Has he truly discovered the Money Pit?" The dismay in her expression twisted Lena's heart.

"Good heavens, no." Lena drew a quick breath to pull herself together. While she had always leaned on Ella in the past, this was not one of those times. She needed to work the situation out for herself. Never mind how much she longed to tell Ella everything—from the latest news about Clarke to what had happened to Bernie to her confused emotions over Sterling.

Instead, she waved a hand in dismissal, holding tight to a smile. "Nothing of the sort. I still don't think he'll find anything if he continues to dig where he is now."

"Then what is it?" Ella reached for Lena's hand and held it tight. "I'm not an invalid, you know. I'm having a baby." She smoothed the bump with her other hand. "He's going to be strong and healthy, so there's no need to worry about either of us."

"Yes. Yes, he is." The familiar sense of knowing crept over her, and Lena believed it beyond a doubt. A strong baby boy. How wonderful.

The knowledge didn't ease the desire to take care of Ella now. They needed to stay the course and remain vigilant, keeping her protected and sheltered so she could focus on herself and the baby.

Lena wouldn't tell her about Bernie, nor would she lie about finding proof to prove Clarke a liar. Yet she needed to tell her something to distract her. That left her only one choice.

"It's not anything to do with Oak Island." Lena said the words quietly. "It's ridiculous, really. Nothing can come of it."

"What?" Ella asked.

"I seem to be…falling for Sterling. For Renwick." She shook her head, her heart thudding painfully at the admission. "Against my better judgment. See?" She held Ella's gaze, desperately needing her to agree. "It truly is ridiculous."

"What is ridiculous about you and Renwick?"

She stared at Ella, surprised by the question. "First of all, he's a duke."

"You're a duke's granddaughter."

"One with no title. Besides, marrying a duke would be terrible. All the obligations and expectations." She shook her head again. "I don't want any of that."

"Understandable," Ella agreed, loosening a knot of worry in the pit of Lena's stomach.

"Worst of all," Lena continued, "I think I like him."

Ella blinked, clearly not following her logic. No surprise when there wasn't any.

"It's one thing to feel some sort of physical reaction—" Lena began.

"You mean attraction?"

Lena nodded with reluctance. "I suppose you could call it that. But when you start to like the man, despite his faults…"

Ella laughed and clapped her hands, clearly delighted. "You like him even though you see his faults? You are in deep trouble."

"Don't say that." Lena jerked to her feet to pace across the room and back, trying to ignore the way her heart was pounding. The way her body tingled when he was near. Caring for Sterling would only result in her being hurt. If he discovered her premonitions, he wouldn't want anything to do with her. "As I said before, I don't want any of this. And I'm nearly sure he doesn't either."

"Nearly?" Ella lifted a brow.

Lena felt her cheeks heat once again. "There has been a moment or two when something that might have been admiration gleamed in his eyes."

"What color eyes does he have?"

"Brown. Not like coffee. More like melted chocolate. Or perhaps melting chocolate that hasn't been stirred, with shades of darker and lighter brown." She sighed only to stiffen at the sound of Ella's laughter.

"You are sunk, my dear." Ella grinned. "When you answer a simple question so eloquently, you are truly sunk."

Lena's heart lurched to her throat. "No. It's only attraction. Temporary and fleeting." She watched Ella, hoping she'd agree. When she did, Lena would know she needed to try harder to keep her distance from Sterling before she became more involved with him. That would keep her from getting hurt.

Ella merely gave her a knowing look. One Lena had received numerous times when Ella knew she was right but chose not to argue. "Time will tell. Besides, what is so wrong with having this 'attraction' toward Renwick? He seems more than suitable."

"He would never have me." Lena was certain of it. She could barely breathe with the pain the thought brought.

Outrage darkened Ella's blue eyes. "Why on earth not? You're perfect. Anyone can see that."

Her passionate defense made Lena smile. "No, I'm not. I have one huge flaw that Sterling would never be able to overcome."

"What might that be?"

"My premonitions." Lena fingered the locket her grandfather had given her, the metal warm between her fingers and offering a bit of comfort. It was a relief to know their grandmother had the same sense if only because it meant Lena wasn't as odd as she'd always felt. She might be different from most but not all. She hadn't told either of her sisters about the connection. For now, she wanted to hold the information close like a precious secret.

"Lena, you can't know how he'd react if you told him." Her brow puckered with concern. "You haven't told him, have you?"

"No. But apparently their cook claims to have premonitions

at times, and he thinks it nonsense."

"He only believes that because he hasn't seen yours." Ella's lips twisted, obviously realizing that wouldn't necessarily change his opinion.

"Eventually, he will. When that time comes, he'll stare at me with repulsion and distrust. Like so many others." She met Ella's gaze. "You know it's true."

"I do not. Nor do you. You're making assumptions, and that is never wise."

"He doesn't trust people to begin with." Lena sank into her chair, wondering if she should've shared all of this with Ella when they were trying to keep her from worrying. Surely, it was better that she worry over this rather than the treasure hunt.

"If you decide your feelings for Renwick are steadfast, then you should tell him the truth."

Lena shivered. She couldn't imagine doing that. Not when the image of him glaring at her came easily to mind. Trusting others was not one of her strengths, nor was it one of his. How ironic distrustfulness was something they had in common.

Too much was at risk with Sterling. She would prefer he never knew the truth. It would be better if she kept her distance from him and hoped these feelings faded.

With that realization, her emotions plummeted once again.

STERLING SCOWLED AS he waited in Brooks's early that evening, hoping Viscount Ludham would make an appearance. How could he have allowed the opportunity to question Lena to slip through his grasp? He'd arranged for a moment alone with her and instead, desire had overcome his good sense.

With a sigh, he realized that thinking of her now brought forth passion again. What was it about her that caught his interest? He gave himself a mental shake. Interest was too tame of a word for what he felt. He'd never experienced anything quite like this.

She was not the sort of lady he'd expected to have feelings for. While intelligent, beautiful, and kind, so were several others he could name. He appreciated her spirit, which her claim that Clarke was mistaken revealed in spades. Her gentleness with Bernie was also admirable, and he didn't think for a moment that Lena only pretended to like Bernie to further any chance with him.

As he pondered the matter, he realized there was no good way to describe the bond he felt with Lena. It was as if they were magnets drawn to each other by a hidden force. The notion was ridiculous, yet he was at a loss to explain it any other way.

Marbury strode across the room, pausing at the sight of Sterling. "Good evening, Renwick." He gave a brief bow.

"Good to see you," Sterling said with a nod before gesturing toward a chair at his table. "Care to join me for a drink?"

"Certainly." Marbury studied him as he sat. "You look less than pleased. Has the investigation of your break-in yielded any results?" His expression changed to one of alarm. "Your sister's injury hasn't worsened, has it?"

Sterling had come across the earl at the Royal Geological Society offices the day after Bernie had been hurt and told him of the incident.

Marbury had been appalled and shared the events that had transpired when he'd helped Ella and her sisters look for their father's stolen journal. He'd also told him what Vanbridge went through when a few artifacts had gone missing from his museum. Sterling had been shocked by the trouble that seemed to have followed the Wright sisters from Oak Island.

"She's slowly recovering. Thank you," Sterling said. "But the investigation isn't getting anywhere. The police have no clues. I didn't realize quite how dangerous searching for treasure could be. Especially when I'm not the one doing the searching."

"Agreed." Marbury ordered a whiskey then asked, "Speaking

of the search, has any further progress been made?"

"Not that I know of." Sterling frowned, realizing it had been some time since he'd heard from Clarke. The man's lack of communication was not helpful. The sooner Sterling's friend was in place to provide a report on Clarke's endeavors the better. He hoped to have word from him in the coming days. "What are your thoughts on Lena's insistence that Clarke is digging in the wrong place?"

"Lena?" The earl grinned. "The two of you truly have become friends, eh?"

"Miss Wright has called on my sister several times." Would that suffice as a reason for using her given name? Rather than wait to see, Sterling repeated his question. "Do you think she's right?"

Marbury hesitated, making Sterling even more curious. "I tend to wonder if she could be."

"Why?"

The earl shifted in his chair as if uncomfortable, the delay in his answer puzzling when it seemed a straightforward question. "She tends to be right about many surprising things."

"How do you mean?"

Marbury shook his head. "I won't say anything more. But know that the Wright sisters are amazing women. You may have already witnessed that for yourself. They are each strong and independent. Perhaps those traits come from their unusual upbringing on Oak Island. They've endured more difficulties than most ladies I've met."

Sterling pondered the earl's remarks, easily able to agree from what he knew of Lena. But he didn't understand Marbury's claim that she was frequently right.

He told himself to put Lena from his thoughts and focus on the break-in as the waiter brought their drinks. That was the priority at the moment.

"How well do you know Viscount Ludham?" Sterling asked Marbury, careful to keep his voice low so as not to be overheard.

"Well enough to know he's an ass."

"Why do you think that?" Sterling detested gossip but knew Marbury wouldn't share anything unless he knew it to be true.

"The man was cruel at school to anyone he thought inferior and hasn't changed. If there's an easier path to riches, he'd be the first to take it, regardless of whether doing so harmed others."

"On that, we agree."

"He's pursued Ella, Norah, and now Lena. He seems astounded they didn't jump at the chance to further their association with him."

Sterling didn't like that news in the least. "Has he been on any treasure hunts?"

"Not to my knowledge. He seems to prefer to remain at home and criticize those who do."

"He is vocal about such things," Sterling agreed. "I overheard an interesting conversation he had with a man named Winslow."

"David Winslow?" Marbury scowled. "I can't say that I like him either."

"Oh?"

"He's much of the same ilk. He befriends those he thinks can gain him something. What was the conversation about?"

"It had to do with the dig on Oak Island." Sterling hesitated, wondering how much to tell Marbury. He tended not to trust anyone, but he was beginning to think he needed assistance to discover what Ludham and Winslow were doing. "I have reason to think Winslow might be more than an acquaintance of Clarke's."

Marbury frowned. "Why not ask Clarke?"

"I haven't decided if I can trust him."

"While I appreciate a certain reserve when it comes to relationships, you're going to have to trust someone eventually," Marbury said.

"You sound like my sister." At Marbury's puzzled look, Sterling added, "She frequently suggests I should learn to trust others." He shrugged. "Difficult when one has often been disappointed."

"But rewarding if one places trust in the right person." Marbury's smile suggested he had found that person. "I'm pleased to say my wife has changed my mind about such things."

The earl's affection for his countess was easy to see, especially when they were together, but even when Marbury spoke of her. The meaning of marriage vows—to love and honor—took on a whole new meaning.

Sterling didn't remember his own mother well as she'd died while giving birth to Bernie. But she had been distant, leaving his care to the nanny. His parent's marriage had been more of a business arrangement. While that wasn't uncommon even in these modern times, Sterling was beginning to think that wasn't what he wanted.

Was his growing attraction for Lena a sign he should consider her as a potential bride? How could he think about the possibility of a future when the issue of Oak Island stood between them?

Her disapproval of Clarke was no secret. While it was easy to believe the dig would soon be over, that wasn't a certainty. He need only look at how long her father had searched to know it wasn't an easy task, despite what Clarke claimed.

Was he ready to trust her? Yes, and yet no. She hadn't done anything to make him think her unworthy. Her affection and concern for Bernie were certainly in her favor. But more than once, an uncomfortable look had come over her expression, as if she were guilty of something. Like she'd been caught in a lie.

Or she had a secret.

That didn't sit well with him. He didn't like secrets. Secrets too often led to betrayal.

Before he could give the matter further thought, Viscount Ludham entered the room.

Marbury noted his entrance as well and raised a brow. "Want some assistance with Ludham?"

"Yes, I would appreciate that." He'd like another opinion on the viscount's response to his questions.

They remained where they were, finishing their drinks while Ludham greeted a few others before settling at a table by himself. It amused Sterling that he ignored both him and Marbury completely.

"Looks like as good of an opportunity as we can expect." Sterling pushed back his chair.

"Agreed. Let us see what he has to say for himself." Marbury stood, as well.

Sterling led the way to the viscount's table. "Ludham."

The man looked between Sterling and Marbury, his expression less than pleased as he slowly rose to bow. "Good evening. I trust you are both well."

"We are indeed." Rather than wait for an invitation, Sterling pulled out a chair. "You don't mind if we join you for a moment." He didn't pose it as a question.

"Not at all." The glare he gave them said otherwise. "Please do."

Marbury and Sterling both took a seat, leaving Ludham no choice but to join them. "Something on your mind?"

"It's more that we are wondering what is on yours," Marbury said.

He frowned. "How so?"

"How well do you know Walter Clarke?" Sterling asked.

"Your treasure hunter?" Ludham leaned back in his seat with an amused expression. "Not well. Why?"

"You and Winslow have been in contact with him."

Ludham stilled. "What makes you think that?"

Sterling opened his mouth to tell him that he'd overheard him, but Marbury interrupted with a warning glance at Sterling. "A friend of a friend."

"Who?"

Marbury shrugged. "I can't remember the name. What truly matters is what he said."

"What might that be?" Ludham asked.

"We wanted to give you the benefit of the doubt and speak

with you directly," Sterling said, rather than answering Ludham's question. "We wouldn't want to rely on rumors."

Ludham's gaze shifted back and forth between them as if trying to decide how to respond. "Rumors about Clarke?"

"And his progress on Oak Island."

"I'm afraid I don't know anything about it. Sorry I can't be of more help."

"We know Winslow is going to see Johnson," Sterling said. "What does he hope to learn?"

Ludham stared, alarm widening his eyes. "Johnson?"

"Surely you don't think the man can provide additional information about where to dig on the island," Sterling said.

"Nothing of the sort." Ludham shook his head, though his demeanor suggested he was lying.

Based on the conversation Sterling had overheard, he knew he was.

Ludham gave a one-shouldered shrug as if relenting. "Winslow happens to be acquainted with Johnson as he went to school with him. I believe he wanted to speak with him about the history of the island, mainly about Captain Kidd."

"Kidd?" Marbury frowned, while Sterling watched him with interest. Everyone knew of Marbury's interest in the pirate. "Surely not in connection with Oak Island."

Ludham smiled but it wasn't especially friendly. "I didn't really pay much attention. You'll have to ask Winslow."

"Why are you and Winslow interested in Clarke's progress?" Sterling asked.

Ludham paused again, hesitating. "It should come as no surprise that Clarke is interested in learning anything that might prove helpful with his search. He asked Winslow to see what he could discover." His gaze met Sterling's. "Even you can't find fault with that, Your Grace."

Sterling held back the urge to say he certainly could. He preferred to be consulted before actions were taken. But when he'd hired Clarke, he'd been aware of his reputation for being independent. He should appreciate that the man had taken the initiative to discover more.

There was more to Clarke's actions than Ludham was sharing. Something wasn't right. He wouldn't claim to have his cook's supposed ability, but he knew when something smelled foul. And this did.

"And?" Marbury prodded. "Has Winslow discovered anything helpful thus far?"

"Not that I'm aware of." Ludham folded his hands over his stomach. Sterling thought his relaxed pose feigned. "I suppose Clarke hopes that Winslow's conversation with Johnson might shed some light."

"Doubtful that Johnson will provide meaningful details that he didn't already try when he was digging," Marbury said. His amused smile seemed to irritate Ludham, based on the way the viscount scowled as he glared at the earl.

Marbury's remark eased Sterling's upset. He was right. Numerous people had looked at length for written evidence of treasure on Oak Island with no success. The chances of Ludham and Winslow making any discoveries seemed unlikely.

However, their efforts made him even more suspicious of Clarke. Sterling doubted Clarke's next report would mention anything about his own attempts to find more information.

With a tip of his head toward Marbury to signal they should leave, Sterling stood. "I appreciate your time, Ludham." He didn't bother to suggest the viscount let them know if anything further was discovered.

Sterling walked out of the club, followed by Marbury, and paused on the steps, glancing about to make certain no one could overhear. "That wasn't particularly helpful."

Marbury shook his head. "No, but one never knows when something learned will be helpful later. Perhaps that will prove true with this as well."

Sterling nodded. "Thank you."

"Happy to help. Now, I'm going to have dinner with my

wife." Marbury bowed. "Good evening, Your Grace."

Sterling bid him good night and stepped into his waiting carriage, but his thoughts remained on the conversation with Ludham. He needed to discover more about what Ludham and Winslow were up to.

Chapter Eighteen

LENA CURTSIED AS she finished a dance at the Harrison ball with Lord Canham, a man who asked her to dance at nearly every ball. He was handsome in a quiet way with brown hair and eyes, as well as an excellent dance partner. But Lena had realized last Season that she liked him in a brotherly manner rather than as a potential husband. She hoped he felt the same. She didn't want to hurt his feelings.

"Thank you, my lord," she said once he'd escorted her back to Norah.

"The pleasure is mine, Miss Wright." Rather than leaving, he remained by her side, seeming content to be in her company.

She cast a worried look at Norah, who raised a brow in response, clearly understanding the problem. The moment made her appreciate having sisters. One didn't always have to explain a situation for them to understand.

How lonely Lady Bernice must be with no sisters, no mother, and few friends. That made Lena even more determined to continue their friendship and serve in the role of an older sister if the occasion warranted it.

Sterling's presence complicated that intent. She'd managed to keep her distance from him for the past two days. Whether doing so had calmed her feelings toward him remained to be seen. She continued to think of him far too often but hoped she'd regained control over her emotions.

She'd spent most of that time going through the letters again and had even made an attempt to compare them with her father's notes on the history of the island. Unfortunately, she hadn't gained any additional insights. She was certain she was missing something, but what?

The map of Oak Island pressed into the paper was a puzzle. Why bother to make the map when Jenkins didn't mention it in his letter? Had he copied the image from another or made it himself from his own exploration of the island?

She hoped to have a word with Vanbridge about it when he arrived to join Norah later this evening. He might be able to help her determine where to search for more clues.

"Fine weather we've been having." Lord Canham's comment reminded her of his presence.

"Yes, yes we have." Lena wracked her mind for something more to say. "Have you been able to enjoy it?"

"I had a nice ride this morning in Hyde Park. I thought you might be there as well."

"Not today." She held back from sharing that she intended to ride the following morning. That might only encourage him to try to find her. She'd rather he didn't.

"Good evening, ladies."

The familiar voice had Lena and Norah turning with joy to see Viscount Worley standing behind them.

"How wonderful to see you, Worley," Norah greeted him. "You've been gone so long we were beginning to fear you didn't intend to return."

"That was a temptation." Worley grinned as he looked them both over in turn, his brown eyes warm with affection. "But how could I resist coming home when both of you are here?"

"You are incorrigible," Lena said with a laugh. "The trip must've been productive, for you look quite pleased."

"It was indeed. The expedition was a success in many ways."

The time away had done him good, she realized as he continued speaking. His dark eyes were clear, and his expression relaxed. His bushy moustache hadn't changed a bit.

His familiar smile made Lena realize how much she'd missed him. His friendship with Marbury had extended to Lena and her sisters soon after their arrival in London. He'd helped them with the search for their father's missing journal as well as the stolen coin. Worley's numerous trips to far-off lands always seemed to fill him in a way that life in London didn't.

Only too late did Lena realize she'd completely ignored Lord Canham. She turned to speak to him, but he'd already departed.

Perhaps it was for the best. Hopefully, he realized she wasn't interested in anything more than friendship.

Soon Vanbridge joined them and greeted Worley with a handshake and a smile. "I look forward to hearing of your expedition once you've had a chance to recover from traveling."

"Actually, Marbury and I are meeting at the Society offices tomorrow to review a few of the artifacts I brought back. Care to join us?"

"I'd be honored." The two men spoke at length while Lena and Norah listened with interest as Worley described one of the temples he'd come upon and the difficulties in reclaiming it from the jungle.

Worley asked how Ella was faring, and Norah shared that she'd visited Ella that afternoon and she was still resting. Their conversation continued, providing Lena with the opportunity she'd been hoping for.

"Vanbridge, might I ask your opinion?" Lena kept her voice low. While Norah knew she wanted to speak to him about the letters, Lena wasn't ready to share the story with Worley. Not until she'd found something of interest. Besides, Worley would surely mention Sterling. The viscount was too observant at times and might guess her feelings for the duke.

"Of course." Vanbridge met her gaze, clearly curious.

"Norah may have mentioned the map of Oak Island I found pressed into the privateer's letter. But there is no reference to it in what he wrote. I feel it must be a clue of sorts, yet I cannot find anything more."

"Interesting. Norah did mention that several of the passages also made you wonder if they could be clues."

She shook her head. "I'm beginning to think I was wrong. While those lines don't fit with the rest of the letters, I wonder if they were merely his attempt to be poetic. But if they are clues, I don't know what they point to."

He gazed into the distance, seeming to consider the matter further, before returning his attention to her again. "I'd be happy to look at them, of course. You've looked to see if any of the other pages have something pressed into them?"

"Yes, to no avail. There are no symbols or other markings that I can see."

"Usually there is a pattern to codes. Both for ease of deciphering and for the person who creates them. Those patterns are what allow them to be solved. Try looking at the letters from different angles or in bright light. Upside down or sideways. Look for repeated words or phrases. That might bring forth results."

Lena nodded. She'd done some of those techniques but more out of frustration than with the hope of actually finding anything. It was time to do so with a different frame of mind. "Thank you. I shall try your suggestions before I bother you with them."

"It's no bother. I enjoy examining such things."

"I can see why," Lena said with a smile. "But it's beyond frustrating when the answer escapes you."

"True. Step away for a time and come back to them. That helps to view the item more objectively. But I'd be happy to look at them."

"I'll bring them over in the next day or two if I continue to be unsuccessful." If there was a clue in the letters, she wanted to find it. Proving Clarke was wrong might upset both Sterling and Lady Bernice, but she didn't want her father's reputation harmed more than it already had been by Clarke's claims. Then there was Ella's condition to consider. Her sister was better, but another article in the newssheet about Clarke's progress could easily change that.

The evening lengthened, and Lena enjoyed a dance with Worley. His skills on the dance floor made him an excellent partner.

"I'm so pleased you've returned," she told him afterward as he returned her to where Norah and Vanbridge visited with friends.

"It's good to be home. At least for a time."

"When will your next adventure take you away?"

He frowned. "Perhaps as early as autumn but more than likely, not until spring. We need drier weather than the summer months offer to make true progress. However, there's a chance we might return in October if the rains hold off."

As they drew to a halt, Lady Bernice joined them.

"Lena, I've been looking for you." Her eyes were bright with excitement behind her spectacles. She glanced at Worley, seeming to just realize he was there. "I'm terribly sorry to interrupt. How rude of me."

"Not at all." Worley dipped his head then glanced at Lena with a question in his eyes.

She quickly made the introductions, doing her best not to look for Sterling. "I'm certain you know Lady Bernice's brother, the Duke of Renwick, since he's a member of the Royal Geological Society." Even the mention of him was enough to cause her cheeks to heat.

Worley visited with Bernie, being his usual charming self and putting the younger woman at ease.

Do not look for Sterling, Lena ordered herself. Before she could stop, she was perusing the ballroom for his tall form. She was both relieved and disappointed not to find him, which only made her scold herself for looking.

"Good evening."

Her breath caught as shivers of awareness ran along her back. Leave it to Sterling to be where she least expected him. She took a firm hold of her emotions and turned to face him, only to have her heart thunder at the sight of him, so handsome in his black evening clothes. His golden hair had been smoothed to the side, though a hint of wave remained. She managed a curtsy despite her trembling knees.

"Good evening, Your Grace." Oh, dear. Keeping her distance for two days hadn't helped in the least. Absence truly did make the heart grow fonder.

STERLING STARED AT Lena as she looked at him with those wide, lovely blue eyes. Eyes that threatened to drown him with the emotion swirling in their depths, making him wonder at her thoughts.

Her blonde hair was twisted in an elegant coiffure that elongated her graceful neck. Her deep green evening gown made her skin glow with vitality. She was beautiful as always and caught his full attention while everything around them fell away. He longed to offer his arm and tuck her hand along his side, declaring her his for all to see.

He blinked, hoping—needing—to break the spell that bound them. Now was not the time to indulge in his attraction to her.

How ridiculous that it took immense effort to force himself to look at those nearby, including Bernie. If he wasn't careful, his sister would soon realize just how much he cared for Lena.

"Good evening, Your Grace." Worley bowed.

Sterling nodded. "You've returned to England's shores at last, eh?"

"For a time. I have much to share at the next Society meeting. Our dig yielded exciting results." Worley glanced between Lena and Sterling, making him wonder what the viscount saw. "I understand you've started a dig of your own."

Sterling wasn't surprised he knew and looked toward Bernie, noting a flush in her cheeks. "Thanks to my sister, yes. Walter

Clarke is leading a dig on Oak Island on our behalf."

Worley looked at Bernie. "Will you have a chance to visit the island while work is underway?"

"I don't believe so. I am not as brave as you are, traveling the world and living in difficult conditions." She glanced at Lena. "Or you."

Lena smiled, though it looked as if it required effort. "Living on Oak Island wasn't nearly as difficult as trying to survive in the jungle." Her smile became genuine as she shifted her attention to Worley. "I certainly admire the viscount for his efforts."

Irritation swept through Sterling, surprising him with its strength. If he didn't know better, he might think jealousy held him in its grip. That couldn't be. Yet as he watched Lena and Worley speak with ease and affection, he couldn't deny it.

He blew out a breath, acknowledging just how much he cared for Lena. Worley was no threat to that. Sterling liked the man and admired his passion for exploration, despite the extreme conditions he endured. He was an excellent storyteller and shared his experiences with humor and self-deprecation.

Still, Sterling didn't care for the way Lena looked at the viscount with admiration. He held back the urge to take her hand and draw her to the terrace so he could have her all to himself. Then again, maybe that was a good idea, regardless of Worley.

He forced himself to listen to the conversation, biding his time until he could ask Lena to dance.

That lasted all of ten minutes before he cleared his throat, unable to take it anymore. "Miss Wright, may I have the honor of a dance?"

"Of course." Pink colored her cheeks, making her look even lovelier.

He gave himself a mental shake. Since when did a blush threaten to weaken his knees? It was almost as if not seeing Lena for the past few days had intensified his attraction to her.

Sterling risked a glance at Bernie, hoping she remained oblivious to his feelings. Otherwise, she would accuse him of stealing

Lena, who was quickly becoming one of her favorite people.

He offered his elbow and attempted to ignore the spear of desire that shot through him when she placed her gloved hand on his arm. Damn if she didn't adjust her fingers as he drew her hand tight against him, sending another ripple of awareness through him.

How odd that these small things, which he was unaware of with others, were magnified with Lena. The realization was unsettling. Why was it that he felt both off balance and...*whole* when he was with her?

The question was for another time, when he was alone and could consider the situation at length. Then again, he'd already examined his feelings without discovering answers. He didn't like feeling out of control of his body or his emotions. It seemed that when he was with Lena, he had no choice.

Sterling glanced at her as they neared the dance floor, wondering if she felt any of what he did. That pretty blush could easily be from embarrassment because he'd asked her in front of her sister, Vanbridge, Worley, and Bernie. Or it could be because she was thinking of their last kiss like he was.

He closed his eyes briefly, wishing he hadn't thought of it. Doing so made him want another and so much more.

"I didn't realize you were friends with Worley," he said as they waited for the other couples to clear the floor. Any subject would do to help clear his thoughts. Even Worley.

"We've known him since we arrived in London. He's helped us on many occasions."

The answer didn't change the jealous feeling that simmered inside him. He wanted to know how deep her affection was for the viscount. "Helped you?"

"He placed his life in danger to aid us." She heaved a sigh that caused him to frown. "Isn't that special, considering most think chivalry dead these days?"

"Were circumstances so dire?" He wasn't about to touch the chivalry remark.

"Absolutely. Life or death. First Ella and Marbury. Then Norah and Vanbridge." She shuddered, but he couldn't tell whether it was real or feigned. "Thank goodness the situations had a favorable outcome."

"With Worley's aid."

"In part. He's a dear."

"Indeed." Sterling clenched his teeth before he said anything further. Worley wasn't the issue.

Then what was?

Himself and his uncontrollable urges when it came to Lena.

He glanced down at her, but that only made the matter worse. She was so beautiful. So appealing. Her long lashes. Those pink cheeks. Her smooth skin. The swell of her breasts just visible along the lace neckline of her gown.

His imagination took hold, and he envisioned her without the gown, in only a thin chemise. His lower body stirred at the image as his gaze held on her.

"Shall we?" she asked, bringing his mind back to the now empty dance floor.

"Of course." He guided them forward, nodding at a few acquaintances as they waited for the music to begin. He forced himself to think of the dance ahead rather than how Lena would look in his bed.

He'd always considered dancing a necessity of his position. Something he needed to learn, regardless of whether he enjoyed it. But as the strains of a violin filled the air with Lena in his arms, he reconsidered that low opinion.

Dancing was underrated.

Waltzing even more so.

Holding her as they moved in time to the music was magic, pure and simple. Their bodies brushed against one another as they turned. An unexpected joy tugged at his heart.

The thought nearly had him taking a misstep. His heart? No, no, no. That couldn't be right. Enjoyable? Yes. But nothing more. How could it be when he hadn't decided whether he could trust the delectable Lena Wright?

Again, he clenched his jaw. This time because of the lie. No purpose would be served in telling himself falsehoods.

He trusted Lena. The true problem was that she didn't trust him. How he knew that, he couldn't say. Perhaps it was the wary look that often shadowed her eyes. He didn't care for it. Especially when it was absent when she looked at Worley.

Noting the cautious glance she gave him again, he smiled, only to see a puzzled expression cross her face. He must've forced it, showing too many teeth or the like. He wasn't quite sure since he rarely bothered to smile. He tried again, pulling her closer as he did so. She stiffened as they turned.

"Is something amiss?" he asked.

"I don't know. Is there?" Her raised brow challenged him to answer honestly.

Dare he tell her the truth? Surely speaking honestly was the best course of action. "Why is it I feel that you don't trust me?"

"I wouldn't say that."

"What would you say?" He swung her into a turn, pleased once again by how well they moved together. Would the same be true if they indulged in a more intimate dance?

The music swelled, saving her from answering immediately. The delay only made him more curious.

"It's not you in particular," she said at last.

"Hmm. You sound less than convincing." He glanced at the open doors to the terrace as they moved past them again. The opportunity to escape was becoming more tempting by the moment.

Her gaze darted about, and a hint of panic flashed in her eyes as if she couldn't determine a way to respond.

"Lena." He waited for her to look at him, hoping that when she did, he'd see the same connection he felt reflected in her eyes. Finally, she looked at him, and his world settled. "I would never hurt you."

Harm could be caused in more than one way. A cruel word.

A hurtful look. His father had found numerous ways to inflict pain. But Sterling knew he would do everything in his power to protect Lena, much like he did Bernie with one exception—his feelings for Lena were far from sisterly.

He drew a quick breath at the thought. Damn. How had it come to that so quickly? They circled near the terrace doors once again, and this time, he couldn't resist. With a bit of skill and determination, not to mention a distracted dance partner, he took a few deliberate steps, and they were in the cool evening air.

"Oh." Lena looked about as if puzzled by how they came to be outside. "We shouldn't—"

"But we are." He kept hold of her arm and guided her toward a darkened corner. "Only for a moment." He glanced back toward the ballroom, pleased to see no one other than a few of their fellow dancers seemed to have noted their escape. Not yet anyway.

That left him free to return his attention to Lena, who blinked up at him in confusion. Amusement caught him—he was confused too.

"Was that a true smile?" she asked as she watched him.

"Yes." He allowed his smile to grow just to please her. What else might he do to make her happy?

"Sterling?" She looked down to where he held her arm and shifted to take his hand between her gloved ones then held his gaze. "I do trust you."

The air left his lungs in a rush. He hadn't realized how much that meant to him until she said it. There was only one way to show her how her words touched him.

"Thank you." He drew her close, gazing into her eyes before taking her mouth with his.

While he meant the kiss to be gentle, he couldn't hold back. Not with the whirl of emotions inside him. Passion took control, and he sought a deeper connection with her. While she might be friendly toward Worley, he wanted more. Friendship was a start, but it wasn't nearly enough.

Her lips opened for him before he could demand it. That made the kiss even more arousing. Her tongue danced with his and time slowed. She wrapped her arms around him, and he knew he'd never felt anything sweeter than this moment.

Never tasted anyone sweeter than Lena.

Now wasn't the time or place to explore what was between them. They had only a few moments. If they were caught, he would be forced to propose and she to accept. Odd, but that no longer sounded so terrible.

Still, he eased back to look into her darkened blue eyes, grazing a finger along the softness of her cheek.

"Sterling?" The familiar feminine voice behind him had him stiffening. But the accusation in the tone had him turning in dismay.

"Bernie," he began, his heart squeezing at the hurt in her expression, her eyes hidden by the glint of the torchlight on her spectacles.

Then his sister turned and fled into the ballroom, quickly disappearing in the crowd.

Chapter Nineteen

L ENA CAUGHT THE flash of pain in Bernie's expression before she disappeared. Knowing she was the cause of it sent a spear of pain through Lena's chest. She should've shared how she felt about Sterling with his sister, or at least hinted at it. Bernie had told her how often ladies had pretended to befriend her only to get close to her brother.

That wasn't the case with Lena. Or at least, not anymore.

Guilt flooded her as she considered the matter further. In truth, she might not have encouraged a friendship with Bernie if she hadn't been trying to find out more about their efforts to dig on Oak Island.

"I'll speak to her," Lena told Sterling.

The glare he sent her had Lena taking a step back.

"No. She's my sister. I'll go after her." With a frustrated shake of his head, he gestured toward the ballroom. "You go in first. It wouldn't do to have anyone see us entering at the same time."

Lena wanted to argue. To protest the look of dismissal he'd given her. But that would have to wait until a better time. With one last glance at him that had her heart longing for what couldn't be, she slipped into the ballroom and made her way around the perimeter of the dance floor to find Norah.

She couldn't resist searching for Bernie as she went. While she understood Sterling's need to be the one to speak to her, she wanted to talk to Bernie as well.

Norah and Vanbridge were in the middle of a conversation with friends when she joined them. Norah's puzzled look as she looked past Lena for Sterling had Lena shaking her head. No doubt she expected Sterling to have escorted her back. Explanations would have to wait until later. She stood to one side to allow the conversation to flow around her while continuing to look for both Sterling and Bernie, to no avail.

What would he tell Bernie? She wished she knew. Yet she could easily guess what he'd say—that the kiss had meant nothing.

The thought was thoroughly depressing.

THE FOLLOWING MORNING, Sterling waited for Bernie to appear for breakfast at her customary time, only to grow even more concerned when she didn't. He'd tried to speak with her at the ball, but she had insisted an explanation wasn't necessary, then claimed to have a headache. He'd escorted her home soon afterward without seeing any glimpse of Lena.

Discussing it during the carriage ride with Aunt Edith listening had been impossible and he knew his attempt to explain upon their return home had been rather convoluted.

How could he tell Bernie about his feelings for Lena when he couldn't describe them to himself? He feared Bernie would think he was making excuses for his behavior.

Perhaps he was.

While he didn't want to jeopardize Bernie's friendship, neither did he want to step away from Lena. He wasn't certain he could keep his distance. Not any longer. In truth, he was eager to explore what was between them.

Marbury and Vanbridge were to blame for his higher expectations of what marriage could be. Their examples filled him with the possibility of having a union that was more than simple duty.

Having a marriage like theirs meant opening himself to trusting others. That meant risking disappointment. Or worse—hurt. How many times had he tried as a boy to win his father's love? His father had always rejected him, finding fault with the way he acted.

Sterling had learned to remain aloof, telling himself he didn't trust others but was that true? Wasn't that just a way of protecting himself from the pain of rejection?

One thing was clear. He wouldn't allow his father to continue controlling him. He didn't know if he had a chance for a future with Lena, but he wanted to continue down that path and see what happened.

Bernie would understand if he explained it to her.

He tossed aside his napkin and stood, striding toward the stairs to take them two at a time. First, he looked in the drawing room but found it empty. Next, he tried his sister's sitting room, only to find no hint of Bernie. Left with no choice, he knocked on her bedroom door.

"Bernie?" His only answer was silence. "I know you're in there." He didn't, but it was his best guess. He waited a few more seconds and was certain he heard the rustle of movement. "I'm coming in."

He waited a moment, then opened the door, unsurprised to see his sister sitting at her desk. "Good morning."

She glanced at him briefly before returning her attention to the letter she was writing. "Morning. Is there something you need?" The fact that she didn't look at him showed the depth of her upset.

As she sat at her desk, her posture perfect, he realized she wasn't the fragile little girl she used to be. She was a woman grown and deserved to be treated as one. But he knew he wouldn't ever lose his need to try to protect her.

"Yes." He walked slowly forward, taking a deep breath with the hope the right words would come to mind. "I need to speak with you. But first I want to apologize."

"Whatever for?" Her quiet voice hurt him more than her anger would've.

He ran a hand through his hair, uncertain what to say. "I should have told you about my feelings for Lena. I'm sorry I didn't."

At last, she set down her pen and turned in her chair to face him. "Yes. You should have."

"I swear to you that I do not intend to ruin the friendship the two of you have."

"Do you truly have feelings for her or is this a fleeting attraction that will soon pass?"

Sterling hesitated. "Would you rather it was? Fleeting, that is?"

Bernie drew tiny circles with her finger on the polished surface of her desk for a long moment. "I care for Lena very much." She paused the motion to meet his gaze. "I would hate to lose her as a friend. But I also worry that's the only reason she is my friend—because of you."

"That's not true. She isn't Lady Susan." That particular young lady had befriended Bernie while they were at their country estate. She'd been visiting a cousin for a few weeks in the area and struck up a friendship with Bernie. It hadn't taken long for both Sterling and Bernie to realize the lady had only done so to get to Sterling.

Bernie had been disappointed and hurt. The incident had shaken her confidence, something she had little enough of to begin with, thanks to their father.

Sterling had hoped her time in Switzerland would help her regain it. While that seemed to be the case, he also knew that a few of the ladies at the finishing school had sought out Bernie simply because her brother was an eligible duke. He hated to know he couldn't always protect her.

"You are right," Bernie offered at last. "But sometimes it's hard to know who to trust."

"We can only rely on our instincts. Those are usually better judges of character than our brains."

Bernie gave a small smile. "Now you are starting to sound like Cook. She always says 'she knows what she knows.'"

"Perhaps that's what she means," Sterling said with a smile.

"How do you feel about Lena?"

Sterling had hoped she'd forgotten the question. "I don't know. I suppose I need more time to say for certain. There is much to admire about her."

"She is very pretty."

"Yes," he agreed, "but there is more to her than her appearance, don't you think?"

"Of course," Bernie agreed. "At first, I only wanted to talk to her about Oak Island." She frowned, seeming to consider the statement further. "I suppose in a way I was using her."

"Talking with others about a common interest is something we all do. It provides a connection where friendships start." He drew closer and reached for Bernie's hand. "Do you forgive me for not telling you about my interest in Lena?"

"Of course." She squeezed his hand. "It was just a shock to see the two of you together on the terrace. Especially when I didn't realize you thought of her or she of you in that regard. However, that doesn't mean you can ruin my friendship with her. Please take care. I don't want to see either of you hurt."

His sister's gentle words had him blinking in surprise. He realized it was true. He'd promised Lena he wouldn't hurt her, but she also had the power to hurt him if she chose. He could no longer imagine not having the pleasure of her company. He enjoyed spending time with her as much as he enjoyed their kisses. That was something he'd never experienced before. His relationship with Lena, whatever it was, was full of firsts.

LENA WAITED UNTIL midafternoon to call on Bernie with her maid accompanying her. Hopefully, by then, Sterling would have had a chance to speak with her and explain. Lena still didn't know quite what she would tell her friend and wished she knew what Sterling had said. She couldn't possibly confess her feelings for Sterling to Bernie when she hadn't told him how she felt.

Confused, for certain.

This was the first time she'd experienced this, and she was still sorting through it. Sorting? Perhaps reeling was a better word.

"Good afternoon, Miss Wright," Foster said as he opened the door with the same warm smile he'd offered the last time.

Lena had yet to become accustomed to it. "Good afternoon. Is Lady Bernice receiving?"

"Allow me to inquire." He gestured toward the reception room for her to wait then greeted Nancy before a footman showed her to the kitchen.

Lena hoped Bernie would see her. In the hours that had passed since that moment on the terrace, she'd realized how much she treasured her friendship with the younger woman.

"Lena."

Lena spun from where she'd stood looking out the window to see Sterling enter the room. Her heart thudded at the sight of him, uncertain what his presence meant. Had he come to tell her that Bernie refused to see her? She dearly hoped not. "How is Bernie?"

"Not especially happy with either of us, but I believe she'll recover."

"Thank goodness. I've been so worried." She bit her lip, wondering whether she could ask what was on her mind. "Did you tell her…"

Sterling watched her with an amused look. "Tell her what?"

Lena sighed in exasperation. "What exactly did you say?"

He walked closer to stand before her, his brown eyes warm, whether from affection or mirth, she didn't know. "That I like you. That I want to become better acquainted with you."

"Truly?" Her entire body flushed. His low voice sent heat pooling in surprising places she hesitated to name. Her heart felt as if it would beat out of her chest. She took a breath to try to regain her balance only to breathe in his scent of the woods on a rainy day.

Her thoughts had been so focused on Bernie that she hadn't prepared for the possibility of seeing Sterling. Hadn't rebuilt her defenses from their kiss last evening.

His eyes darkened, making her wonder if he felt the same desire she did. Then he bent his head to claim her mouth with his, and she had no doubt. His lips were warm and firm. She swore she could feel the heat of his hand where it rested on her waist, despite the layers separating them.

The clearing of a throat had her jerking back. Embarrassment took hold when she realized Foster had returned.

Sterling remained where he was, blocking her from the butler's view, which gave her a moment to collect herself. At last, he turned to face the butler.

"Lady Bernice would be pleased to greet Miss Wright in the drawing room," the servant said.

"Thank you, Foster." Sterling turned back toward Lena.

Lena risked a glance at the butler, only to stiffen in shock when he smiled then bowed. It almost seemed as if he approved of what he'd witnessed. What would Sterling think if he knew?

"Shall I escort you upstairs?" Sterling offered.

"I think it best if I speak with her alone first if you don't mind."

Sterling considered her request, then nodded. "I do believe you're right. Foster will show you to the drawing room."

The butler's polite mask had returned though a small smile lingered before he turned away to lead the way up the stairs to the doorway. "Miss Wright to see you, my lady."

Bernie stood by the window, her expression wary as Lena thanked Foster then entered the room.

"Bernie, I am so sorry." Lena walked forward until she stood before her. "Can you possibly forgive me?"

Bernie shook her head. "There's nothing to forgive."

"Of course, there is." Lena tightened her lips. "We should've mentioned our…interest in one another rather than allowing you to discover it in such a manner."

"I won't deny it was a surprise."

"It has been to me, as well."

"Truly?" Bernie's brow puckered as she looked closely at Lena.

"Very much so." Lena risked a glance over her shoulder to make certain Sterling hadn't joined them. "I'm still not certain what to make of it."

"When you say 'it,' to what exactly are you referring?" Bernie's head tilted to the side, sunlight glinting off her spectacles.

Lena huffed out a breath. "I have no idea. I seem to be attracted to your brother in an unexpected way."

"Do you love him?"

The pointed question caught Lena off balance, making her breathless. Was this love? This longing to be with him, the desire to kiss him, to wax poetic about the color of his eyes, and simply talk with him when they were together. She feared it might be. How could she admit it to Bernie when she couldn't admit it to herself?

"I don't know. I suppose that's one of the reasons I didn't say anything to you. This is still so new. We're exploring what we feel for one another. It's important that we take our time to see if it's real and lasting."

"Hmm." Bernie's lips twisted, and she took a step closer. "There's something I need to know, and I would appreciate your honesty."

Lena hesitated. "I'll do my best to answer."

"Did you befriend me so you could further an assignation with Sterling?"

"No." That Lena could answer without hesitation.

Bernie heaved a sigh of relief. "I'm so pleased you said that."

"Regardless of what happens between myself and Sterling, I would like us to remain friends."

"You sound doubtful. As if there's a chance nothing will come of it."

Lena bit back the urge to tell her just how unlikely it was that anything would. Not because of a lack of attraction on her part, but because of the secret she kept. Even now, when she was truly beginning to understand the depth of her feelings for Sterling, she couldn't imagine telling him about her ability. She reached up to grasp her locket with her gloved fingers, its presence giving her a faint hope.

Was it possible that if her grandmother had found love with her grandfather despite her gift, Lena could too? She gave herself a mental shake. It was far too soon to consider such an outcome.

"I don't know how what's between your brother and me will end. But I hope that whatever happens, you and I can remain friends." However, Lena knew that would be difficult. Seeing Bernie would make her think of Sterling. If their relationship ended, Lena didn't think she could come to Renwick House. Not when that might mean she'd run into him.

"Your hope is mine as well," Bernie said with a smile. "I suppose I can understand you not telling me. When one feels a certain awareness, it's often better to keep it a secret. To hold tight to the idea before sharing it with anyone else."

Lena's eyes narrowed. "You almost sound as if you speak from experience."

Bernie caught her lower lip between her teeth as she adjusted her spectacles. "I didn't say that."

"But someone has caught your notice." Lena didn't need her gift to understand what Bernie wasn't saying.

She pressed a finger against her lips, seeming to debate what to share with Lena. "I confess that thoughts of Viscount Worley have filled my mind since you introduced us last evening. He's so kind. So amusing. He doesn't speak to me as if I've just left the schoolroom, but as a woman who knows my own mind."

Lena's heart squeezed. "Bernie, do not allow your feelings to be taken by him. It's true that he's exactly as you say. But matrimony is not in his plans." She struggled to explain. "He will always be a good friend to us, but that is all." She shook her head as Bernie started to protest, not wanting to be the one who told her the full truth. "Count him as a friend but look elsewhere for love. That is all I can say."

Bernie's shoulders lowered. "How disappointing. I don't pretend to understand how you know this, but I will do my best to see if someone else catches my eye."

"There's no rush," Lena reminded her. "You have years before you think of marrying anyone."

"True." Bernie smiled. "Besides, if anything does happen between you and Sterling, I will finally have the sister I've always dreamed of. I don't want to marry and leave if that proves true."

Lena could hardly breathe at the idea of her and Sterling having a future together. That seemed impossible at this moment, no matter how much she cared for him.

The longer she waited to tell him about her gift—if she ever did—the better. She would enjoy this time with him as best she could and hope her secret didn't drive them apart.

Chapter Twenty

Treasure Location Confirmed on Oak Island!

Walter Clarke, famous treasure hunter and explorer, has confirmed that he's found the elusive Money Pit, a shaft rumored to hold untold riches in gold and jewels.

"I knew it was only a matter of time before we found success, but I am pleased it came so quickly. How unfortunate that David Wright spent decades digging without anything to show for it."

When asked what Clarke attributed that to, he added, "I fear Wright didn't truly understand how pirates think or the signs that indicate treasure."

Clarke also stated he has a plan to circumvent the supposed flood tunnels using special pumps to keep out the seawater. "Discovery of treasure is imminent. Mark my words. We are poised for success."

White-hot fury shot through Lena as she finished reading the article.

"How dare he?" She tossed aside the paper and bolted to her feet to march to the window, well aware of her grandfather's watchful gaze.

"Indeed," he agreed, his tone grim.

It was bad enough that Clarke insisted he'd found the Money

Pit, but to mention her father's name and suggest he was basically a failure was nearly more than she could bear.

"Clarke has clearly overstated his progress." Her grandfather's matter-of-fact statement had her spinning to face him.

"Then you still think I'm right?" Hope speared through her. Somehow, having her grandfather believe in her meant more than she'd expected.

He drew closer, his gaze holding on her, his expression giving nothing away. "Do you still *feel* he's wrong?"

"Yes. At least, I think so." Yet her confidence faded as she probed her thoughts without success. She didn't feel anything at the moment. What if her earlier feeling no longer applied? What if Clarke had, indeed, found the Money Pit, and she was only embarrassing herself and her family by denying it?

She closed her eyes as defeat took hold. If only she knew for certain. "I'm not sure. I haven't felt anything since the last article."

"Don't be so hard on yourself." He placed his hand on her shoulder, lending comfort. "Your grandmother found that if she cleared her mind and settled her emotions, the feeling often came. Wanting it too much made it elusive and kept it out of reach."

Lena nodded, knowing that to be true. She drew a long, slow breath to release the anger that held her. She closed her eyes to better focus on her grandfather's calming touch and reached for the locket, appreciating the way it warmed between her fingers. Her earlier tension fell away as her thoughts settled, then cleared.

In a rush, the familiar shiver came. Along with it, a deep certainty. Her eyes popped open to meet her grandfather's. "He's lying." She couldn't help the hesitation that filled her as soon as the words were out. "How can that be? Why would he be so bold as to say he found it when he hasn't? To what purpose?"

The duke released her as he considered her question. "He must feel pressure to do so. But surely Renwick isn't pressing him to make a discovery within a certain timeframe." He shook his head. "I don't know. You didn't see anything specific that might explain his motivation?"

Lena more closely considered the feeling she'd received. How she wished she had a vision that accompanied the sensation as her grandmother had. But she didn't. She could only use what she was given.

"I don't know anything more," she said at last. "Only that he's not digging in the right shaft. But I don't know which one is the real one, or if there even is a Money Pit. I just think he won't find success where he's working now."

Her grandfather nodded. "Then we'll move forward with what you do know. Why don't you send a message to Norah and ask her and Vanbridge to meet us at Marbury's? The earl may not want Ella to know about the latest article, but I'm not certain he can keep it hidden from her for long."

Lena nodded even as relief filled her. Being with her sisters would make this easier for all of them.

After she finished the message to Norah and then requested a footman deliver it immediately, her thoughts turned to Sterling. She wished she could warn him. That she could think of a way to tell him Clarke was lying and wasn't to be trusted. But she'd already done that with little effect because she had no proof. Now that this news story had been released, Sterling would think she'd been wrong.

But deep inside, she knew she wasn't, despite her lingering doubts about her gift. She couldn't understand what Clarke could gain by doing this, but he was lying.

Within the hour, all of them were seated in the drawing room with the exception of Ella. Marbury had decided against telling her the news until they discussed it first. He reluctantly shared that her contractions had resumed, concerning even the doctor. Marbury didn't want to tell her anything that might be upsetting.

Norah immediately looked at Lena. While Lena was worried about Ella, she still believed she and the baby would be fine and hoped Norah understood that from the nod she offered. But whether Clarke's announcement would change that remained to be seen.

"What do you propose be done?" her grandfather asked of everyone.

Marbury paced the length of the room, his distress obvious. Lena's stomach tightened at the depth of his concern. Obviously, she wasn't alone in her worry that this would upset Ella.

Lena studied the faces around her, but no one seemed to have an answer. Norah clenched her hands in her lap, her eyes holding on her husband as if hoping he had a solution.

"If only I had found proof," Lena whispered. "But now I realize that even if I did, I wouldn't hand it over to Clarke."

"Perhaps that's it," Vanbridge said as he stared at Lena.

"How do you mean?" Norah asked.

Marbury halted his pacing to draw nearer.

"What if Clarke said all that to try to force our hand? He's obviously in a hurry to make a discovery. Lena has stated to many that Clarke is wrong. He must've heard that. Maybe Clarke has decided that if Lena is so certain he's wrong, she must know what is right. What better way to make us come forward with our evidence than to declare he's found the Money Pit?"

"You might be right, as convoluted as that sounds." Marbury ran a hand over the back of his neck as he nodded. "I'm certain he's not the only one who must think we discovered new information. It would be logical. How else could we say Clarke is wrong unless we know what's true?"

Lena appreciated his use of "we" but that didn't reduce the weight of responsibility that sat heavily on her shoulders.

"The question is, what do we do about it?" the duke asked, one brow cocked. "He seems to be doing his damnedest to ruin David Wright's reputation."

Lena and Norah shared a surprised look, both stunned to hear their father's name come from their grandfather. To realize he didn't want his late son-in-law's reputation ruined any more than they did was a pleasant shock.

The duke glanced between them and lifted one shoulder in a half-hearted shrug. "You loved him as did my daughter. That matters to me, even if I disagree with his and Bethany's actions when they eloped. That is in the past and can't be changed. But I don't want to see any of you hurt by this."

Lena and Norah rose to press a kiss to each of his cheeks.

If Lena didn't know better, she'd think a hint of a blush crept over his face. But his smile as he looked at them melted her heart.

"Thank you," she whispered.

"Yes," Norah agreed. "Thank you."

"Yes, yes." He waved a hand in the air as if to dismiss their gratitude even as he shifted in his chair. "Of course. How shall we proceed?"

Lena's thoughts raced. There had to be something more they could do than simply wait. "What if we send an anonymous message to the reporter, stating that Clarke is lying?"

Marbury shared a look with both her grandfather and Vanbridge. "That could be helpful if the reporter will share it."

"We'll make it convincing enough that he'll be compelled to write about it." Her grandfather's eyes narrowed as if he were considering how that could be done.

"If it's controversial, chances are the reporter will want to print it." Norah's eyes gleamed with hope. "Controversy sells papers."

"I have a few details that Renwick happened to share with me," Marbury said, his gaze on Lena.

Her stomach tightened, wondering what they could be. The fact that he'd told Marbury but not told her was disconcerting. "What sort of details?"

"He overheard Viscount Ludham speaking with another man named Daniel Winslow about Clarke and his dig. I wouldn't want to give any names to the reporter since we have no proof, but if we suggest that someone in London knows more than they're saying, and provide hints to their identity, it could lend credence to our claim."

Vanbridge nodded. "I like it. Especially since we'll be fanning the flames. Clarke might do something even more drastic and show his hand."

"Nothing ventured, nothing gained." The duke's smile lifted Lena's spirits.

"I haven't told Renwick this as I haven't seen him," Marbury continued, "but I heard that Winslow is deeply in debt. He's been gambling heavily to try to regain his footing, but it's only sunk him deeper."

"Desperation might cause him to act unwisely." The duke nodded. "Hopefully, he will soon prove himself guilty along with Clarke and anyone else involved."

"What will Renwick think of our plan?" Lena asked. As much as she wanted to silence Clarke, she didn't want to hurt Sterling or Bernie if it could be avoided.

"I'll have a word with him before we proceed," Marbury said. "I tend to think he will approve as he would like to flush out the truth about Winslow and Ludham just as much as we would. And if Clarke is lying to him, he'll want to know that, too."

Lena hoped Marbury was right. At any rate, something had to be done about Clarke before he ruined everything that she and her sisters had worked so hard to do to honor and protect their father's memory.

TWO DAYS LATER, Lena searched Hyde Park for Bernie. Bernie had invited her for an early morning ride so they could avoid the crowds that filled the park later in the day. After having nearly lost Bernie's friendship, Lena realized just how much it meant to her. Finding time for them to do something together was more important than ever.

After Bernie learned about the information Lena and her

family had sent the reporter at *The Times*, would she change her mind about wanting to be friends?

Lena dearly wanted to tell her, but Marbury suggested she wait. He intended to speak with Sterling today. Then Sterling could share what he wanted with his sister.

If Bernie didn't join her this morning, Lena supposed that would be a sign the lady knew what was happening and didn't appreciate it.

Lena hoped that wouldn't be the case. She glanced behind her, noting her groom directly behind her, but there was still no sign of Bernie.

She hadn't ridden far when the sound of hooves galloping toward her had her turning expectantly, only to see Viscount Ludham approaching on the black stallion she'd seen him ride before.

"Good morning, Miss Wright." His overly bright smile made her uneasy.

"Viscount Ludham." Lena couldn't help but glance back at her groom to make certain he remained nearby.

"I hope the day finds you well." Ludham guided his horse to walk beside hers, not bothering to ask if he could join her.

"Indeed, it does." She had never liked the man. He'd pursued both of her sisters and herself without them giving him any encouragement. Rather than getting to know them, he offered ridiculous compliments that made Lena uncomfortable.

She wondered if their being granddaughters of a duke attracted him. While aware some considered her and her sisters attractive, appearance shouldn't be the only factor that drew a suitor.

"I've noted you riding with your grandfather on other occasions, but I am pleased to find you on your own this morning." The viscount's brown hair was clipped short, his dark eyes lit with interest as he studied her.

"We ride together quite often." How interesting that Ludham hadn't approached them then.

"The latest news on Clarke's endeavors on Oak Island sounds quite promising. I hope you aren't finding it too upsetting."

Lena debated how much to say. Just how involved was Ludham in the matter? Would telling him how wrong she thought Clarke was increase the chances of bringing the matter to a conclusion? If only she'd asked Marbury for more details.

This chance might not come again. What harm could come from using it as best she could?

She forced a laugh. If she was going to do this, she intended to take it as far as she could to rattle the viscount. "There is no possibility that Clarke has found the Money Pit." She shook her head, keeping her smile in place.

"What makes you think that?" The tightness in Ludham's voice was unmistakable.

"Obviously, you've never been on the island, or you wouldn't have to ask. I don't pretend to know what game Clarke is playing, but he's about to make a fool of himself and all of those with whom he's associated." She cast the viscount a look out of the corner of her eye to gauge his reaction.

His narrow lips pursed as if he'd taken a bite of lemon, making his displeasure obvious.

She couldn't resist pressing further. "The shafts that have been dug over the years are numerous. Searchers were either looking for the Money Pit or attempting to find a way to dig around the flood tunnels that protect it. I don't believe for a moment that Clarke has stumbled upon the proper shaft this quickly. In fact, I'm certain of it."

Ludham drew back on his reins, and her mount slowed as well. "How are you so sure?"

She smiled again, holding his gaze, allowing the certainty of her sense of knowing to fill her. "I will only tell you that I have no doubt."

Before he could question her further, Bernie arrived with her groom behind her. She frowned at Viscount Ludham, clearly not wanting him there. "Good morning."

"Lady Bernice." Ludham dipped his head. "What a pleasure to see you." He seemed to be making a concerted effort to regain his composure, though his expression was still pinched.

Bernie glared at him from behind her spectacles, seeming less than impressed by his greeting. "Ludham."

The viscount seemed to grasp the fact that Lena and Bernie had planned on riding together this morning as he glanced between them. "Were you two expecting one another?"

"Yes," Bernie replied without hesitation. "Though I often ride at this hour, Miss Wright accepted my invitation to join me this morning."

"How nice." His tight smile suggested it wasn't. "Now I have the pleasure of the company of two beautiful ladies."

Bernie cast her eyes toward the sky as if she found his comments ridiculous.

Lena tried to hide a smile, pleased to see Bernie saw through the man's attempt at flattery. She didn't want the younger woman to be taken in by a compliment, regardless of who gave it.

"I'm certain you have more important matters to attend to," Lena said. "Lady Bernice and I wouldn't want to take your time."

"Nothing of the sort. I'm happy to accompany you."

"I must insist." Lena allowed some of her true feelings for the man to show. At least, that was her hope. She drew back on her reins, pleased when Bernie did the same. "Have a pleasant day," she told the viscount.

"Goodbye," Bernie added with a firm tone.

"Very well. Apparently, the two of you have much to discuss." With a nod and a disgruntled look, Ludham departed, jerking on the reins of his stallion.

Lena watched him ride away with relief.

"I can't say that I care for him." Bernie scowled as she watched him, too.

"Good."

"Good?" Bernie looked askance at her.

"Because it means you are an excellent judge of character." Lena smiled as she kneed her horse forward.

Bernie rode alongside her. "Who could enjoy his company when he's insincere and irritating?"

Lena laughed. "Who indeed?" Relief flooded her that Bernie didn't seem upset. Did that mean Marbury had spoken with Sterling and gained his approval for their plan?

She hoped so. When she knew for sure, it would ease her worry. Perhaps she should've been the one to speak with Sterling. But how could she when she knew he'd ask why she felt so certain? That was a question she couldn't answer.

STERLING DETESTED GARDEN parties. They seemed pointless. Flowers and plants were all well and good, but only if they were his, so he could enjoy them at his leisure. Nor did he care to visit idly when he had other, more important matters on his mind.

Yet he stood at the Morrison garden party with a glass of lemonade in hand, keeping an eye on Bernie. Aunt Edith was there as well, but after his sister had been hurt, he couldn't help but worry, especially since he hadn't determined who had done it. He'd been displeased that she'd gone riding the other morning without him, but she had stated the groom had remained close, plus she'd met Lena who also had a groom accompany her.

He had been pleased when Marbury had advised him of the plan to send the reporter who had written of Clarke's recent supposed success information to the contrary. Sterling was weary of Clarke's claims and didn't think he could believe them. His acquaintance, Richard Norton, was scheduled to arrive on the island in two days. Sterling already had a good idea of what Norton would find—that Clarke had exaggerated his progress and the potential for success. If that were true, the dig would soon come to an end.

Watching over Bernie wasn't the only reason he was here, he admitted to himself. There was also the possibility Lena would come. His spirits lifted at the thought. Three days had passed since they'd been together. He was baffled by how much he missed her.

It would be both torture and a joy to see her at a crowded event where the chance of them having a moment alone seemed unlikely. Then again, he was becoming adept at stealing time with her. The crowded garden party would certainly provide a challenge, he thought as he studied the bustling paths of the expansive garden.

When his gaze caught on the small maze at the far end, he smiled with satisfaction. The area held the potential for a quiet moment with Lena. Where else might work? He had located two more possibilities when the lady herself came into view.

His heart leapt. His pulse quickened. All others fell away.

He was definitely enamored of her.

She wore a pale pink silk gown with a deeper pink underskirt. Piping of the same shade circled the neck, cuffs, and waist. A matching hat and parasol completed her attire. A hint of the same color also tinted her cheeks as she leaned close to Lady Havenby, who walked at her side and smiled.

Lena looked like a breath of fresh air, a cool drink on a hot summer's day. He gave himself a mental shake even as he sought a comparison more worthy of her beauty. But it wasn't just her appearance—it was how she made him feel.

He wished he better understood it. That he could define it. Perhaps there was a hint of magic that surrounded them. In truth, there was no other explanation for the emotions running through him.

Then despite the crowd, she saw him as if somehow sensing his presence. The link they shared couldn't be dismissed.

"Go on," Bernie whispered.

"What do you mean?" Sterling asked, though he already knew.

"I won't leave Aunt Edith's side," his sister promised, an amused look on her face. "Go be with Lena."

"Are you certain?" He glanced around to make certain no threats lurked nearby. How ridiculous.

"Positive." She nudged him with her elbow. "I'll catch up with you both in a while."

He gave into her urging and left her in Aunt Edith's care. After handing his glass to a passing footman, he moved toward Lena, easing his way along the busy pathways until he reached her.

"Lena." He drank in her beauty. "You are so lovely."

Her eyes widened, and she glanced toward Lady Havenby, but the lady was already speaking with someone else. "Thank you. It's a beautiful day, isn't it?"

He didn't want to speak about the weather or the garden. He just wanted to—

To what?

He tried to sift through the unfamiliar emotions that churned inside him. He had yet to determine exactly what he wanted. How he should proceed.

"Sterling?" Questions lingered in her beautiful blue eyes. "Is something amiss?"

"No. All is well." He drew a breath and offered his arm, not caring who saw them. "Shall we enjoy the garden together?" Now wasn't the time to act or say something he might regret. For now, he would enjoy his time with her. There was no rush to move forward on his feelings. With a deep breath, he pushed back the sense of urgency filling him that said otherwise.

"I'd like that very much." She took his arm, and they joined the other guests who meandered slowly along the path.

"Oh, what beautiful roses." Lena leaned forward to smell the deep pink blooms, and he couldn't help but note what a pretty picture it made.

The moment etched into his mind as the truth took hold—he loved her. The realization made his mouth dry, his palms damp.

But there was no other explanation for how he felt. They didn't have to talk or do anything special when they were together. He just wanted to be with her. The world settled into place when she was at his side.

Admitting the truth to himself was one thing. But he wasn't prepared to admit it to anyone else. Not even her. Not until he worked through the idea and had time to become accustomed to it. As a person who had always planned out his days, he needed to carefully consider the future. To weigh the advantages and disadvantages of his actions. This situation was no different. He should proceed with caution, not reckless abandon.

But when Lena looked up at him and smiled, his heart did a somersault, and it was all he could do to keep a declaration from spilling out.

Lena raised a brow as if somehow sensing his unease. He shook his head, denying anything was wrong, so she continued along the path. She stopped to admire a bright purple hyacinth along with a whimsical fountain that featured frogs in ridiculous poses.

"I think you should consider adding something similar in your garden," she teased, making him smile, something she frequently did.

To think she used to call him His Grumpiness. The moment made him realize that he was already a better person for having her in his life. It also made him wonder what else might happen if they shared a future together.

"I will certainly consider it." He would if it made her happy.

As they continued, he began to relax. Seeing the garden through her eyes was a completely different experience. The flowers were brighter. The elaborately trimmed hedges more interesting. Perhaps there were advantages to garden parties he hadn't seen before.

A passing footman offered glasses of lemonade, and they found themselves speaking with a few others while they enjoyed the cool beverage.

"Is Bernie here?" Lena asked as she perused the crowd.

"Yes." He tipped his head toward where Bernie and Aunt Edith stood.

After they finished their drinks, he offered his arm again, ignoring the interested looks of some guests, and led the way along a different path that happened to lead to a small copse of trees.

"It's difficult to believe we're still in London," Lena said as she looked about. "This reminds me of the garden at my grandfather's country estate."

"Do you go there often?"

"Not often enough. It's so peaceful there. The skies are bluer and the air clearer."

"More like you experienced in your childhood." He realized his mistake too late and silently muttered a curse. He'd meant to avoid the topic of Oak Island, not wanting it to interfere with what was turning out to be an idyllic afternoon.

"Yes, more like that." Her expression grew somber. "I miss parts of it. The ocean for certain, although it was never peaceful. Still, walking along the shore always seemed to calm me."

"Were you often upset?"

Her eyes widened in alarm then darted about as if she'd realized what she'd said and regretted it.

"Sometimes I feel restless. Time alone helps." The smile she gave him didn't reach her eyes.

He reviewed the conversation in search of the cause for her sudden upset but couldn't find it. It almost seemed as if she hadn't wanted to reveal her need for a way to calm herself.

Didn't everyone have that same need? He certainly did.

"I enjoy riding when I'm upset," he said, hoping to ease her tension. "Riding in the country is preferable, but a ride in Hyde Park is helpful, as well."

She nodded, her relief obvious. That only made him wonder all the more. Perhaps he didn't know Lena as well as he thought. The realization confirmed that he was right to wait to act on his feelings. They both needed time to learn more about each other.

Sterling pushed aside his impatience and told himself there was no rush. Any time spent with Lena was a pleasure. He only hoped she'd soon feel comfortable enough to tell him what caused the reserve that so often came over her expression.

✦ ✦ ✦

Chapter Twenty-One

THE LAST THING Lena wanted to do with so much already on her mind was attend another ball. But Marbury had called that afternoon to advise her that he felt their efforts to shake Ludham and Winslow were working. The news article questioning whether Clarke had truly found anything had appeared the previous day, and he was certain the success of their plan was within reach.

"I ran into Ludham at the Society offices, and he acted strangely," Marbury had told her. "He seemed preoccupied and rather angry. Quite out of character for the viscount."

"That's wonderful news."

"It could be, yes. I am going to Brooks's later to help spread the rumor that Clarke isn't going to be successful. If you have the opportunity to do the same at the ball, we might be able to push them further. But do be careful. There is always the chance that Ludham or Winslow will do something drastic if they think Clarke's hope of success is dwindling."

Lena had only to remember what happened to Bernie to realize the danger. This was not a matter to be taken lightly. Since Norah and Vanbridge had another engagement, it was up to Lena to see what she could do at the ball.

Not being able to see Ella was one more reason to force the matter to a conclusion as quickly as possible. Marbury had kept the latest news from his wife and told her that Lena was under the weather and not able to visit. Keeping her distance was painful, but Lena knew her sister would immediately sense something was wrong. Ella's contractions had slowed but not halted completely. The entire situation couldn't be over soon enough.

The distance the issue put between her and Sterling continued to bother her. Though they were united in uncovering what it was that Ludham and Winslow were doing, the search on Oak Island remained a barrier between them. She didn't see how they could move forward—whatever that might mean—until Clarke's lies were revealed.

There was a chance Sterling wouldn't be in her future once this was over. He might resent the part she played in revealing Clarke's deception when all was said and done, despite wanting to end Clarke's duplicity. The fact that he and Bernie weren't attending the ball this evening worried her. Bernie's note had only said that she was tired and intended to stay home, which meant Sterling wouldn't come either.

"Is all well, my dear?" Lady Havenby asked as they waited in the reception line outside the ballroom.

"Yes, of course." She managed a smile. "I'm just worried about Ella."

"As am I. The poor dear. Marbury is being so protective of her."

"Which looks sweet from where we are but is probably driving Ella crazed." Lena could well imagine Ella's frustration.

"So true," Lady Havenby agreed.

They greeted their hosts. Lady Masterson had always been kind to Lena and her sisters, having been a friend of their mother's.

"I know I say this every time I see you and your sisters, but you look so much like your mother," Lady Masterson said after giving Lena a warm hug. "She would be so proud of you three."

"I hope so." Though Lena wondered what her mother would

think of their current dilemma. She had no doubt Lady Bethany would be as angry with Clarke's claims as her daughters were.

That was an excellent reminder of how important her efforts were. Lena intended to tell anyone who would listen how ridiculous she thought Clarke's most recent claim was. Hopefully, that would help place more pressure on Winslow, Ludham, and Clarke to act, revealing whatever scheme they had planned.

"I wanted to ask your thoughts about the new search on Oak Island," Lord Masterson said. "Do you think Clarke is truly close to finding treasure?"

Lena felt the weight of stares from several interested guests. She paused for dramatic effect. "No, I don't. In fact, I know he's digging in the wrong place." She shook her head, trying to look amused. "I wonder how long it will take before he realizes it?"

"You sound so certain." Lord Masterson's eyes narrowed with curiosity. "Why is that?"

She leaned a bit closer as if to tell him something in confidence but didn't lower her voice. "Let us just say that I have privileged information."

"Of course, you do." Lord Masterson nodded. "How interesting."

Lena smiled knowingly then glanced around only to stiffen at the sight of Viscount Ludham a short distance behind her in the receiving line.

The intensity of his dark gaze caused a hint of fear to skitter down her spine. Had she gone too far? Yet she'd said nearly the same thing to him in Hyde Park. Did the fact that she'd said it in a public setting make a difference?

Lady Havenby touched her arm, bringing her attention back to the moment. "Thank you again for having us," the lady told the Mastersons.

They continued to the ballroom and paused just inside the doorway.

"Care to share what that was about?" Lady Havenby's brown eyes held on Lena. "Do you truly know that Clarke is lying about his progress?"

Lena hesitated. She hadn't seen Lady Havenby since they'd decided to spread news about Clarke's false claims. Nor did the lady know about Lena's gift. Though she was a dear friend, she liked to gossip. She was never malicious about it but adored being the one who knew everything first. Lena and her sisters had learned not to share too much with her. However, at times, her propensity to gossip was an advantage.

"We are fairly certain he is." Lena tried to think of a reason she could give Lady Havenby that didn't involve her gift and was also true. "You see, Lady Bernice found some old letters in their attic that contain some interesting information. I've had the chance to read them myself. While we'd like to spread word that Clarke is wrong, we don't necessarily want anyone to know about the letters."

"Of course." Lady Havenby nodded. "The situation could easily turn dangerous. Treasure hunters can be quite ruthless at times."

"Exactly."

"But it would be remiss of me not to share your opinion of Clarke's efforts with others." Her knowing smile caused Lena to laugh.

"Yes, it would," Lena agreed. "The more who start to question Clarke, the better."

"I'm pleased to be of assistance." She glanced over her shoulder. "I do believe I see Lady Dyke. She might be interested in hearing that."

Lena touched her arm to gain her attention. "Many members of the Royal Geological Society have placed wagers on the outcome. I would hate to see them lose money."

"Even more reason to help share the news in case her son did. Leave it to me." Lady Havenby winked then moved several steps away to speak with the other lady.

Lena glanced around to see whom else she could speak with, only to see Ludham nearby again. She looked away, hoping he hadn't overheard her conversation with Lady Havenby. She didn't have much time to ponder the concern as Lord Canham arrived and asked for his customary dance.

She managed to work the information into their brief conversation, though the lord didn't seem particularly interested.

Viscount Worley soon arrived, and she danced with him, too. Marbury had already spoken to him, and Worley was doing his part to further spread their opinion.

Nearly a half hour later, Worley returned to her side. "I do believe you've managed to make the topic one that everyone is speculating about this evening."

"Perfect." She looked over her shoulder, wanting to be more careful who might overhear her this time. "Ludham was here earlier, but I haven't seen him since. Have you?"

"Can't say that I have. Perhaps he didn't like the talk involving Clarke's doomed attempt and left."

Lena hoped so. Time passed slowly after that. She danced several more times and spoke with a few friends, many of whom asked after Ella. She didn't tell them of the worry over her contractions, but only said she was doing well.

She turned to see where Lady Havenby was, only to find Viscount Ludham standing beside her. Her stomach tightened with distaste as his gaze swept boldly over her.

"Good evening, Miss Wright. Might I have the honor of a dance?"

Though tempted to refuse, she wanted the chance to talk to him further about Clarke.

"Of course." She glanced at Lady Havenby, who nodded even if her lips pursed in disapproval.

Ludham offered his arm, and Lena forced herself to take it. Unfortunately, the musicians began playing a waltz after they took their place on the dance floor.

As had happened the last few times she'd danced with Ludham, he held her too close and made her worry that he'd step on her toes. Rather than simply leading, he pulled her about as if she were a doll, completely ignoring the rhythm of the music.

She didn't care for his lack of technique, but this was her chance to push him about the treasure hunt. "Have you placed a wager on Clarke's success like many other members of the Royal Geological Society?"

"I have." He smiled, but it wasn't particularly warm. "I look forward to winning."

"Oh? Are you so certain of the outcome?"

"I would be even more so if you would consider sharing what you know."

"Why would I tell you if I knew anything?" She allowed disbelief to color her tone.

"Because you want Clarke to fail as much as I do."

Lena nearly took a misstep. "You want him to fail?" She couldn't wrap her mind around his statement. Not when they'd been so certain Ludham was working with Winslow to find the location of the Money Pit.

Ludham pulled her into a spin-turn before replying. "Clarke stole an opportunity I had to search for treasure several years ago. I will never forgive him."

Lena mulled over the information, wondering if it was true. She didn't trust Ludham and wasn't about to start now. He might be telling her this just to learn what she knew.

"I only speak from the experience of having lived on the island for so long and watching my father search. There is no possibility Clarke has discovered anything this quickly, let alone the Money Pit."

Ludham's eyes narrowed. "I don't believe you. I insist you tell me what evidence you have."

"If I had proof and gave it to you, what would you do with it?"

Ludham smiled grimly. "I will show Clarke for the scheming fool he is. I will ruin him and make certain no one ever hires him again. His career will be over."

Lena shivered at the determination in his voice. She tended to believe what he said. "If you wait long enough, he will soon be revealed as a liar."

"That's not nearly enough. His treachery requires a higher price. I insist you tell me what you know."

Lena was grateful for the numerous couples surrounding them. Otherwise, she might have feared for her safety. Had he heard her mentioning the letters to Lady Havenby? "As I said I am only speaking from my own experience." She paused, then boldly asked, "What part does Winslow play in this?" She held her breath, wondering if Ludham would tell her.

"Clarke has promised Winslow a significant cut of the treasure if he can provide any helpful clues. Winslow is desperate to do so to keep his creditors away. He seems to think it's the only way out of his financial mess."

Lena had heard enough. Learning anything more might put her at risk. Still, she couldn't let it rest until she understood the whole story. "You're willing to betray Winslow?"

"Please." He scoffed. "Winslow is no one. No title. No fortune. He'll never amount to anything. I've known him for several years as we're both members of the Explorer's Club. He was well into his cups one evening and told me that he and Clarke have been friends since childhood. Winslow is envious of the man's success and feels it should've been his. That is something on which we both agree. When I happened to mention that I knew you and your sisters, he was certain you could help. It has been simple enough to pretend to aid him in looking for clues as to where the treasure is. Meanwhile, Clarke is setting himself up for failure."

"Why is Clarke overstating his results? Why not wait to see what he can find?"

"His ego demands nothing less. He adores being in the limelight, as do most treasure hunters. When a reporter contacted him after being told about the dig, he couldn't resist giving an interview."

The music drew to a close, and Ludham looked closely at her.

"I've shared what I know. Why don't you honor me by doing the same?"

"I appreciate what you've told me," she began, still uncertain if she could believe everything he said. "But as I told you from the start, I only speak from experience. Even if I came across a map of the treasure, I'm not sure I'd give it to anyone."

It was almost a relief that she hadn't found anything. Handing over information about the location of the treasure to anyone other than her father seemed like a betrayal to his memory.

Perhaps in time, a treasure would be found on Oak Island, but she didn't want it to be discovered so quickly. Keeping Clarke from saying disrespectful things about her father would be enough for now.

"I ask you to reconsider," Ludham said, seeming unable to take no for an answer and making her think he knew about the letters. "We both want the same thing. I will make Clarke look like the fool he is, just as you want."

"I appreciate that. But I don't have anything that would help." She didn't care for the way his dark eyes glittered and was anxious to return to Lady Havenby.

"Who does?" His eyes narrowed as he studied her. "Renwick? Or perhaps his sister?"

Lena frowned, alarm filling her at the direction of his thoughts. "Don't you think they would've already shared anything they found with Clarke?"

"Clarke is making Renwick look like a fool. I think it unlikely that the duke will aid him now. In fact, I would guess Renwick will soon call an end to the search and remove Clarke from the position."

"If he does, that will grant your wish."

"No, it won't." Ludham's fierce expression had her taking a step back. "Clarke will simply find a new endeavor and another wealthy person to finance it. I want him ruined."

"I can't help you."

"Then I'll find someone who can." Ludham spun on his heel

and strode out of the ballroom.

Lena's thoughts whirled as she watched him depart. While she appreciated that he seemed to have the same goal as she and her family did, the viscount's determination was a threat not to be taken lightly.

STERLING LOOKED UP from his breakfast to see Bernie striding into the room wearing a riding habit and a bright smile.

"Good morning," she said.

"You seem to be in fine spirits this morning." He set down the newssheet. When she'd told him she didn't feel well enough to attend the ball the previous evening, he'd been worried.

"Indeed, I am. Nothing like a good night's rest to restore a person. Now I'm looking forward to a ride."

He pushed back from his chair. "I'll go with you." Never mind that he had already been on one earlier.

"Nonsense." She waved a hand in dismissal. "I'm sure you've already gone, and I don't want to interrupt your breakfast. I want some fresh air and don't plan to be gone long."

"Are you certain? I'm happy to join you."

She kissed the cheek he offered. "You are a dear. But it's not necessary. The groom is accompanying me. I will see you soon."

He watched her depart, relieved to see her acting more herself. He knew the situation with the treasure hunt on Oak Island was wearing on her as it was him. He was done with Clarke and his lack of truthfulness. When Bernie returned, he would speak to her about shutting down the treasure hunt and relieving Clarke of his duties. The man obviously had his own agenda, and Sterling wanted no part of it.

He returned to his breakfast and his newssheet for a time and was just preparing to see to the correspondence awaiting him in his study when he heard voices in the corridor.

Foster appeared at the doorway. "I'm sorry to disturb you, Your Grace, but Miss Wright is calling and asks for a moment of your time."

Surprise caught Sterling as it was well before calling hours. Did this mean she had news on Ludham or Winslow? "Show her to my study."

Foster bowed and departed, and Sterling went to his study, anxious to hear what Lena had to say.

The butler announced her, and her maid remained at the door as Lena entered, her expression somber.

"Forgive me for calling so early, but I spoke with Viscount Ludham last evening and wanted to share what he said."

Though Sterling was eager to know what she'd learned, he took a moment to draw in Lena's presence. Once again, he had missed her. Today, she wore a simple blue muslin gown that made her eyes all the more stunning.

However, the worry in their depths had him gesturing toward one of the chairs before his desk. She remained standing as if too restless to sit.

"How is Bernie?" she asked. "She sent me a message telling me she didn't feel up to attending the ball last evening."

He nearly smiled at her consideration. It came as no surprise that she, too, was worried about Bernie. Her worry for his sister touched him. Especially when he knew that it had nothing to do with him, but because she liked Bernie as a friend.

"She is feeling much better. Well enough that she left to go for a ride not a quarter of an hour ago."

"Oh, good." She nodded, but the news didn't remove the crinkle of her brow. "As I was saying, I danced with Viscount Ludham last evening."

Sterling didn't care for the jealousy that had him clenching his jaw at the thought of the two dancing. He would have preferred to be Lena's only dance partner. That showed just how much he'd come to love her.

"The viscount said he's not truly helping Winslow. Instead,

he wants to see Clarke fail."

Sterling frowned, shaking his head. "That doesn't make any sense."

"Clarke took an opportunity from him several years ago, and he has never forgiven him for it. He intends to make certain Clarke's career is ended and wanted to know how I knew Clarke was digging in the wrong place."

She hesitated and looked away.

"Oh?" He couldn't imagine the reason for her sudden discomfort.

She cast him a wary glance, still saying nothing.

He waited to see if she'd say more, hoping the cause of her concern became clear.

She looked away as she continued to explain, as if suddenly interested in his bookshelves. "I told him it was only because of my experience on Oak Island. That I had no proof. But he didn't seem to believe me. He wants to find something to prove Clark is lying, which of course would damage his reputation. Ludham has been using Winslow for that same purpose, although Winslow thinks they are working together to help Clarke succeed."

"And Winslow is hoping Clarke will give him a share of the treasure if he finds it," Sterling guessed.

Lena looked at him at last. "Exactly."

"Interesting." Sterling considered this new information but didn't think it changed his decision. "I haven't told Bernie, but I think the time has come to end the search for now. Clarke is obviously not the right person to lead the dig. He can't be trusted."

The relief on Lena's face tightened his chest.

"While I have never met the man, I can't say that I like him." She sank into the chair and released a deep breath.

"Clearly I should have done this sooner if it was bothering you that much."

Her beautiful blue eyes widened in surprise. "You would do that for me?"

Sterling ignored the maid standing at the door and moved around his desk to sit beside Lena. Hoping the maid couldn't see, he took Lena's hand in his. "When I started the search, I didn't know you and your sisters. Therefore, I didn't give any thought to how upsetting all of this would be. I only wanted to give Bernie something to do. She seemed listless when she returned from Switzerland, and I thought this would give us something to do together. But not at the expense of hurting you."

Lena's hand tightened on his, and she blinked rapidly, suggesting just how much his words meant to her.

"Oh, Sterling." To his surprise she drew back her hand, her body stiffening as her eyes became unfocused and her face pale.

"Lena?" She didn't respond, and he was almost certain she couldn't hear him. It was as if she were under some sort of spell.

Then she gasped, her startled gaze meeting his. "Bernie."

"What about her?"

"She's in danger." Lena jerked to her feet, her hands clenched in fists, and her focus darting about the room. "Where did you say she was?"

Sterling stood, thoroughly confused. "She is riding. In Hyde Park."

"Hurry. She's in danger." Lena reached out and gripped his arm tightly. "Go to her now, before something happens." She drew back a step and pressed her gloved fingers to her mouth as if keeping from saying anything else.

"I don't understand. How—"

Before he could finish the question, Lena shook her head. "There's no time to waste. She needs you."

He didn't understand what was happening, but he knew for certain he trusted Lena with his life—and his sister's. With one last look at her, he ran from the room.

Chapter Twenty-Two

LENA WATCHED STERLING rush out the door, desperate to follow and help in any way she could. But she had her carriage, while he would be on horseback. She'd only slow him down. Besides she didn't know anything else. Not where in Hyde Park or who or what.

She pressed a finger to her pounding temple, wishing she had answers. But as was so often the case, she knew nothing more.

"Miss?" Her maid entered the study and looked at her with a worried expression. "Are you all right?"

Lena wanted to shake her head. She wasn't. Not in the least. Though she hoped and prayed for Bernie's safety, and that Sterling would find her in time, the truth of what she had just done sank in.

This was not going to end well, regardless of the outcome.

If Sterling discovered she was right, and Bernie truly was in trouble, he might be thankful, but he'd want to know how she knew his sister needed help. He might even conclude that Lena was working with Winslow and Ludham.

And if he found nothing, and Bernie was fine, he would think her crazed. That she had made up the story for no reason.

"We should go," she told Nancy and stepped toward the doorway, only to halt.

As much as she wanted to run, to return home rather than

face Sterling's reaction, she couldn't. She wouldn't. What mattered right now was Bernie's safety.

"No." Lena turned around to look over the empty study, her thoughts racing with concern for her friend. "We will wait for the duke's return to make certain Lady Bernice is well."

"Of course, miss," Nancy said.

Lena noted the hint of approval in her tone, yet it was little comfort. She gestured for Nancy to have a seat on a bench near the bookshelves, then sat as well, her body quivering with the need to take action.

Perhaps she should follow Sterling now. Waiting for their return was going to be painful. Especially when she knew beyond a doubt that she had just lost any chance she had for a future with him.

She should have kept her gift hidden. But how could she when she felt Bernie was in danger? If only she'd thought of an excuse as to why she believed that.

Already she could imagine Sterling staring at her with suspicion, once again. The look that said he didn't trust her. That was the foundation of any relationship. How could she expect trust from him when she hadn't had enough faith to share her secret?

She reached for the locket her grandfather had given her and held it tight. What had her grandmother done in situations like this? Lena was certain the lady had handled it with more grace and courage than herself. The thought only made her feel worse.

She'd been forced to choose between her feelings for Sterling and Bernie's safety. That was no choice at all. Lena closed her eyes and said a silent prayer for their safe return. That was as much as she could hope for.

STERLING RODE AS if his life depended on it. Or rather, as if Bernie's did. He couldn't imagine why Lena suddenly thought his sister was in danger, but the terror darkening her eyes and pinching her expression had been enough to convince him.

A glance over his shoulder showed a groom following him, though he was falling back, his horse unable to keep up with Sterling's. He should have asked Lena for specifics about Bernie's location and why she thought his sister was in danger, but it was too late now.

He knew Bernie's usual route and hoped she hadn't deviated from it this morning. He took some comfort in knowing that a groom accompanied her as well. Perhaps his frantic ride would be for naught. He'd come upon her, and she'd look at him with a puzzled expression.

He dearly hoped that was the case.

He entered Hyde Park at a gallop, pushing his steed even harder once he reached the open meadows. He ignored curious stares from the few other riders he passed, grateful the park wasn't overly busy at this hour, as it allowed him to make good time. He looked for Bernie, thankful he knew what she was wearing, which made the search easier.

He hadn't ridden far into the park when he saw her and Thomas, the groom. His blood chilled to see they weren't alone. Another man on horseback rode directly behind them. The three entered a wooded area and then soon disappeared into the trees.

That wasn't part of her normal route. His chest tightened at the realization that if he'd been a few minutes later, he might not have found her.

Sterling slowed his horse to a trot as he entered the woods, looking frantically for them. There, just ahead, he caught sight of her bright blue attire. He wound through the trees, hoping to get closer before whoever was with her realized he was there.

Bernie glanced over her shoulder in his direction, her spectacles glinting. Even from this distance, he could see her face was taut with fear. Then her attention returned to the stranger as if she hadn't seen Sterling. She said something, but he was too far away to hear.

It took only another moment to see the man's profile—Winslow.

Sterling's heart lurched at the sight of a pistol pointed at Bernie and the groom. The servant stared at the weapon, seemingly frozen with shock and of little help.

Sterling halted his horse and dropped silently to the ground, doing his best to hide behind the trees. After he looped his reins around a low branch, he risked another look at the three.

Winslow hadn't heard Sterling's approach thus far. Perhaps he was so focused on Bernie that he didn't hear anything else. Sterling reached for the riding crop tied to his saddle. Certain Winslow would either see or hear him at any moment, he gripped the makeshift weapon and hurried through the trees with as much stealth as possible.

Bernie's gaze caught on him as he neared, causing Winslow to look in his direction as well. Sterling gave the man no time to react but ran forward to strike Winslow's outstretched arm with the crop.

Winslow cried out in pain, dropping the weapon to the ground on the other side of his horse, too far for Sterling to reach.

"Damn you." He glared at Sterling, his haggard appearance much different than the last time Sterling had seen him. "You are ruining everything."

"Ruining your attempt to steal information to help Clarke?"

"That's exactly what he's doing," Bernie declared, her eyes glittering with anger. "He insists I know something that will aid him and refuses to believe otherwise."

"Don't you think if we did, we would've shared it with him?" Sterling demanded.

"When I told him you'd both been seen with one of David Wright's daughters, he was certain you were holding something back." The man jerked at the reins of his restless horse. "Then I heard about the letters Lady Bernice found, and I knew you had discovered some clues." He looked between Bernie and Sterling as his horse threatened to rear. "This isn't over."

"Yes, it is, Winslow," Sterling said and reached for the man's reins.

Winslow jerked them away, then with one last glance at the pistol on the ground, he spun his mount and kicked it into a gallop, fleeing the scene.

Charles, the other groom, arrived, leading Sterling's horse.

Sterling took the reins and then pointed toward Winslow. "Follow him but keep your distance as he could be dangerous. I want to know where he goes."

The servant did as he requested, leaving Sterling to look over Bernie, his heart pounding madly at the memory of the gun pointed at her. "Are you all right?"

Bernie nodded as she blinked rapidly. "He insisted I tell him what I discovered in the letters. I explained there were no details about the location of the treasure in them, but he didn't believe me." She pressed her hand to her heart as if hoping to calm it.

Sterling was tempted to do the same to his own. Instead, he glanced at Bernie's groom. "Thomas, are you well?"

The man nodded, seeming to regain his composure. "Yes, Your Grace. He came upon us so suddenly. I'm terribly sorry." He shook his head, clearly overwhelmed by the unexpected experience. His gaze fell to the pistol.

"Escort Lady Bernice home and take this with you." Sterling retrieved the gun and handed it to Thomas. "I'm going to see if I can catch up with Charles and Winslow."

"Sterling, be careful." Bernie's eyes were dark with worry behind her spectacles.

"I will. You do the same." He glanced at them both. "There's always a chance Ludham will make an appearance." Lena had said the viscount wasn't truly working with Winslow, but Sterling was still not certain what to believe.

"Yes, Your Grace." Thomas nodded at Sterling's order.

Sterling leapt onto his horse and took off at a gallop. But within a few minutes, he realized Winslow and Charles had disappeared. He'd have to wait for the servant's return to learn the outcome.

He took some comfort that he already knew where Winslow lived and the places he frequented. With effort, he should be able to locate him if the groom was unsuccessful. Bernie's welfare was more important than tracking Winslow through the woods.

After one last look in the direction he thought they'd gone, he turned his horse toward home, patting its neck and keeping a slower pace.

The near miss of the moment began to sink in, chilling him to the bone. If Winslow was desperate enough to draw a weapon on a lady just to gain information about the location of possible treasure, chances were that he would've been willing to use it.

He shuddered at the thought of Bernie injured again, or worse. Thank goodness Lena had warned him. But how had she known Bernie was in danger? One moment they had been discussing Ludham's confession, and the next she'd been urging him to go after Bernie.

He didn't pretend to know how that had come about, but he intended to find out.

LENA ROSE TO pace Sterling's study, growing more worried with each minute that passed. Foster had looked in on her a few times to see if there was anything she needed. He'd also escorted Nancy to the kitchen to visit with the other servants while she waited.

They should've returned by now. Had Sterling arrived in time? Was Bernie well?

She pressed a hand against her knotted stomach, knowing Sterling would demand answers when he returned. She told herself she should appreciate this time alone as it allowed her to collect herself and prepare an answer. But at this point, she'd rather face Sterling's questions and be done with them.

The only response she could offer was the truth.

As suspicious as Sterling was, she held little hope that he'd accept her answer. Just when she thought they were forming a deeper connection, this had happened. She feared it would drive a wedge between them. Trying to explain her gift was impossible. She need only think of how Mrs. Johnson, her father's partner's wife, had reacted, crossing herself as if Lena were evil or the like. She wasn't the first to respond that way. What people didn't understand, they feared.

Her family were the only ones who'd accepted her gift. How unfortunate that none of them were here at the moment. She sighed. Now wasn't the time to feel sorry for herself. Her focus needed to remain on Bernie.

The sound of voices in the corridor sent her heart racing. She hurried to the door in time to see Bernie step inside, speaking to Foster. Lena's knees were weak with relief as she rushed toward her. "Bernie?"

Bernie's eyes widened in surprise at the sight of her. "Lena? I didn't realize you were here."

Sterling hadn't told his sister. Not yet. Perhaps it was best if Lena allowed him to explain to Bernie how he'd come to find her. "Are you all right?"

"Yes, yes." Bernie walked toward her only to frown. "Wait. How did you know something was wrong?"

"I was speaking with Sterling just before he left." Lena didn't wait for Bernie to question her statement but leaned forward to hug her, grateful she was well. "What happened?" she asked as she pulled back.

Bernie was obviously still confused based on her furrowed brow but responded to the question. "A man approached me in Hyde Park. He insisted I knew where Clarke should be digging on Oak Island."

Lena gasped. "Do you know who it was?"

"Sterling called him Winslow." She shook her head. "When I told him I didn't know anything, he pulled out a gun and ordered me to come with him."

"Oh, Bernie. How terrible." Lena held Bernie's arms, hoping to comfort her. "You must be beside yourself. Let's get you a chair." She glanced at Foster, who watched with a concerned expression. "Will you have tea sent to the drawing room?"

"Of course, miss." The butler hurried toward the kitchen.

"Excellent idea," Bernie said. "My brother should return at any moment, I hope."

The hint of doubt in those last two words squeezed Lena's chest, her worry for him mounting. She wrapped an arm through Bernie's and guided her toward the stairs. The idea of a gun pointed at her friend had Lena taking a deep breath. Thank goodness she'd warned Sterling.

"You must have been so frightened," Lena said as she guided her up the stairs and into the drawing room.

"I couldn't think what to do." Bernie's voice trembled, telling Lena that something stronger than tea was needed.

She glanced around the room as she escorted Bernie to the settee, then strode toward the decanters and glasses on the side table. She splashed some brandy into a crystal glass and returned to Bernie's side. "Drink this."

Bernie reached for it with hands that trembled even more than her voice, confirming Lena's choice of beverage. Still, Bernie eyed the glass warily. "I don't think—"

"I insist," Lena said. "Drink it all. To help with the shock. I promise you'll feel better."

Bernie took a sip and grimaced, but at Lena's expectant gaze, she emptied the glass then shuddered. "Oh, my."

"Well done." Lena set aside the glass. "Tell me the rest."

"I was arguing with him, telling him that I didn't know anything. He kept talking about the letters, but I explained that both you and I had looked at them and found nothing of importance."

Winslow had gone too far. Unease spread further through Lena at the danger in which her friend had been. At the danger Sterling could be in.

"Then Winslow told us we had to go with him into the

woods." Bernie's breath came faster, and Lena put a hand on hers, hoping to comfort her.

She looked at Lena with gratitude and then drew a deep breath. "Sterling arrived in the nick of time. Otherwise, I don't know what we would have done. He used his riding crop to force the man to drop the gun. Then the man fled. The groom and Sterling went after him."

Alarm filled Lena. She dearly hoped he didn't take any unnecessary risks. She delicately probed her thoughts but came up with nothing. Did that lack of anything mean Sterling was unharmed or was her gift failing her once again?

Before she could decide, Sterling strode into the room, causing both women to draw a breath of relief. His gaze shifted between Bernie and Lena. "Bernie, how are you feeling?"

They both rose as he neared and took Bernie's hands in his.

"I'm fine." She smiled tremulously as she looked at Lena. "Thanks to you and Lena's comforting presence."

Sterling's gaze shifted to Lena, and her heart began to beat out of her chest. She could see the questions in his eyes but didn't want to answer them.

Not when she knew it would be the beginning of the end.

Then she gave herself a mental shake. The end had already come the moment she'd told him Bernie was in danger. There was nothing she could do to change the situation.

She lifted her chin. She had nothing to be ashamed of. She had done what she thought best and would do it again if given the chance. She looked away from his assessing gaze and returned her focus to Bernie. "I am so relieved you're all right. You'll want to rest, so I'll be going."

"Wait." Sterling's firm tone brooked no argument. His expression softened briefly as he looked at Bernie before hardening as he returned his attention to Lena. "Allow me to see Bernie settled, and then I will speak with you."

Bernie glanced back and forth between them as if confused.

Sterling didn't give her a chance to ask what was happening

but took her arm and guided her toward the door. "You'll want to change clothes. I'll have tea and toast sent to your room," he said, his voice fading as they walked down the corridor.

Lena blew out a breath, the urge to leave nearly overwhelming. But no. She would answer his questions as best she could, then leave. How unfortunate that she hadn't had a chance to say goodbye to Bernie. She didn't expect to see her friend again any time soon.

Lena didn't have to wait long, although her nerves were stretched taut by the time Sterling returned, his expression unreadable.

"Thank goodness she was unharmed," Lena said. Anything to break the uncomfortable silence.

"Thanks to you."

Lena's breath caught, but one look at his expression suggested he was not feeling any form of gratitude. In fact, his eyes were positively chilly.

The realization caused her to brace herself. "I'm so relieved. I'm sure you have questions." As much as she dreaded the conversation, she also wanted it over.

"I do." He held her gaze. "Are you working with Ludham and Winslow?"

Her heart pinched to think he believed that of her. How could she blame him when it was the logical explanation for her knowing Bernie was in trouble?

"No, I am not." She answered without hesitation, though she doubted that would help.

His brow furrowed. "Then how? How did you know Bernie was in danger?"

It had been a long time since she had told anyone about her gift. But never had it mattered more. "At times, I have what you might call a feeling. A premonition of sorts." Her entire body tensed as she tried to explain the inexplicable. "It doesn't come often. But when it does, I often sense trouble."

"Are you referring to some sort of second sight?" Doubt

colored his tone, his dark eyes sweeping over her from head to toe. As if he didn't believe her. As if he didn't know her.

She held tight to her courage. While relieved he was familiar with the term, that didn't ease her hurt.

"Yes. I don't have a vision that comes to mind. I only know something is amiss. Not always who or where or what." His eyes hadn't warmed in the least.

Still, she forced herself to continue. "I felt that Bernie was in trouble. Thank goodness you knew where she was and how to find her."

Sterling turned away, causing a lump to form in her throat. "I'm sure you'll forgive me if I have difficulty believing all this."

Lena bit back a retort. If he truly cared for her and trusted her, then his response would have been different. Her heart ached for what might have been, stealing her breath.

She had to leave before she told him how much she cared for him. After all, what mattered was that Bernie was safe.

She turned to go, only to turn back. "I know this is difficult to understand or believe, but it's the truth." When he didn't respond, she clenched her fist, hoping to hold onto her composure. "I had your and Bernie's best interests at heart. I hope you can find a way to believe that at least."

Once he had time to think about what she'd said, he wouldn't want anything to do with her. He obviously didn't care for her in the same manner she cared for him.

"Bernie is strong and will recover from her fright," she managed. Then she strode toward the door, relieved to see Nancy waiting, her eyes wide with sympathy.

Lena took a sip of a breath to keep sobs from coming. She needed to stay strong, even though she knew that when she stepped out of the house, she would leave her heart behind. With Sterling.

"Lena, wait!"

She ignored his request and ran down the stairs as fast as her feet could carry her. Before she did something ill-advised like turn around and tell Sterling she loved him.

Chapter Twenty-Three

STERLING SAT WITH Bernie while waiting for the police to arrive, pleased she didn't seem overly distraught by the ordeal. He asked her exactly what Winslow had said, so he could share it with the police and hopefully spare her the interview.

Bernie's focus was on the favorable outcome rather than what could have happened. He hoped that didn't change. She hadn't asked why he'd come after her, but she eventually would. He wasn't certain how to respond when she did.

All he could think of was that pistol pointed at Bernie. The image knotted his stomach with anger. It would take seeing Winslow caught to help ease the knot. Until that happened, he couldn't think about talking to Lena though she was ever in his thoughts.

Never mind that his heart ached that she hadn't stopped when he'd called out to her. What would he have said if she had? Would he have told her that he loved her? He blew out a breath at the thought.

He told himself that he didn't have time to consider Lena's claim of intuition. He had Bernie's welfare to see to, answering the questions the police were sure to have, and Winslow to catch.

Yet what Lena told him never left his thoughts. Nor would he forget the moment she'd had the premonition or whatever she called it. The glazed look that had come over her eyes. The way she had seemed to briefly lose awareness of everything around her.

Something odd had happened in those few seconds. He didn't understand it and wasn't certain if he wanted to.

There was no doubt she had saved Bernie. But the fact that Lena had been telling him about Ludham's true intent only to suddenly have a premonition about Bernie struck him as too much of a coincidence. His mind had difficulty understanding that she simply had a "feeling" that his sister was in danger. Believing someone meant trusting them.

Did he trust Lena?

He had thought he did until that moment. It was difficult to overcome his suspicious nature when his father had drilled it into him for as long as he could remember. His mind insisted he keep his distance, but his heart ached for her. Telling himself that his focus needed to remain on Bernie didn't change that. However, he needed to be practical. Sorting out his feelings for Lena would have to wait until he ended the danger Winslow presented.

When Foster advised him the police had arrived, he left Bernie with her maid and Aunt Edith for company and went downstairs.

"Thank you for coming so quickly," he said as the same two men who'd come last time entered his study and bowed. He wasn't certain whether to be relieved or pleased they were familiar.

"Of course, Your Grace," Detective Inspector Stephens said. "How unfortunate that another incident occurred."

"We understand your sister was threatened at gunpoint?" Captain Thomason asked, seeming anxious to get down to the business at hand.

Sterling gestured for the men to sit and then explained the events.

Once again, the inspector took notes, asking Sterling to repeat a few points. He seemed very interested in the description Sterling provided of Winslow and the places he thought the man could be found.

"There's one thing I don't understand, Your Grace." Inspector Stephens glanced at his notes before looking back at Sterling. "You mentioned you didn't accompany your sister on the ride in Hyde Park, yet you managed to save her. What made you decide to look for her?"

Sterling paused, uncertain how to respond when he had no intention of mentioning Lena's involvement. How did she answer questions like this? She couldn't tell the truth, or some might think her mad. The realization was a sobering one. The protectiveness he felt toward her didn't surprise him given the depth of his feelings for her. "I simply changed my mind."

"How interesting that you arrived just in time." The inspector's tone remained respectful, but the question in his eyes was undeniable and had Sterling shifting in his seat as the urge to offer more took hold.

"I had a bad feeling. Something told me I should go after her." His empathy for Lena increased even more.

Both the captain and the inspector nodded.

"A bit of intuition, eh?" the inspector suggested. "I've experienced that as well. Always pays to follow your gut." He closed his notebook and stood, as did the captain. "We will keep you apprised of our progress."

"Thank you."

"I'm certain it goes without saying, but I'd advise you and Lady Bernice to take care. Since Winslow didn't get what he wanted, he might try again."

"The same concern crossed my mind," Sterling said. Hearing the inspector state it only made him more worried.

The two men left, and Sterling turned to stare out the window. He would make the staff aware of the danger and put extra footmen on duty until Winslow was caught. Surely, Bernie wouldn't mind remaining home for the next few days. It shouldn't take longer than that for the police to locate and arrest Winslow.

Once more, Sterling was filled with gratitude that Lena had told him Bernie was in danger. He didn't understand her ability, but it must be difficult to manage without giving away her gift. Warning others of potential danger meant sharing why. Stating you had a feeling wouldn't always be enough. His conversation with the police made that clear.

The fact that Lena had trusted him enough to reveal her ability was something he didn't take lightly. But his reaction to it had been less than ideal.

He realized he was being a coward by ignoring his need to speak to her. He wanted to thank her again and ask her to explain more. He wanted to better understand her ability, and he wanted to see the light of affection return to her lovely eyes when she looked at him.

One thing Sterling knew for certain—regardless of her gift, he loved her and wanted her in his life. Did he dare hope she might feel the same?

PRETENDING ALL WAS well when it wasn't took a toll on Lena as the day passed slowly into the next. For one of the few times since her sisters had married, she was glad they no longer lived at Rothwood House.

It was difficult enough to mask her emotions during her brief visits with Ella. Her sister thought Lena's quiet mood was due to the danger Winslow presented, and Lena let her. After all, that was certainly part of her upset. Ella didn't ask how Sterling had reacted to her telling him about her gift as if sensing it wasn't anything Lena wanted to talk about.

Her grandfather had noted her distress when he saw her in the front entrance upon her return home. He'd taken one look at her face, escorted her into his study, and insisted she tell him what happened.

"I-I was at Renwick's, sharing what Ludham told me last night. That he wants to make Clarke look like a fool." Lena heaved a shuddering breath. "In the middle of our conversation, I had a premonition that Lady Bernice was in trouble."

"Did it prove true?" he asked, his expression full of concern, warming the chill around her heart.

"Yes. She was riding in Hyde Park with her groom when Winslow confronted her with a gun and demanded she tell him where the Money Pit was. Luckily, Renwick arrived in time to save her."

"They're both unharmed?"

"Yes." Only her relationship with Sterling was injured. Over before it had hardly begun.

"Did he catch Winslow?"

"Unfortunately, not."

"It's concerning to think how desperate Winslow has become. You and your sisters need to take care. We need to advise Marbury and Vanbridge of the situation."

She'd left that task in his capable hands.

That Sterling didn't contact her came as no surprise but hurt all the same. She had sent a note to Bernie, expressing hope that she was recovering from her fright. Bernie had sent a polite reply that she was. Lena was disappointed she didn't mention Sterling. Then again, why would she?

With a sigh, Lena attempted to focus on the embroidery for Ella's baby's gown when Norah strode into the drawing room, tossing her reticule and gloves into the nearest chair. "What on earth is going on?"

Lena blinked, realizing too late that she hadn't prepared what to say when she finally did see her sister. "I thought Grandfather told you."

Norah sat beside Lena, much to her dismay. Hiding her emotions would be more difficult with Norah so close. "He told us that Winslow threatened Lady Bernice with a gun and that Renwick arrived in the nick of time to save her. But I know there is more to the story. Especially since you seem to be avoiding me."

"Nothing of the sort," Lena denied. "I only wanted some time alone." She hoped that was enough of an excuse to satisfy her sister.

"Lena." Norah studied her so closely that Lena finally had to look away. "Please tell me what happened. You know I will do my best to help." Norah reached out to squeeze her hand.

The sympathy in her expression was all it took to bring tears to Lena's eyes.

Norah leaned forward to hug her. "What is it? I truly will do anything to help."

Lena returned her embrace even as her tears fell, her emotions getting the best of her. "You can't. No one can."

Norah drew back, her expression filled with alarm. "Tell me."

"I was at Renwick House, telling Sterling what Ludham had told me. That he had only been aiding Winslow with the sole purpose of seeing Clarke fail." She swallowed hard. "And then I had a feeling." She sniffed and wiped away a tear, reminding herself that she had done the right thing. That didn't stop her tears. "I realized Bernie was in danger and told him. I'm so glad I had the premonition and he arrived to save her."

"Oh, Lena." The fact that Norah understood her upset was both comforting and discouraging. Her reaction confirmed Lena's fear. That the moment had marked the end of her association with Sterling and Bernie.

"I am so sorry," Norah said. "I know it's of little comfort, but it was bound to happen sooner or later. Better that he find out now before…" Her voice trailed off as if uncertain how to continue.

Lena didn't know either. All she knew was that her heart ached for what might have been. She had no idea if Sterling had felt the same. Now, she would never know.

"Did you explain everything?" Norah asked.

"In part. Enough to make him realize this wasn't a one-time

occurrence. It's silly of me to be so upset when nothing could have come of our relationship anyway."

At that, Norah stiffened, a look of outrage on her face. "How do you mean? Ella and I had high hopes that the two of you were coming to an understanding. He would be lucky to have you in his life. What difference does it make if you have an extra sense?

Lena managed a smile at her sister's fierce defense of her. "You know it's not that simple. I can't always hide it. What if something happened while we were with others?"

"The same thing that happens now. We find a way to explain it."

Lena shook her head. "The bigger problem is that Sterling is slow to trust others. Just when he was beginning to trust me, this happened. He even asked if I was working with Ludham and Winslow."

"Then he is a fool. He should know in his heart that you would never deceive him."

Lena's breath caught. "But didn't I? I didn't trust him enough to tell him about my gift. I am as much to blame as he is."

Norah sank against the cushions as the truth of what Lena had said sank in. "You're right. You should have. But there are reasons you didn't. Strong, valid reasons. If you explain, he might understand."

Lena pressed a hand against her mouth as she considered the suggestion. "I don't know if I have the courage. What if he thinks even more poorly of me than I fear?"

"Then he is not the right man for you. That much I know." Norah held her gaze. "Please tell me you will consider it. Love is worth fighting for."

While Lena knew that to be true, she didn't know if she dared to tell Sterling what was in her heart.

Chapter Twenty-Four

LENA DONNED HER favorite ball gown—an emerald green that gave her much-needed confidence. The gown was in the princess style with no bustle and a slim silhouette. The bodice had gold and green stripes and was trimmed in lace.

She put on her grandmother's locket, rubbing the smooth metal for luck. Nancy rolled her hair into a loose chignon at the back of her neck, leaving several wispy strands to curl around her face.

"You look lovely, miss," the maid said with a smile as she stepped back to admire Lena's appearance in the mirror.

"Thank you, Nancy."

The Willingham ball was this evening. Another message to Bernie had confirmed that she and Sterling planned to attend, though Bernie said she wouldn't truly enjoy any functions until Winslow had been caught. Marbury had told Lena that rumors suggested the man had fled to the Continent. He hadn't returned home, and his few remaining servants had left. The police continued to search for him to no avail.

Lena didn't blame Bernie for still being worried but hoped the ball would provide an opportunity to speak with Sterling. To apologize for not trusting him with her ability sooner. If that went well, she intended to share what was in her heart with the hope he might feel the same.

Butterflies danced in her middle at the thought. She hoped nerves didn't get the best of her. But she'd had plenty of time to think during the past two days. Norah was right. Love *was* worth fighting for. She need only look at her sisters to see just how true that was.

At this moment, the chance for a future with Sterling felt as far out of reach as a star in the night sky—bright, full of promise, but untouchable.

She shook aside the dismal thought and focused on her plan. If she didn't try, she would forever regret this chance. That much she knew for certain. But regardless of how Sterling reacted, she realized how much she'd changed in the past few weeks.

While her gift of premonition would always set her apart, she now felt at peace with it. Especially when she reflected on how helpful it had been of late. Gifts should be welcomed and acknowledged just as her grandmother had done. Not demanded nor rejected. The timing of her intuition was rarely ideal, but she hoped she now had the peace of mind to allow her ability to grace her and those she cared for whenever possible.

Whether Sterling would understand remained to be seen. If they were to have the chance for a future together, he would have to accept her *and* her gift.

She took comfort in knowing Norah and Vanbridge would be at the ball as well. Norah would be pleased if she learned of Lena's plan, but Lena wasn't certain if she'd tell her. Her questioning looks would make Lena even more nervous.

Within the hour, Lady Havenby came for Lena and they arrived at Willingham House. Nerves continued to plague Lena, making her doubt her plan and sending chills along her body.

"What is it?" Lady Havenby asked, her voice sounding as if she were speaking to Lena from another room as they alighted from the carriage.

"Nothing." Lena frowned, trying to determine what was happening. The feeling dropped away before she could take a firm hold of it. She cleared her thoughts, but it remained elusive.

Was she merely nervous or was her intuition trying to tell her something? Wishing wouldn't make the feeling come. All she could do was open herself to the gift.

As they climbed the stairs lit by torches and entered the open doors of the townhouse, a light-headed sensation had her blinking to clear her dizziness. She drew a deep breath to regain her balance, relieved when it worked.

"Are you certain?" Lady Havenby asked, clearly worried. "You've gone pale."

"I'm fine." Lena forced a smile and looped her arm through the older woman's. She intended to embrace her gift but also wanted to keep it hidden. The balance was a difficult one. "Excited for the evening is all."

"If you're sure…" At Lena's nod, the older woman smiled. "I have no doubt it will be a delightful ball." She leaned close. "Tell me, do you hope to dance with the Duke of Renwick again?"

"I do." The thought of it had her stomach dipping as if she'd taken a misstep. She hoped for not just a dance but a few minutes to speak with him more than she could say.

After greeting their hosts then continuing into the ballroom, Lena reminded herself it was unlikely that he was already there as the hour was still relatively early. That didn't keep her from looking over the crowd for his tall, commanding form.

To her delight, he stood across the room near Bernie and Mrs. Easton, listening to his sister, his expression somber as usual. His elegant evening clothes and aristocratic features caused another dip in her middle.

Bernie looked wonderful, much to Lena's relief. Her animated face showed no hint of distress as she gestured with her hands.

But it was Sterling who caught her attention once more. As if feeling the weight of her regard, he looked up and met her gaze. Her breath caught as she waited, wishing he'd give her a sign— something to indicate he was pleased to see her. That there was a chance her crazy plan to win his heart might work.

He smiled. Only a hint of one with the corner of his mouth

curling slightly. But that was more than enough to cause her heart to dance with joy.

Maybe this evening would be the beginning of the rest of her life. Maybe he felt half of what she felt for him. Hope welled within her, nearly bringing tears to her eyes.

"The duke should attempt a smile on occasion," Lady Havenby whispered to Lena as she frowned at Sterling.

"He is smiling," Lena protested. She supposed it was so subtle that those who didn't know him well might not see it. But she did.

"If you say so." Lady Havenby's expression remained doubtful. "I shall eagerly wait to see if he asks you to dance."

"As will I." Lena's gaze returned to Sterling, who continued to watch her with a steady regard. Was that heat in his eyes, or was she imagining things from across the room?

Before she could decide, she felt a presence at her elbow.

"Good evening, Miss Wright," Lord Canham said. "May I have the honor of a dance?"

Though Lena wished to refuse since the only man she wanted to dance with was Sterling, she nodded. "I would be delighted. Thank you." The opportunity to speak with Sterling would arrive if she was patient.

However, she lost track of Sterling and Bernie over the next half hour as she danced several times and greeted friends. Norah and Vanbridge hadn't arrived, making her wonder about their delay.

After returning to Lady Havenby's side a fourth time, she could wait no longer to speak with Sterling. As she scanned the ballroom for him, a footman appeared at her elbow.

"Excuse me, miss. I have a message for you." The liveried servant bowed then offered her a small slip of paper.

"Thank you." Anticipation swelled through her as she took it, holding it with reverence. Could it be from Sterling? Had he found a way for them to steal a few moments together?

The servant stepped away, leaving Lena to glance at Lady

Havenby, pleased her chaperone hadn't noticed the delivery of the message. Lena kept her back to her and opened the message.

Meet me on the terrace.

S

Lena studied the words, uncertainty filling her rather than joy. She couldn't explain her doubt. She'd never seen Sterling's handwriting. But she didn't think it was from him. Who else could have sent it?

A chill crept over her as the music faded from her awareness.

It wasn't from Sterling. She knew that beyond a doubt. Then the answer struck her—*Winslow.*

Fear stole her breath as the sound of the music rushed back into her awareness, seeming overly loud. What should she do?

She glanced around the ballroom as panic threatened, only to realize she needed to pretend excitement in case Winslow watched. She didn't dare find Sterling to tell him what she knew, or they'd never catch the man. If she had the chance to end this tonight, she intended to take it.

"Lena, you look lovely this evening."

She turned to find Viscount Worley beside her with his customary smile. "Worley. Thank goodness. You're just in time."

"Oh?" His brow raised in question, his gaze holding hers even as his smile faded. "What's wrong?"

"Winslow asked me to meet him on the terrace." She forced a smile, doing her best to act as if nothing was amiss. She was certain Marbury had told Worley about Winslow's recent activities. "He could be watching. Pretend I told you something amusing."

Worley chuckled then offered his arm as a cold gleam appeared in his dark eyes. "We will go find him together."

"No. If you accompany me, he will surely flee."

"I'm not allowing you to see him alone." The steel in Worley's tone was so unlike him that she studied him in surprise.

"There's no other way. I'll distract him so you and Sterling can—"

"Is Renwick here?" Worley glanced about. "There he is. By the refreshment table."

Lena did her best to allow her gaze to casually take in the room, at last seeing Sterling. Her heartbeat sped. She wanted the chance to aid him and Bernie if she could. Thank goodness Norah and Vanbridge hadn't arrived. Norah would know in a heartbeat what Lena intended and wouldn't approve.

Time was of the essence.

Keeping her polite smile, she turned away from Sterling to face Worley. "Please tell Sterling what's happening, but not until I have stepped onto the terrace."

"No. That is a terrible plan." The heated words caused Lena's smile to falter. "Winslow could take you away before we arrive."

"Smile, Worley," Lena reminded him. "Remember? He could be watching."

Temper showed through the viscount's smile. "I'm not leaving you unattended with Winslow, Lena."

"Fine." Lena released a frustrated breath as she considered other options. "You proceed toward the terrace doors, so you'll be nearby when I step out."

"I have a better plan. I've been here numerous times and am familiar with the house. I'll go out through another entrance and see if I can find Winslow to make certain he doesn't escape."

"Worley," Lena began, fear for her friend threatening to take hold, making her realize that her plan held risk. "Promise you'll take care."

"I will if you will." His smile softened. "Determine another way to alert Renwick. I'll see the two of you outside." With a dip of his head, he departed, meandering slowly through the crowd in the direction of the corridor that led to the card rooms.

Lena didn't look at Sterling again, but instead, moved a few steps toward Lady Havenby, certain she could count on her assistance.

The lady finished speaking with a friend and glanced at Lena. "Are you enjoying yourself, my dear?"

"I am. But I wonder if I could ask an urgent favor."

"Of course." The lady's eyes lit with interest.

Lena debated what to say. Sharing that she wanted to meet a man on the terrace, who was more than likely armed and dangerous, seemed unwise. Lady Havenby would never allow her to carry out her plan. Yet the lady adored being in the thick of any excitement. Lena and her sisters had witnessed that after having had more than their fair share of alarming escapades after coming to London.

A portion of the truth would have to do.

"Renwick, Worley, and I are hoping to catch Winslow, the man who threatened Lady Bernice," she whispered.

Lady Havenby's eyes went wide. "How do you intend to do that? Is he here?" She started to glance about, but Lena reached for her arm to stop her.

"He might be watching us at this very moment, so we must pretend all is well," Lena warned as she smiled.

Lady Havenby quickly did the same. "What do you want me to do?" The thrilled look on the older woman's face couldn't be denied.

"Could you please make your way to Renwick and advise him that we need him on the terrace?"

"Surely, you're not going out there." Lady Havenby frowned, clearly displeased with the idea. "That could be dangerous."

"Worley is doing so." Lena hoped that would satisfy her. After all, it was true. Never mind that she hadn't responded directly to her remark.

"Very well." She nodded. "Shall I find Renwick now?"

"Yes. He's near the refreshment table. Remember to proceed slowly and act as if nothing is amiss. We must assume Winslow is watching."

"You may count on me." With a lift of her chin, Lady Havenby started in Sterling's direction, greeting a few acquaintances as she went.

Lena blew out a relieved breath. Now it was her turn to act. For once, her gift had proven to be of assistance right when she needed it. Perhaps Sterling could find it in his heart to care for her and accept her as she was if she helped catch Winslow.

She moved toward the terrace, forcing a smile as if she were excited at the thought of meeting Sterling and ignoring the knot of fear in the pit of her stomach.

STERLING WATCHED LADY Havenby approach, disappointed to see Lena wasn't with her. Each time he'd located Lena and started in her direction, along with Bernie, they'd been interrupted. He wasn't leaving Bernie's side this evening. Not when Winslow hadn't been found.

The look he'd shared with Lena earlier had sent his pulse racing. His body reacted each time he saw her. He caught himself—it wasn't only his body that reacted. It was his heart. He loved her with all that he was.

The past two days had given him ample time to realize he couldn't imagine a future without Lena. He might not fully understand her intuition, but he trusted her and wouldn't allow anything to keep them apart.

Yet it was impossible to make plans for their future until Winslow was found. Once that happened, he would advise Clarke he was shutting down the treasure hunt on Oak Island.

He'd received a report from Richard Norton stating that Clarke was digging in four different shafts and had plans to start two more. The famed treasure hunter was scrambling, taking shortcuts where he shouldn't in an effort to find the supposed treasure quickly. Two of the men he'd hired had already quit, claiming unsafe conditions.

The dig had caused more problems than Sterling had thought

possible. Halting the project would remove a major obstacle that kept him from Lena. After that, he would share what was in his heart.

He was anxious to put his plan in motion. Did he dare share the details with Lena this evening or should he wait until he'd completed it with the hope his actions showed her how much he cared? Attempting to explain in a crowded ballroom seemed impossible.

Before he could decide for certain, Lady Havenby reached his side.

"Good evening, Your Grace." She gave a rather hurried curtsy while he bowed.

"Good evening."

She greeted Bernie and Aunt Edith before returning her attention to Sterling. "I wonder if I might have a moment of your time."

Alarm filled him as he noted her forced smile even as concern tightened her features. "What is it?"

"Miss Wright asked that I advise you that Viscount Worley needs you on the terrace to aid him in capturing Winslow."

"What?" Shock had him responding more loudly than he should've.

"Smile," she demanded, keeping her own. "We must assume he's watching." The drama in her tone would've been amusing under other circumstances.

"I do not smile." That was no longer completely true. Not since Lena had entered his life.

"Oh. Yes, of course." Her ready agreement annoyed him, much to his surprise. "It would look quite out of character if you did."

"Humph." He intended to change that just as soon as he got his hands on Winslow. He glanced at Bernie, who was conversing with Aunt Edith. "Might I ask for your assistance in return?" he asked Lady Havenby.

"Of course." Her face lit with delight. "It is quite exciting to be needed so much this evening."

He frowned, not certain what she was speaking about. But he had no time to ask. "Would you remain with Lady Bernice and Aunt Edith? They're rather nervous after what happened."

"All the more reason that Winslow is caught this evening." The lady gave a decisive nod. "I would be honored to remain with them until your safe return."

"Thank you." Sterling turned to Bernie and Aunt Edith. "I need to step away to take care of something." When alarm flared in Bernie's eyes, he did his best to reassure her. "I will return shortly, but meanwhile, Lady Havenby will remain at your side."

Rather than wait for their questions, he walked toward the terrace, forging a path through the crowd as best he could. Luckily, most moved out of his way. He truly did need to do something about his reputation as being grumpy, based on the way several of the other guests hurriedly stepped aside.

He reached the terrace doors, but there was no sign of Lena. He looked about again, questions circling through his mind. What was Winslow doing at the ball? How did Lena know he was here? And how did Worley think to capture him?

However, neither Lena nor Worley were in sight. His heart pounded painfully in his chest at the realization that Lena must be outside.

With Winslow.

The thought of her in danger threatened to halt his thoughts. He eased out the doors, doing his best to shove aside his worry and focus on the task at hand—catching Winslow.

The night was dark, the air pleasantly cool after the warmth of the ballroom. If torches had been lit for guests who needed a breath of fresh air, they were now extinguished. No doubt that was Winslow's doing.

Sterling eased along the wall, out of the circle of light spilling through the doors, willing his eyes to adjust to the dark. The faint sound of voices caught his ears. Still there was no sign of Lena.

It took only one more step for him to realize one of the voices belonged to a woman. *Lena.* Fear clutched his senses. He drew a slow breath to will it away and make sense of the situation.

"I don't have any information to give you," Lena said, her voice barely above a whisper.

"That's a lie. You've discovered the location of the Money Pit. It was in those letters Lady Bernice keeps going on about."

Sterling continued to ease forward as quietly as possible, hoping the darkness hid him. He couldn't see anyone. Where was Worley?

"The letters mention Oak Island, but they don't mention the treasure."

"Tell me the truth," Winslow demanded. "Surely you want the treasure to be found. That would prove your father had been justified in digging all those years."

"Even if I knew, I wouldn't share it with you."

Sterling grimaced at her belligerent tone. Was she trying to get herself killed?

"What does Ludham have to do with all this?" Lena asked.

Winslow scoffed. "He departed for America yesterday. Apparently, his father has a holding there in need of repairs that he wants Ludham to oversee. I said good riddance as he wasn't any help to me."

Sterling took another step past a tall bush and the pair came into view. Or rather, the vague outlines of them did. The night was too dark to see much else. Hopefully that meant he was hidden, too.

"You must know something." Winslow's tone was growing frantic. "Why else would you continue to tell everyone that Clarke is digging in the wrong place?"

"Because he is." The certainty in Lena's hushed voice was undeniable.

Damn if Sterling didn't believe her. The memory of his conversation with Marbury at the club came to mind. "She tends to be right about many surprising things," Marbury had said.

Suddenly, it all became clear. Lena saving Bernie from falling into the fountain at the garden party. Lena discovering Bernie injured in his study. Lena urging Sterling to go after his sister because she was in danger.

Her ability was more than just feelings. She truly had a gift of premonition.

But Winslow was having none of it. "Don't force me to use this." He raised his arm, and the outline of a pistol became visible, sending fear spearing through Sterling once again.

"Treasure is not worth killing over." The calm authority in Lena's voice was impressive.

"It is when you have creditors barking at your heels day and night."

"Gambling is a nasty habit. Especially when you have no money to spare. Don't expect sympathy from me."

Sterling was nearly close enough to make a move. Two more steps and he'd be able to lunge for Winslow. That is, if Lena didn't encourage the man to shoot her first. While Sterling admired her spirit, he wished she'd take more care.

"I don't want your sympathy. I want the location of the Money Pit. Now."

Sterling cleared the bush and rushed toward Winslow, keeping his focus on the pistol. He shoved the man's outstretched arm upward as Winslow cried out in surprise. "Run, Lena!"

She didn't move, seeming transfixed by the scene unfolding before her.

Winslow lurched back and wrenched free from Sterling's grasp. "Damn you, Renwick."

Sterling didn't bother to respond. Instead, he threw a punch in the direction of the voice as it was too dark to see his face. His aim proved true, and his fist hit flesh with a satisfying smack.

Winslow stumbled back but quickly regained his footing. "You'll pay for that, Your Grace." He said the term with a snarl.

Sterling was painfully aware of Lena's presence and Winslow's gun waving wildly. He reached for Winslow again but couldn't catch his arm. He shoved Winslow back, making certain he stood between the man and Lena. "Stop, Winslow. You've taken this too far."

"Clarke promised me a share of the treasure." Winslow's voice took on a pleading tone. "Finding it will solve all my problems."

"No, it won't." The voice came from behind Winslow and caused the man to spin to face it.

That was the opportunity Sterling needed. He leapt toward Winslow, taking him to the ground. Still Winslow struggled and tried to escape Sterling's grasp.

"Give it up, Winslow," Sterling demanded, using his weight to keep him in place.

"No!" The desperation in his tone had Sterling stiffening. Then the weapon discharged, sending a muffled blast into the quiet night.

Chapter Twenty-Five

"No!" Lena's heart stopped. She was sure of it.

Though Sterling had told her to run, there was nothing that could've forced her from his side. With the blast of the gun still ringing in her ears, she gasped as the two forms on the ground stilled.

"Sterling?" She rushed forward, terrified even as she prayed he wasn't hurt.

A third figure—Worley—knelt beside them. "Renwick?"

A moan filled the air and one of the men moved.

"Yes." Though Lena was thrilled to hear Sterling's voice, he sounded odd.

"Lena, find some light," Worley requested.

"Of course." Before she could rise, several people filed onto the terrace, bringing torches with them.

"What's going on here?" Lord Willingham asked, holding a light aloft. "I thought I heard a gun discharge."

"You did, my lord," Lena affirmed. "Winslow threatened me with a pistol. Renwick and Worley saved me." Her voice trembled as she shared the news, but her focus remained fastened on the men on the ground, both in dark suits, making it impossible to discern who was whom or which one was hurt.

More light flooded the terrace, along with additional guests. Gasps, murmurs, and cries of fright filled the night air as the crowd realized someone might have been shot.

To her relief, Sterling sat up and then glanced at the still form beside him.

Worley placed a hand on Sterling's shoulder. "Are you all right?" Then he pulled his hand away to stare at it, blood glistening in the light. "You're not all right."

A lady screamed at the sight of the blood, causing Lena's heart to pound even harder.

"A flesh wound, I think. Winslow managed to pull the trigger before I could get the pistol away from him." Sterling moved his shoulder as if to prove it wasn't serious despite the blood on his suit coat. He handed Worley the weapon, and the crowd's murmurs grew louder.

Worley took it with a shake of his head, then glanced behind him and gave it to Vanbridge.

"Lena?" Her brother-in-law stared at the gun then at her, eyes wide. "You're unhurt?"

"I'm fine." Well aware of the onlookers who stared in shock, she watched Worley assist Sterling to stand, while two other men tended an unmoving Winslow.

"I believe he struck his head when we were struggling," Sterling said.

"Send for the police and the doctor," Willingham ordered one of the footmen who stood nearby.

Winslow stirred, moaning, then was hauled to his feet He didn't look at any of them as he was led to a nearby stone bench but hung his head, whether in pain or defeat, Lena didn't know.

She turned from the man and drew closer to Sterling, wishing she could tell how badly he was hurt. The torn fabric of his suit coat and the blood made it impossible to think clearly. "You could've been killed."

"But I wasn't. All is well." Sterling took her hand, seeming to ignore the people watching them. "You're unharmed?"

"Yes. I—"

"Sterling?" Bernie's frantic tone as she forced through the

crowd, with Mrs. Easton and Lady Havenby behind her, had both turning to face her.

"I'm fine, Bernie," Sterling reassured her.

"Winslow?" She looked about, pressing a hand to her mouth as she saw him on the nearby bench.

"Caught." Sterling gave a single nod. "No need to worry about him any longer."

Norah joined them, hugging Lena twice for good measure that she hadn't been hurt. After explanations were given again, the majority of the guests returned to the ballroom at the behest of Lady Willingham.

Vanbridge and Worley stood on either side of Winslow along with Sterling until the police arrived a few minutes later. Lena told them what happened and gave them the note Winslow had written.

Sterling spoke with them, as well, then left Vanbridge and Worley to oversee things once the doctor arrived. Lena, Bernie, and Mrs. Easton waited in a nearby sitting room while the physician saw to Sterling's injury in Willingham's study. Lena was certain Sterling allowed the care only as an example to Bernie.

Soon he joined them, a scowl on his face. "It hurts worse now than it did before he tended it."

Bernie gave him a pointed look as if to say, "I told you so" but wisely held her tongue.

Norah came in to inform them that Winslow had been taken away. "He insists Clarke is to blame even though he was the one who held the gun." Her frown made her disgust with the man obvious.

"It certainly makes me wonder just what Clarke told him." Sterling shook his head. "I don't suppose we'll ever know as it's unlikely Clarke will admit to anything. However, I will be shutting down the treasure hunt tomorrow."

"You will?" Lena asked though Bernie showed no surprise.

Sterling's gaze held on her, a wealth of emotion swirling in his eyes. "I have already found the true treasure. One that I never expected."

Lena drew a quick breath, her entire body filling with hope.

Norah seemed to understand the look on Sterling's face as he looked at Lena and turned to Bernie. "Lady Bernice, let us return to the ball. Lord Canham was asking after you."

"He was?" Bernie's eyes widened behind her spectacles as if she was excited by the lord's interest. "You're certain you're all right, Sterling?"

"I'm fine."

"I'm so relieved." Bernie stepped close to press a kiss on his cheek then moved toward the doorway. "Aunt Edith, are you coming?"

"Which one is Lord Canham?" she asked as the two ladies stepped out of the room.

Norah hugged Lena for what must've been the third time. "I'm so relieved you're all right."

"As am I." Lena smiled despite the tension taking hold at the prospect of speaking alone with Sterling.

"Good luck." Norah mouthed the words out of his view.

Lena nodded, appreciating her sister's support as well as the fact that she knew they needed a few moments alone.

"Don't be long, Your Grace," Norah said with a stern look at Sterling, which made Lena laugh. "People will note your absence."

"I will do my best to protect your sister's reputation from harm," Sterling said with a smile.

"I'm happy to hear that." Norah departed as well, leaving the door slightly ajar.

Lena turned to face Sterling, emotion clogging her throat. "I'm so relieved you weren't hurt worse."

"When I saw Winslow pointing that pistol at you—" He broke off with a shake of his head as if unable to complete the thought, then moved to take both her hands in his. "You shouldn't have taken the risk of going outside."

"The message from Winslow nearly fooled me. But I was certain it wasn't from you."

He lifted a brow. "Did you know or did you sense it?"

"Perhaps both." She hoped it didn't matter how she knew the things she did. She looked at their joined hands before meeting his eyes again. "I'm sorry I didn't trust you sooner with the truth about my ability. I hope you can forgive me."

"Trust is not easy for me to give. But you have mine, Lena. You also have my heart."

"Oh, Sterling!" Lena squeezed his hands as joy filled her. "You have mine as well. I love you so much."

"I love you as well. With all that I am. You are everything I could hope for in a wife and more than I deserve. Your kindness, thoughtfulness for others, honor, and intelligence are qualities everyone should aspire to. You are beautiful inside and out. In your actions and your heart. I am a better man for knowing you. You truly are the treasure I never hoped to find." He dropped to one knee, causing Lena to gasp. "Lena, would you do me the honor of becoming my wife?"

While some women might be surprised by a proposal so soon after the ordeal they'd just endured, Sterling's timing was perfect for Lena. What they'd been through proved that each moment they had together was precious, and the sooner they started their life together, the better.

"Yes! Oh, Sterling, I can't imagine a future without you in it."

"Despite my grumpiness?" he asked with a grin.

"That nickname no longer applies." She touched the corner of his mouth, loving his smile.

He stood to take her into his arms, moving slowly, suggesting his shoulder was painful. "You have made me the happiest man alive. You're going to make a wonderful duchess."

Lena wound one arm around his good shoulder. "Do you think so?"

"I know so." Then he took her mouth with his, the kiss full of promise.

Lena's heart lifted as if on wings, fluttering in a most delightful way.

Epilogue

Six months later...

STERLING WOKE SLOWLY, still becoming accustomed to the feel of the warm, silky body entwined with his. He loved it.

The happiness that made his chest feel as if a hot air balloon resided inside him was also new. He loved it, too.

More than either of those, he loved the woman tucked against him in the circle of his arms. He smiled, something he did more and more frequently since their marriage nearly a month ago.

He turned his head to glance at the clock, realizing they'd slept in. The night had been a late one spent in each other's arms. Already he knew he would never get enough of his lovely wife. His heart filled to overflowing as he looked at her.

Lena's long, pale hair spilled across the pillow, and her cheeks were pinkened with sleep. The curves of her breasts were just visible along the edge of the sheet.

The past few weeks had been the best of his life. They'd taken only a brief honeymoon as Lena hadn't wanted to miss the birth of her nephew. Nor had she wanted to leave Bernie since his sister was still learning to navigate social events. Bernie adored having Lena as part of the family. Even Aunt Edith had seemed more relaxed now.

Lena had been right about the timing of the birth of the baby, along with numerous other things. He loved the pleased smile that came over her face when one of her feelings proved true as if she was privy to a secret no one else knew.

Lucky him that she so often shared them.

Unable to resist, he pressed a kiss to her temple, then her cheek. Her soft sigh was more arousing than he could've guessed. What could he do but continue this gentle awakening of his wife?

His duchess.

The possessive thought only added to his desire. He moved his arm from under her head then pressed a trail of kisses along her jawline and down her neck to the swell of her breasts.

She shifted, offering another one of those sighs that had him hardening further. He drew the sheet down until her pink-tipped breasts came into view. Now he was the one to sigh.

"Sterling?" Her voice was husky with sleep.

"Yes, my love?"

She opened her eyes and smiled sleepily. "I love it when you call me that."

"Good, my duchess." He lowered to take a nipple in his mouth.

"I like that, too." She arched against him.

"The title or this?" He kissed her other breast.

"Yes," she answered and giggled when he ran his hands along her ribs. "I mean, I like being yours and I like what you're doing."

"Excellent. He kissed her belly as his hand grazed along her silky thigh. "I like both as well."

She ran her fingers through his hair, and he reveled in her touch. "Do we have time for this?" she asked, slightly breathless.

"We don't have to be at your grandfather's for well over an hour," he murmured, hoping she'd agree.

They were joining her family for a late breakfast, including Ella and the baby. It would be Alex's first outing, and Lena was excited to see him and her sisters again.

"Plenty of time," she whispered. The last word was more of a moan as he found the curls at the apex of her thighs.

He ran a finger along her already slick folds, his body demanding he pick up the pace. But Sterling refused to rush things. While continuing the caress, he eased up and kissed her sweet lips, loving the way she shifted restlessly against him.

When she took his hard staff into her hand, he shuddered with need. "Lena."

"Yes, my love?" She smiled, her legs parting to allow him better access.

"You're right. I like the sound of that, too," he managed. Then he lost his train of thought completely as her fingers threatened to send him over the edge.

"Sterling?" At his partial grunt, she said, "You should hurry." She released him to hold his hips, trying to draw him onto her.

"Or perhaps you should," he countered. Before she could respond, he laid back and lifted her to straddle him.

"Oh." She considered the position briefly, a hint of wonder in her eyes. "How interesting." She moved, quickly grasping how to make the most of it.

Then she leaned close and kissed him, the tips of her breasts grazing his chest even as her hair cascaded around them. The heat of her moist center beckoned, and Sterling adjusted himself to fit into her opening.

With a gasp, she eased down onto his manhood, holding still as if adjusting to their fit. Soon, she found a slow but steady rhythm that had him doing his best not to find release before she did. Knowing the end was near, he touched her center once more, loving the way her sky-blue eyes darkened as passion took hold.

"Sterling!" Her body jerked with pleasure, sending him over the edge as a thousand stars exploded inside him.

He held her tight as they returned to earth together. "I love you, Lena. So much."

"And I love you." She shifted to his side and propped on her elbow to look at him. "If not for you, I would never have come to accept my gift. I always felt torn when a feeling came over me. A mix between wanting it and willing it away. I can't begin to explain the peace you've given me. I feel whole now. All because of you."

"The same holds true for me. You've given me a balance I never had before. Thank you, Lena." He kissed her.

"I'm forever yours," she whispered.

"The two of us. Forever and always."

Her eyes narrowed as she looked at him, a smile on her lips. "Would it be so terrible if we were just a few minutes late?"

Before he could answer, she kissed him again, and he was lost.

LENA GRINNED AS she and Sterling entered the drawing room at her grandfather's house. What else could she do when her family, with the exception of her grandfather, gave them a knowing look as if guessing the reason they were late?

"Good morning," she managed despite the blush heating her cheeks.

"My apologies for our tardiness," Sterling added.

Everyone returned the greeting while Lena walked directly to Ella who held baby Alex. She hugged Ella and brushed a finger along Alex's round cheek, hoping he woke soon. "You look wonderful," Lena said to her sister.

"Why, thank you. I feel wonderful." Her sister glowed with happiness as she looked down at her son. Marbury sat beside her with the same besotted look upon his face.

The sight of the three of them so enamored with each other brought tears of joy to Lena's eyes. She looked at Norah, unsurprised to see the same tears in her sister's eyes.

As her gaze held on Norah, a chill crept over her scalp and the conversation fell away to a murmur. She drew in a quiet gasp as a premonition took hold. Norah was expecting.

Lena blinked, wondering if her sister knew. It took only a moment to see the truth on her sister's face. She did. Lena glanced at Vanbridge and his grin, along with the light of excitement in his eyes, told her he knew as well.

Unable to resist, Lena leaned down to hug Norah but didn't say a word. It was her news to share when and where she chose.

Then she moved to her grandfather and greeted him with a kiss on his cheek. He beamed as he looked at all of them, his pride obvious.

When Sterling sat beside Lena, he leaned close. "Are you well?"

To know that he knew her well enough to understand when she had a premonition warmed her heart. "I am," she reassured him, and he smiled in return.

Davies arrived to announce breakfast was ready, and they all made their way downstairs, chatting as they went.

Once they were settled, Davies served glasses of champagne while a footman brought out silver-covered trays of food.

After everyone had been served, her grandfather cleared his throat, gaining their attention. "Thank you for coming this morning. We have much to celebrate." He swallowed deliberately as if emotions were threatening to gain the better of him. "Not only do I have three wonderful granddaughters, but I also have three amazing grandsons-in-law, and now a great-grandson. I am truly blessed." He shook his head as if he could hardly believe it. Then he turned and retrieved three small blue velvet boxes bound with white ribbon from a tray Davies held. He stood to hand them to his granddaughters.

"What is this, Grandfather?" Ella asked as she took the box with one hand, still cradling Alex with the other. Already she seemed adept at managing the tasks motherhood required.

"A gift to remind us that treasure is not always where we think. For some, it might be lost forever, buried in the ground. But my treasures are here in this room. I know I didn't welcome you the way I should've upon your arrival in London, but I want you to know that I love each of you." He gestured toward the boxes. "Open them. Please."

Lena glanced at Sterling then opened the lid to find a large pearl pendant with three diamonds sparkling above it. "It's beautiful."

"So beautiful," Ella agreed.

"Gorgeous." Norah pressed a finger to her lips as if to hold back tears.

"The pearls are from a necklace I had made for your mother but never had the chance to give her. I think she would be pleased to know you have them. The three diamonds represent the three of you. I-I—" He broke off and took a deep breath, blinking several times. "I can't imagine my life without you all. Thank you for making me so happy."

Lena and her sisters all stood and hugged the duke, the four of them linked in a way Lena knew would stand the test of time.

"To finding lost treasures," he said with a teary smile.

"Here, here!" They all cheered.

Lena looked over her shoulder at Sterling, her heart incredibly full, grateful to have not one but two dukes in her life.

About the Author

Lana Williams is a USA Today Bestselling Author with over 35 historical romances filled with mystery, adventure, and sometimes, a pinch of paranormal to stir things up. Filled with a love of books from an early age, she put pen to paper and decided happy endings were a must in any story she created.

Lana spends her days in Victorian, Regency, and Medieval times, depending on her mood and current deadline. She lives in the Rocky Mountains with her husband, and a spoiled lab, and loves hearing from readers. Stop by her website and say hello! There, you can find links to connect with her on Facebook, Twitter, or Instagram.

Website: lanawilliams.net
Facebook: LanaWilliamsBooks
Twitter: LanaWilliams28
Instagram: authorlanawilliams